The Three

Vol.

Mrs. Oliphant

Alpha Editions

This edition published in 2023

ISBN : 9789357944885

Design and Setting By
Alpha Editions
www.alphaedis.com
Email - info@alphaedis.com

Contents

VOL. 3

CHAPTER I.

ALICE'S FATE.

ALICE SEVERN was very innocent and very young,—just over sixteen,—a child to all intents and purposes,—as everybody thought around her. Old Welby, who had taken to meddling in the padrona's affairs, with that regard which the friends of a woman who is alone feel themselves entitled to display for her interests, had been pressing very earnestly upon Mrs. Severn's attention the necessity of preparing her child, who had an evident and remarkable talent, to exercise it in public.

'Few people, indeed, have their way so clear before them,' he had said repeatedly. 'It is the finest thing in the world to have a girl or boy with a decided turn. If you could but see the parents who come to me with sons who don't know what they would be at; and the idiots think they may be made painters because they care for nothing in earth or heaven. But here is this child with a talent. Of course, if it were a talent for our own art, we might know better how to manage it; but such as it is, it is a gift. Never undervalue a gift, my dear madam. Providence itself points out the way for you. You have only got to train her for her work.'

'But, Mr. Welby,' pleaded the padrona, 'she is such a child. How could I send my little maid out into the world to appear in public! I could not do it! It would drive me out of my senses. My child! You forget what kind of a creature she is.'

'I don't in the least forget,' said the R.A. 'She is very pretty, too, which is a pity; but you should be above foolish notions in that respect,—you who are so well known to the public yourself.'

'Not so very well known,' said the padrona, with a half smile; 'and then it is only my name, not me. And even if it were my very self, why it would only be me still, not her. I am old, and what does it matter? But my lily, my darling! Mr. Welby, you are very kind, but you do not take the circumstances into consideration;—you do not realise to the full extent what the consequences would be.'

'I don't know what you mean by the full extent,' said Mr. Welby; 'but this I see as clear as daylight, that some time or other the child will probably have her bread to earn. I say probably. She may marry, of course, but the papers tell us people have given up marrying now-a-days. You can't live for ever, ma'am; and still more certainly you can't work for ever. And the child has actually something in her fingers by which she could earn money, and provide for herself with the greatest ease. Besides, a musician is not like a singer, or a dancer, or anything of that sort. She comes on and sits down before her piano, and never pays any attention to her audience. She need not even look at them unless she likes. She has only a little curtsey to make, and so is off again. It is positively nothing. She may marry, of course, but that would be no protection against poverty. And what's the alternative? A lingering, idle sort of life at home; saving scraps, and making her own gowns and bonnets; or, perhaps, giving music-lessons to tiresome children whom she would hate. You should not, my dear Mrs. Severn, do such injustice to your child.'

'Indeed, I am the last person to do her injustice,' said the padrona, half angered, half saddened, with tears in her eyes. It was a very trenchant style of argument. 'If I were to die, or if I were to fail in my work!' Mrs. Severn said to herself, with one of those awful throbs of dread which come upon a woman who is the sole protector and bread-winner of her children. Such a thought was not unfamiliar to her mind. It came sometimes at chance hours, stealing upon her suddenly like an evil spirit, and wringing her heart. It set her now, for the hundredth time, to count up the little scraps of resource they would have in such a terrible contingency, the friends who would or might be kind to them. 'If I might but live till Edie is twenty!' was the silent prayer that followed. It did not seem possible that so long as she did live she would be unable to work. This frenzy of dread was but momentary. Had it lasted, so sharp and poignant was it, the life which was so important might have been put in jeopardy; but fortunately Mrs. Severn's mind was as elastic as mind could be, and rose again like a flower after the heavy foot had pressed it down. Yet, Alice,—could she be doing injustice to Alice? These arguments had without doubt made a certain impression upon her. Let but this summer be over, she said to herself. It would be time enough certainly when the child was seventeen,—one more year of sweet childhood and leisure, and undisturbed girlish peace. And then the grateful thought came back upon the mother of Mr. Rich's commission which she was working at, and her year's work which was secure. Could there be comfort greater than that thought? And the morrow would care for the things of itself.

While such discussions went on,—for they were frequent,—Alice moved about the house, a soft, domestic spirit, with light steps and a face like a flower. Every day it became more like a flower. The sweetness expanded, the husks of the lovely blossom opened, the woman came gliding noiselessly, so that nobody around perceived it, out of the silken bud of the girl. She was clever at her needle, as her mother had boasted, and made and mended with the homely natural satisfaction of a worker who is conscious of working well; and she was housekeeper, and managed the accounts, and ordered the dinners, proud of her importance and the duties of her office; and she saw the children put to bed, and heard them say their prayers. The homeliest, most limited life,—and yet what could the world give that was better? Not Nelly Rich's leisure, and gaiety, and luxury; not Mary Westbury's tedious comforts and occupations. Alice for her part had everything,—and the piano, and the talk of nights added to all. And yet her mind was not undisturbed, as her mother fondly thought. A little secret, no bigger than a pin's point, had sprung into being in the virgin heart;—not worth calling a secret,—not a thing at all, in short,—only a murmur of soft, musing recollections,—dreams that were not half tangible enough to be called hopes. As, for instance, what was it he meant when their eyes met that afternoon as she played to him? how was it that he remembered so well every time he had seen her,—even her dress?—questions which she asked and then retreated from, and eluded, and played with, and returned to them again. And would he go to India? Would he come back to Fitzroy Square? So misty was the sphere in which all this passed that the one question seemed to Alice as important as the other. What if he might come again some afternoon, flushing all the fading sky with new tints? What if he should go away and never be heard of more? All this was in the child's mind when her mother resolved that this summer at least Alice should be left in undisturbed peace. The old story repeated itself, as everything does in this world,—the everlasting tale of individual identity, of isolation and separation of nature between those who are dearest and nearest to each other. The mother would have given her life cheerfully for her child, but could no more see into that child's soul than if she had been entirely indifferent to her. And Alice, the most loving and dutiful of children, went sweetly on her way, shaping out her own individual life, and never suspecting in that any treason to her earliest loves, or any possible break in her existence. It all turned on the point whether a young Guardsman, who,—with all kindness towards Frank Renton be it said,—was not equal to either Alice or her mother, should call, or should not call, next time he might be in town. Certainly a very trifling matter, and almost concluded against Alice beforehand, as may have been perceived.

I cannot take it upon me to say if he had never come that Alice would have broken her heart. Her heart was too young, too fresh, too visionary, to be tragically moved. She could have gone on looking for him, wondering if he would come, quite as capable of expecting that he would suddenly appear out of the depths of India as that he would come from Royalborough. She had so much time to spare yet before beginning life for herself that the fanciful delight of wondering what he meant by a look or a word, was actually more sweet to her than anything tangible could have been; but yet if he had never come again, a pathetic chord would have sounded among the fresh harmonies of her being,—perhaps a deeper note than any which had yet been awakened in her, at least a sadder one. She would have looked for him and grown weary, and a certain languor and melancholy would have come into her life. Already she had more pleasure in thinking than she had ever been known to have,—or at least she called it thinking,—and would sit silent for hours wrapped in soft dreams, forgetting to talk, to the great disgust of little Edith, and wonder of Miss Hadley, who was the sharpest observer in the household, and guessed what it all meant. But still Alice could have no reason to complain had Frank Renton never more made his appearance in the Square. She would never have dreamt of complaining, poor child; she would have sighed, and a ray of light would have gone out of her life, and that would have been all;—and she had so many rays of light that there might well be one to spare!

It was not thus, however, that things turned out. Not much more than a week had elapsed when Frank again made his appearance in the Square. He had not said much to himself about it. He pretended to himself, indeed, that it was a sudden thought, as he had some time to spare. 'One might as well go and bid them good-bye,' he said aloud, the better to persuade himself that it was purely accidental. He had seen Montague, and had all but concluded with him about the exchange, though he had still been quite doubtful on the subject when he came up to town. Yet the sight of the other side, and the reality given to the matter by the actual discussion of it as a thing to be done, had an effect upon him which nothing else had yet had. It was made at once into a matter of fact by the first half-dozen words he exchanged with Montague of the 200th. And now it was all but settled, whatever other conclusions might follow. The suddenness with which this very serious piece of business had been concluded, or all but concluded, had filled Frank with a certain excitement. He did not know how he should announce it at home,—how he should tell it to his friends. But he had done it. No doubt his mother would weep, and other eyes would look on him reproachfully. Not that any eyes had a right,—an absolute right,—to reproach him; but still——! Frank's mind had been very much agitated and beaten about for some days past. That interview with Nelly had been hard upon him. He had not said all, nor nearly all, that he had been expected to say; but still he had said something which had drawn the indefinite bond between them a little closer. He would owe to her, he felt, after what had passed, some sort of embarrassing explanation of the reasons which had induced him all at once to make up his mind and choose India and work, instead of what was vaguely called his good prospects at home. These good prospects he knew, and everybody knew, herself included, were,—Nelly and her fifty thousand pounds; and it would be as much as saying, 'I have given up all thoughts of you,' when he told her of his sudden determination. He had said nothing about going to India in that last interview. On the contrary, he had been rather eloquent on the subject of staying at home. And now he would have to explain to her that India and freedom had more charms for him than she had, even when backed by all her advantages. It was not a pleasant intimation to make; neither was the thought pleasant of telling his mother, who would have still more occasion to reproach him. 'Go to India, when you might have fifty thousand for the asking, and heaven knows how much more!' Mrs. Renton would say; and would feel herself deeply aggrieved by her son's backsliding. He had been beguiled into all this by the talk of Montague of the 200th, and his own errant, foolish inclinations. It had seemed to him like an escape from himself, and he had taken advantage of the chance;—but it was terrible to contemplate the immediate results. And he had an hour or two to spare, and a little music had always so good an effect upon him! Besides, it would not be civil to go away without taking farewell of Laurie's friends. The 200th were to go in three months. There would be little further time for anything but the business of his outfit. Frank turned his steps towards the Square with the resolution, declared,—to himself,—that this should be the last time. He would see them once more, as civility required, and then all would be over. He would put all such nonsense from his mind, the folly of thinking of either;—for was it not folly to entertain such an idea at his age?—and go away and enjoy his freedom. He would be twenty-one before the regiment set sail, which was no doubt a serious age, and the beginning of mature manhood; but still few men without money married so early. And Frank did not want a wife, though he had thus got himself into such difficulties with two girls at once. The clear course was evidently to set himself free from such premature entanglements, and take refuge in distance and novelty, and rejoice in his escape.

By what strange chance it was that the padrona should have gone out that special afternoon, taking Miss Hadley with her, is what I never could explain. Things do occur so sometimes in this curious world, where everything happens that ought not to happen. Alice was alone, all by herself in that shadowy, silent drawing-room. It was a thing which did not occur thrice in a year. And lo! Frank Renton's visit to say good-bye must happen on one of these rare occasions! Alice was not playing when he was ushered in. She was sitting at work close to the piano, though that too was not usual to her. She had gone in with the intention of practising, but the charm of thinking had been too strong for her. Even her work had fallen on her knee in the soft, profound stillness and loneliness which of late had come to be so sweet to her. She was thinking of him, asking herself once more those sweet, vague, fanciful questions. It was so pleasant, in her new mood, to feel herself all alone, free to think as she pleased, and lose herself in dreams for a whole, long, enchanted afternoon. And just at that moment, as good or evil fortune decided, Frank Renton was shown into the room. He himself was struck dumb by the chance, as well as Alice. She looked up at him, poor child, with absolute consternation. 'Oh, I am so sorry mamma is out!' she said; and notwithstanding the stir and flutter of her heart at the sight of him, she was quite in earnest when she said so. Mamma being out, however, made all the difference between conscious safety and calm and the uneasy dread which she could not explain. What was she afraid of? Alice could not answer the question. Not of him, certainly, of whom she believed every good under heaven. Of herself, then? But she only repeated her little outcry of regret, and could give no reason for her shy shrinking and fears.

'Is she?' said Frank; 'but I must not go away, must I?—though your tone seems somehow to imply it. Let me stay and wait for her. I have come to say good-bye.'

'Good-bye?' said Alice, faltering. The child grew cold all over in a moment, as if a chill had blown upon her. 'Are you really, really going to India, after all?'

'After all? after what?' said Frank, turning upon her so quickly that she had no time to think.

'Oh, I meant after——. I thought——. People said——. But, no, indeed; I am sure I never believed it, Mr. Renton; it is such stupid talk; only I was a little surprised,' said Alice, recovering herself. 'I mean, are you really going to India,—after all?'

Frank laughed. He was at no loss now as he had been with Nelly Rich. 'I see that is what you mean,' he said, looking at her with softened, shining eyes, and that delicious indulgence for her youth and simplicity which made him feel himself twice a man; 'and you may say after all. There are some things I shall be glad to escape from, and there are other things,' said Frank, rising and going close to her, 'there are other things——'

He did not mean it,—certainly he did not mean it,—any more than he had meant going to India, when he came up that morning to town to talk the matter over in a vague, general way; but, somehow, as he stood in front of her, leaning over the high-backed chair on which she had placed her work, gazing into the sweet face lifted to him, which changed colour every moment, and was as full of light and shade as any summer sky, a sudden sense of necessity came over him. Leave her?—Was there anybody in the world but the two of them looking thus at each other? Did anything else matter in comparison? 'What is the use of making any pretences?' cried Frank; 'if you will but come with me, Alice, going to India will be like going to heaven!'

She sat and gazed at him with consternation and wonder and dismay; growing pale to the very lips; straining her wistful eyes to make out what he meant. Was he mad? What was he thinking of? 'Go with, you?' she faltered, under her breath, incapable of any expression but that of amaze. Her wondering eye sank under his look, and her heart began to beat, and her brow to throb. The suggestion shook her whole being, though she had not quite fathomed what it meant. And then the crimson colour rose like a sudden flame, and flew over all her face. The change, the trouble, the surprise, were like so many variations in the sky, and they combined to take from the young lover what little wits he had left.

'Would it be so dreadful?' he said, bending down over her. 'Alice, just you and I. What would it matter where we were so long as we were together? I know it would matter nothing to me. I would take such care of you. I should be as happy as the day was long. I want nothing but to have you by me, to

- 8 -

look at you, and listen to you. I do not care if there were not another creature in the world', cried the youth; 'just you and I!'

'Oh, don't speak so!' cried Alice, trembling in her agitation and astonishment. 'Don't, oh, don't! You must not! How could I ever, ever leave mamma?'

'Then it is not me you object to?' cried the lover, in triumph, taking her hands, taking herself to him in a tender delirium.

This was how it came about. With no more preparation on either side, with everything against it,—friends, prudence, fortune, Nelly,—every influence you could conceive. And yet they did it without any intention of doing it,— on the mere argument of being left for half-an-hour alone together. True, it took more than half-an-hour to calm down the bewilderment of the girl's mind, thus launched suddenly at a stroke into the wide waters of life. She looked back trembling upon her little haven, the harbour where she had lain so quietly a few minutes before. But we can never go back those few minutes. The thing was done, and nobody in the world could be more surprised at it than the two young, rash, happy creatures themselves, holding each other's hands, and looking into each other's faces, and asking themselves,—Could it be true?

CHAPTER II.

A STRUGGLE.

THERE are moments in life which are so sweet as to light up whole weeks of gloom; and there are moments so dreadful as to make the unfortunate actors in them tremble at the recollection to the end of their lives. Such a moment in the life of Frank Renton was that in which he suddenly heard the padrona's knock at her own door. He had been as happy as a young man could be. He had felt himself willing, and over again willing, to give up everything without a regret, for the sake of the love he had won, and which was, he said to himself, of everything in earth and heaven the most sweet. This he had said to himself a hundred times over as he hung over Alice in the first ecstasy of their betrothal. He could not imagine how he ever could have doubted. Going to India would, as he had said, be going to heaven. Where he went, she would be with him. He should have her all to himself, free from any interference. They would be free to go forth together, hand in hand, like Adam and Eve. What was any advantage the world could give in comparison to such blessedness? He was in the full flush of his delight when that awful knock was heard at the door.

At the sound of it Alice started too. She clung to him first, and then she shrank from him. 'Oh, it is mamma!' she cried, with sudden dismay. Then there was a pause. Frank let go the hand he had been holding. Nature and the world stood still in deference to the extraordinary crisis. He turned his face, which had suddenly grown pale, to the door. And they heard her talking as she came up the stairs, unconcerned, laughing as if nothing had happened! 'It will be a surprise to Alice,' she said audibly, pausing in the passage, at the dining-room door. And Alice shuddered as she listened. A surprise! If the padrona could but know what a terrible surprise had been prepared for herself!

And then she came in upon them, smiling and blooming, her soft colour heightened by a little fresh breeze that was blowing, bright from the pleasant unusual intercourse with the outside world. 'I am sorry you did not come with us, Alice,' she said. 'It is not so hot as we thought it was. Ah, Mr. Renton!' and she held out her hand to him. Upon what tiny issues does life hang. If Alice had not thought it too hot to go out, all this might never have happened. And the mother to speak of it so lightly, thinking of nothing more important than the walk, ignorant what advantage had been taken of her absence! To the two guilty creatures who knew, every word was an additional stab.

'I came up again to-day about the same business,' said Frank, faltering.

Alice bent trembling over her work, and said nothing. She did not go, as was her wont, with soft, tender hands, to untie the bonnet and take off the shawl, taking pride in her office as 'mamma's maid.' She put on an aspect of double diligence over her work, though her hands trembled so that she could scarcely hold her needle.

Even Mrs. Severn's unsuspicious nature was startled. She turned to Miss Hadley, who had come in behind her, and said, half in dumb-show, with a certain impatience, 'What does he mean by coming so often?'

'No good,' answered Miss Hadley, solemnly, under her breath; which laconic utterance amused the padrona so much, that her momentary uneasiness flew away. She sat down smiling, turning her kind face upon the trembling pair. 'Poor Laurie's brother!' she said to herself. That was argument enough for tolerating him and showing him all kindness.

'Alice, how is it you are so busy?' she said. 'I think you might order some tea. Though it is not so very hot, it is pleasant to get into the shade. I hope your business has made progress, Mr. Renton,' she added, politely. As the padrona looked at them it became slowly apparent to her that something was wrong. Alice had not liked the task of entertaining a stranger all by herself; or——! But of course it must be that. It was ill-bred of him, even though he was Laurie's brother, to insist on coming in when there was nobody but the child to receive him. Mrs. Severn began to feel uncharitably towards the young man. Alice flushed one moment, and the next was quite pale. She was reluctant to raise her eyes, and neglected all her usual *petits soins*. When she had to get up to obey her mother, it was with a shy avoidance of her look, which went to the padrona's heart. What could be the matter? Was she ill? Had he been rude to her? But that was impossible. 'Is there anything wrong, my darling?' she said, half rising from her seat.

'Oh, no, mamma!' said Alice, breathlessly, in a fainting voice.

The padrona gave Miss Hadley a look which meant,—Go and see what is the matter; and then with a very pre-occupied mind turned towards Frank to play politeness and do her social duties. 'I hope your business has made progress,' she repeated, vaguely; and then it became apparent that he was agitated too.

'Yes,' he said; and then he came forward to her quite pale and with an air of mingled supplication and alarm which filled her with the profoundest bewilderment. 'Oh, Mrs. Severn, forgive us!' he cried. He would have gone down on his knees had he thought that would have been effectual; but he did not dare to go down on his knees. He stood before her like a culprit about to be sentenced; and she looked at him with eyes in which alarm and suspicion began to glow. There was something wrong; but even now the mother to whom her child was indeed a child did not guess what it was.

'Us!' she said; and somehow a thought of Laurie struck into the maze of her thoughts. He could not have done anything, poor fellow, in his exile, to call for forgiveness in this passionate way. 'I cannot tell what you mean,' she cried. 'What have I to forgive? And who are the sinners?' and she tried to laugh, though it was difficult enough.

'Mrs. Severn,' he said, 'I would not, believe me, have taken advantage of your absence, not willingly. She is so young. I know I ought to have spoken to you first. I did not mean it when I came——'

'She?' cried the padrona, with a little cry. Not yet did she see what it was; but instinct told her what kind of a trenchant blow was coming, and all the blood seemed to rush back upon her heart.

'Yes,' said Frank, rising into the calm of passion, 'I found her all by herself. And I loved her so! From that first moment I saw her,—when you called her, and she came and stood there,' he cried, pointing vaguely at the door; 'and I had come to tell you I was going away. And she was sorry. It all came upon us in a moment. How could I help telling her? I loved her so! Forgive me for Alice's sake.'

The padrona sat gazing at him for some moments with dilated eyes; then suddenly she hid her face in her hands, and uttered a low, moaning cry as of a creature in pain. All at once it had come upon her what it meant. Frank standing there, full of anxiety, yet full of confidence, was bewildered, not knowing what this meant in reference to himself. But the truth was that Mrs. Severn was not thinking of him, had no room in her mind for him at that terrible moment. It was her child she was thinking of,—Alice, who was here half an hour ago, and now was not here, and could never again be, for ever. It all burst upon her in an instant, not anything remediable, as a thing might be which was independent of the child's own will, but voluntary, her own doing, her choice! Something sung and buzzed in her ears; her eyes felt hot and scorched up; sharp pulsations of pain came into her temples. 'My child!—my baby!—my first-born!' she said to herself. It was as if the earth had shaken beneath her feet, and the house had crumbled down about her. Her whole fabric of happiness seemed to shrink up; and yet it was not so much—not so much that she asked; not anything for herself, not the ease, the comfort, the leisure, the pleasures, so many had. Was she not content, more than content to work late and early, to spare herself in nothing, to labour with both hands, as it were, never grudging? Only her children, that was all she asked to have! And here was the first of her children, the sweetest of all, her excellency and the beginning of her strength, her companion, and tender consoler, and sweet helper—gone! She gave a cry, a half-smothered moan, such as could not be put into words. And all this time Frank stood before her, pale, somewhat desperate, but courageous, knowing that however the mother might be against him, the daughter was for him,—and trusting in his fate.

When the padrona at last withdrew her hands from her face it struck her as with a sense of offence that he should still be standing there. Why did he, a stranger, stand and gaze at her misery? What right had he? And then she remembered that it was this boy whom her child had chosen out of the world, to give up her home for him. In her heart, at that moment, the padrona hated Frank. She raised her head, and even he, though he had no love in his eyes to enlighten him respecting the changes in her face, saw that the lines were drawn and haggard, the colour gone, and that a look of age and suffering had fallen upon her. But she commanded herself. She spoke after a minute with an effort. 'Mr. Renton, this is a very serious matter you tell me.' she said; 'my daughter is a child,' and then she had to stop and take breath, and moisten her dry lips. 'She is too young,—to judge what is best,—for her life. And so are you,' she added, looking at him with a certain pity for the boy who was so young too, and Laurie's brother to boot; 'you are both too young to know what you are doing. You should not have disturbed my Alice!' she cried, suddenly, unable to keep in the reproach. 'Such thoughts would never have come into my darling's mind. You had no right to disturb my child!'

She got up as she spoke in a blaze of momentary excitement,—anger, grief's twin brother, rising sudden into the place of grief. She made a step or two away from him, and began to collect Alice's work and fold it up with her trembling hands, turning her back upon him, as if this sudden piece of business she had found was the most important matter in the world. Then she turned round, raising her hand, with an outburst of natural eloquence. 'She was only a child,' she cried; 'as much a child as when she sat on my lap. She had not a thought that was not open to me. I have worked for her almost all her life, watched over her, nursed her, smiled for her when my heart was breaking,—and all in a moment, for a young man's vanity, my child is to be mine no longer. Why did you not come to me fairly, like an honest enemy, and warn me what you meant to do?'

As she spoke, standing before him with her arm lifted in unconscious action, almost towering over him in the greatness of her suffering and indignation, Frank stood lost in astonishment. Mothers, so far as he knew, were glad to get their daughters off their hands. Such was the tradition in all regions he had ever frequented. He had expected difficulties, no doubt, but not of this kind. It was with a certain consternation that he gazed at her, asking himself what it meant. It was all real, there could be no doubt of that. But yet,—he was in Fitzroy Square. It was not a duke's daughter he had ventured on engaging to himself, but a humble artist's, who everybody would have thought would have been glad enough to have her child provided for. This Frank knew, or, at least, he believed he knew, was the light in which the matter would have been regarded by sensible people. And he, though Belgravia no doubt might have scorned him, was no such contemptible match for the daughter of the painter. He stood surprised and discomfited, not knowing how to reply to a woman who addressed him so strangely. Perhaps it would be best to let her have it all her own way, and exhaust her indignation without contradicting or opposing her; but then the passion in her face moved the young man.

'I never thought of coming as an enemy,' he said, with some heat. 'I have loved her ever since I saw her. I am not to blame for that.' How could he be to blame? He had done naught in hate, but all in honour. And thus the mother and the lover stood confronting each other, rivals; but in a conflict which for one of them was without hope.

Then there was an interval of silence,—a truce between the foes. Frank mechanically turned over and over the books which lay on a little table against which he was leaning, and the padrona threw herself into her chair trembling in her agitation. Again and again her lips forced themselves to speak, but the effort was a vain one. She had not the heart to speak. What was there to say? If Alice's heart was gone from her, then everything was gone. It was not as in old days, when she could have forbidden an unsuitable indulgence with the certainty that after the pain of the first few minutes the smiles would come back, the little heart melt, and the child be herself again. Here was a serious trial now, and the padrona's heart was sick. She sat, not even looking at him, with her head turned to one side, and her mind full of bitter thoughts. This silence was worse than anything for Frank. He bore it as long as he could, standing with his eyes fixed upon her, expecting the verdict which was to come. Then, as she did not speak, he summoned up all his courage. He made a few steps forward, so as to bring himself before her eyes, and thus addressed her, with as much steadiness and calm as he could command;— 'Mrs. Severn,' he said, 'could you not put yourself in my position? I did not mean to betray myself. I meant to say good-bye, and go away, and never trouble you more. But she was sorry, God bless her! She looked at me, and pitied me, and I did not know what I was saying. I will not tell you a lie, and say I regret,' cried Frank, with excitement; 'but I will say I am sorry I had not the chance of speaking to you first. Surely, surely, you will not refuse her to me for that!'

'Refuse her to you!' said the padrona, with an unconscious contempt; 'refuse her to you! You cannot think it is you I am thinking of. Oh, young man, how little you know! There is the sting of it! I would give everything I have in the world she had never seen you; but you make me work out my own sorrow. Can you believe I would hesitate a moment if it were only refusing you?' she cried, with a gesture unconsciously full of scorn, throwing, as it were, something from her. Frank had never been spoken to in such a tone before. He had been an important personage at Richmont. Not so would his prayer have been received there. The wounded *amour propre* of his youth made itself felt in his displeasure. He went to the nearest window, and stood staring out into the street, disgusted with himself, and half disgusted, if the truth must be told, with all the circumstances. He had been a fool in thus committing himself. He had behaved like a fool in every way, and this was his reward;— not rejection even, but scorn!

'But I can't refuse her anything!' the padrona said with a sigh, that came out of the very bottom of her heart. There was the sting of it. She could not turn away, as impulse would have made her, the lover whom she felt to be her enemy. There was the child to be considered. It was no plain and easy matter to be decided upon in an arbitrary way. Fathers and mothers have refused their children's wishes before now for their good. Daughters have been even shut up in their rooms, starved, imprisoned, bullied into giving up the undesirable suitor, as everybody knows. But these courses were not open to the padrona. She could no more have stood by and seen her child suffer than she could have flown. The one was as much an impossibility of nature as the other. She could not refuse Alice the desire of her heart. Oh, gentle heavens! to think it could be the desire of that tender creature's heart to go away from her home where she had been cherished since ever she was born,—from her mother, who had loved and shielded her for all her sixteen years,—away to the end of the world with a young man, whom six months before she had never seen! And she not a woman with any weariness in her heart, nor a girl of adventurous instincts, curious and longing for the unknown, but, on the contrary, the purest womanly domestic child, caring little about all the noises of the great world without,—only sixteen, a soft, contented creature, happy in all the little business of her limited life! There was the wonder,—a thing not new, familiar every day;—and yet ever miraculous, a wonder and a portent to the padrona, as if it had never happened before.

It was just then that Alice came faltering into the room. She had cried and leaned her head on Miss Hadley's breast when she was questioned what was the matter; but she would not tell even that faithful friend until mamma knew. Her faithful friend, indeed, was at no great loss. Her eyes were sharp enough to make up the lack of all suspicion in the innocent household. She divined the truth, and she also divined the scene that must be going on in the drawing-room. 'I knew this was what would come of it,' she allowed herself to say,—which was but natural; and she led Alice back to the door, though it was against her will. 'My love, these two will never agree without you.' she said, and stayed outside with that purest self-denial of the secondary spectator, burning with curiosity and interest, yet giving way to the chief personages concerned, which is so often seen among women. She would not even go into the dining-room, where she might have seen or heard something, but stayed outside in the passage, having carefully closed all the doors. So far as she herself was concerned, Miss Hadley was not Frank's enemy. When a man spoke out she respected him, as she always said. It was only when he shilly-shallied that she had a contempt for him;—and to have one of them provided for would no doubt be a great matter. Such, taking

Frank's theory of what was proper and natural, was Miss Hadley's way of thinking; but she knew only too well how impracticable Mrs. Severn could be.

Alice went in faltering, changing colour, ready to sink to the ground with innocent shame-facedness, but as much unaware of the struggle going on in her mother's mind as if she had been a creature of a different species. When she had made a few steps into the room, she paused, and gave a quick timid glance at the two, who were both stirred by her approach. The padrona rose, and gazed at her child, who had thus left her side, while Frank started forward to place himself by her. This was the last touch, which the mother could not bear. She darted to Alice's side, put him away with her hand, took the girl into her arms, and holding her fast, gazed into her face. 'Alice,' she said, 'is it true? Never mind any one but me. Look at me,—at your mother, Alice. Tell me the truth,—the truth, my darling! Can it be? Do you want to go with him, and leave us all,—the boys, and Edith, and all that love you? Is it true? Do you want to leave me, my child?' cried the mother, in a voice of anguish. And she stood holding her fast, reading the answer before it came in her eyes, in the modulations of her lips,—elevated to such a height of passionate feeling as she had never known before in all her life.

Nor was it a less trial for the young inexperienced creature, knowing nothing of passion, who was held thus in the grip of despair. Fortunately, Alice could not understand the full force of the tempest in her mother's heart. 'Oh, mamma, how can you think I want to leave you?' she cried, with tears; and Frank, listening, felt with a pang that he was cast aside. Then she paused. 'But, oh, mamma, dear!' said Alice, with a soft, pleading, breathless tone, melodious like the cooing of a dove,—'oh, mamma, dear!'—and she slid her tender arm round her mother's neck, changing her attitude to one of utter supplication,—'you have Edie and the boys, and my dearest love for ever and ever. And he has nobody; and he says,—— Will you only hear what he says? It is not fancy. He wants me most.'

It was not more than a minute that they stood thus clinging together, but Frank thought it an hour. He was left out of the matter. It was they who had to decide a question so momentous to them. And then he became aware that the padrona had cast her arms round her child to support herself, and was weeping wildly upon Alice's shoulder. No need for any further questions. They had changed characters for the moment. The girl's slight figure tottered, swayed, steadied itself, supporting with a supreme effort the weight of the mother's yielding and anguish; and Alice gave him a look over that burthen,—a look of such pain and sweetness and confidence, that Frank's heart was altogether melted. 'Look what I have to bear,—what I have to give up for you!' it seemed to say;—a pathetic glance; and yet there was in it the triumph of the new love rooting and establishing itself upon the ruins of the old.

When the padrona came to herself she called Frank Renton to her. It was not that she had fainted or become unconscious; but that, when a woman,—or a man either for that matter,—is suddenly called upon to sound the profoundest depths of suffering within her,—or his,—own being, a mist comes upon external matters, confusing place and fact, and above all, time, which goes fast or slow according to our consciousness. It might have been years, so far as she could tell, since she came in cheerfully from her walk, fearing no evil. She had been engaged in some awful struggle against her spiritual enemies, principalities and powers, such as she had never yet encountered; and all unprepared, unarmed for the conflict! She came to herself, lying back in her chair exhausted as if with an illness, without strength enough left to feel the full force of any calamity. She called Frank Renton to her, holding out her hand. 'Sit down here and let me speak to you,' she said. 'I am to listen to what you have to say. And I will listen,—but not now. Such a thing had never entered into my mind. I thought the child was safe for years. I thought she was all mine,—my consolation. I have had so much to do, it seemed but fair I should have a consolation. But there is nothing fair in this world. And now it is you who have her heart, and not me,—and I don't know you even. To be sure you are Laurie's brother. Mr. Renton, if you will come back to me another time, when I have got a little used to it, I will hear everything you have to say.'

'Thanks!' said Frank, not knowing what answer to make, being utterly confused in his own mind, and as much out of his depth in every way as a young man could be. And he would have taken the hand she held out to him in token of amity,—but Mrs. Severn was not equal to any such signs of friendship.

'It will be for another time,' she said, sitting upright in her chair, and drawing back a little. 'If I had received any warning;—but you have only met two,—three times;—is that all?' she said, with a sudden spasm in her voice.

'And at Richmont,' said Frank, divided between offence and humility. Alice had left the room again, and the two were alone.

'And at Richmont,' the padrona repeated with a heavy sigh. 'I might have known. But you don't know my child,' she added, with sudden energy. 'You have seen her pretty face and heard her music, and it is those you care for,—that is all. And there are others as pretty, and who play as well. You cannot know my child.'

'Look here, Mrs. Severn,' cried Frank, driven wild in his turn; 'I have loved her since the first moment I saw her under those curtains. Was it my doing? I was listening to the music, not thinking of any one; and you called Alice, and she came. And I have been struggling against it ever since. I will tell you the truth. I was to marry money,—everybody had made up their minds to it. I was to have a rich wife and give up India, and live a life that would suit me much better at home. That is the truth. And I tried,—tried hard to carry it out. But I had seen Alice, and I could not. To-day when I came I meant to try to say good-bye. I meant it honestly, upon my life. And that other girl is prettier, if you will speak so,' cried the young man, with a kind of brutality, 'than Alice. Judge if it is only for that——'

'Then you will repent,' said the padrona, blazing up into an inconsistent jealousy and resentment. 'Believe me, Mr. Renton, it is far better to carry out your intention, and leave my penniless girl alone.'

The young man started up with a muttered oath. The moment of passion was over, but that of mutual exasperation had come. The light of battle kindled in the padrona's eyes. She would have been glad to be rid of him at any price; and yet,—inconsistent woman,—though she hated him for loving Alice, the thought that he had struggled against that love, the thought that her child had been put in competition with another, set her all a-flame. 'By heaven, you do me injustice!' cried Frank. 'Why will you misunderstand what I say? Let me tell you everything from the beginning. Is it just to judge me unheard? I am Laurie's brother, whom you are fond of; and Alice is mine as well as yours. She has no doubt of me. Why cannot we be friends, we two? I should be your son——'

'It must be for another time,' said the padrona, letting her voice relapse into languor.

The sense of exhaustion had been thoroughly real when she expressed it before; but now, it must be allowed, it was exasperating. The elastic soul had touched the ground, and rebounded ever so little. But she had rebounded in a perverse, and not an amiable way. It was not the calm of despair, but an active wretchedness in which there was hope. And Frank, too, got set on edge, as she was, and left the house with but one soft word from Alice to console him as he went, flaming with opposition and resentment. He could turn the tables on her yet, if he were to try. He could make her regret her interference, if he would. And then a visionary Alice glided into the young man's imagination, holding out her soft arms. Vex her because her mother was vexatious to him? Ah, no! not for the world!

CHAPTER III.

EXCHANGED INTO THE 200TH.

FRANK was not in spirits to go to his club, or anywhere else, after the events of the afternoon. He made a rush for the train instead, thirsting for the quiet of his quarters, in which, at least, he could lock himself in, and be free from intruders. With the same desire for solitude, he ensconced himself as usual in a corner of a railway-carriage, hoping there, at least, to be able to indulge his thoughts in peace. But it was a summer's day, not yet dark, so that he could not hide himself; and his consternation may be imagined when, in two or three minutes, he heard the voice of Mrs. Rich asking for the Royalborough carriage. 'Bless us, there is Mr. Renton, Nelly!' she said, a minute after, for Frank had given a start at the sound of her, and probably caught her eye by the movement, though he had sunk the next minute into the profoundest shade. But, after this, there was nothing to be done but to jump out, and make himself useful to the ladies, and give up his hoped-for solitude. Nelly, of all people in the world, to face him at such a moment! To Frank it seemed as if fate were against him. He had to go through the usual round of salutations, and express his satisfaction at meeting them, while all the time he fretted and fumed. It was not even as if they had been three, which is a safe party. Mrs. Rich had a companion, a lady of about her own age, who was going to Richmont with them, so that Nelly was left to Frank. Neither her mother nor she thought it a bad arrangement. She made her way to the farther window, and seated herself, leaving Frank no alternative but the seat beside her. And she was very lively and full of animation,—a bright, smiling creature, pleasant to look upon. It would be impossible to describe Frank's feelings as he seated himself beside her, with a gap of two vacant seats between him and the elder ladies at the other side, and the noise of the train to favour a *tête-à-tête*. 'Come and tell me what you have been about,' said Nelly. 'Are you always running up and down to town, you idle Guardsmen? I never go but I see heaps of you. Tell me what you have been about.'

'You had better tell me what you have been about,' said Frank; 'that would be more interesting. Shopping? or picture-seeing? or,—oh, I perceive, the flower-show. I had forgotten that.'

'You were not there,' said Nelly, quickly,—'for I looked. There was Lord Edgbaston, and I don't know how many more, who are always to be seen everywhere,—but not you.'

'I was engaged on much less pleasant business,' said Frank, to whom it suddenly occurred that here was an opportunity to tell some portion of his news. It could not be told too soon, especially considering all that had happened since.

'Less pleasant!' repeated Nelly. 'They are very slow and stupid, I think, unless one has some one to talk to one likes. As for the flowers, one can see them anywhere. I had Lord Edgbaston, your charming friend, Mr. Renton; and he was not lively. I don't suppose his talents lie in the way of talk.'

'He is a very good fellow,' said Frank, with a certain tenderness, thinking how soon he should have left all these pleasant companions. His heart melted to them, and his voice took a lugubrious tone.

'How doleful you are!' cried Nelly, laughing; 'one would think you were going to cry. What has been going on? Tell me; has some one been unkind? And I declare you are quite pale. I am getting very, much interested;—do let me know.'

'I don't know that you will be at all interested when you hear,' said Frank, with a certain desperation. 'I have just been settling matters about my exchange into the 200th. They are to sail for India in three months, and it is not cheerful work.'

'To sail for India in three months!' said Nelly. The change that came over her face was indescribable. A half-amused incredulity, then the startled pause, with which she might have said, This is too serious a matter to joke about; and then consternation, anger, mortification. She grew pale, and then brilliantly crimson, till the colour dyed as much as could be seen of her clear, dark skin. She had a right to look at him with eyes of keen inquiry;—not a right to interfere or find fault,—but yet a right to ask the question. He had gone so far that she had, at least, that claim.

'Yes,' he said, with an exquisite discomfort, such as would have been punishment enough for worse treachery than he had perpetrated, 'I have been putting it off and wasting my time, beguiled by pleasanter things. But to-day matters became urgent, and I settled it. I could delay no longer,' he said, with apology in his tone; 'it is not a cheerful piece of work, as I say.'

Nelly did not answer a word. She was struck dumb. That other day, under the lime-trees, he had certainly said not a word about India. He had not, indeed, said all which the opportunity might have justified him in saying. He had been unsatisfactory, and had made a very poor use of the opportunity. But still he had not so much as hinted at anything which could explain this. She sat in her corner, bending towards him a little, as she had been before he made this startling intimation. What could it mean? Could he intend to ask her to go there with him? Nelly's heart gave a sudden bound at the thought. She was so adventurous and eager for change that India itself would not have frightened her. Could that be what he meant? She did not change her position, but sat still, turning towards him in a listening attitude, with her eyes cast down, and a certain sharpness of expectation in her face. The idea was quite new and startling, but it was not unpleasant. She waited, with a tingling in her ears, a sudden sense of quickened pulsation and tightened breath, for the next words he should say.

But at that moment dumbness, too, fell upon Frank. His lips grew dry; his tongue clave to his mouth. He turned a little away, and began to play unconsciously with the little cane in his hand, flicking his boot with it. It seemed to him as if all his powers of speech were exhausted and not a word would come. If only there might be a stoppage at some station, or an accident, or anything! He would have welcomed any incident that would have interrupted this horrible pause. And not a word would come to his lips. He tried to make up some ordinary question about the flower-show, but it would not do. He sat in a frightful consciousness,—afraid to look at her, wondering what she was thinking of it, how she would receive it. And the train was one of those nice, quick express trains, which stop only at Slowley junction. The poor young fellow thought he would have gone mad with that awful pause and stoppage of talk, and the everlasting iron murmur and clank of the wheels.

It was full five minutes before any one spoke, and that at such a time, of course, seemed as a year. Then it was Nelly who resumed the conversation, in a tone clear and distinct, with a modulation of contempt in it which set Frank's nerves on edge. 'I do not see why it should not be cheerful work,' she said; 'no doubt you like it or you would not have done it; but it is sudden surely, Mr. Renton?' And Frank, who did not look at her, who was busy still with his cane and his boot, felt that she was looking steadily at him.

And he was aggravated at the tone. It was the second time that afternoon in which he had been contemptuously spoken to;—by Mrs. Severn, first of all, who had certainly no right to do it, and who had taken pains to make him understand how little importance he was to her, what small hesitation she would have had in cutting him off from all good offices. And now Nelly, who might have an excuse, adopted the same tone. Naturally, it was the one who had some justification for her scorn who bore the brunt of both offences. He looked up at her, and met full, as she had not expected him to meet, the look of restrained resentment, indignation, and wounded feeling, with which she regarded him. Though he was in the wrong, he met her eyes with more fortitude than she could exercise in meeting his. He it was who had been the traitor, and therefore he took the upper hand. 'I am surprised you think it sudden,' he said, fixing his eyes upon her so resolutely that Nelly's could not bear the gaze. 'I have been in negotiation about it more or less since ever I knew you. The opportunity has been sudden, but not the intention.' Thus the man, being unmoved by anything but a passing compunction which he had overcome, got the better of the woman whose heart had been touched ever so little. He looked full at her, and he looked her down.

'But I thought you had changed your mind,' said Nelly softly, with an effort to preserve her calm.

'Oh no, never!' answered Frank, in his majestic way. And then she turned her face round to the window, and gazed steadily out. It was not that she was in love with him,—not much. But she was a girl who had had every toy she ever longed for in all her life, and now for the first time she was denied. She turned to the window, and sudden tears sprang into her eyes. Her own impression was that she was struck to the heart. Her lip quivered; there was a painful feeling in her throat. She had been so bright, so lively, so full of enjoyment,— and now the revulsion came! But she was proud enough not to make any very distinct self-betrayal. She did not mind showing him that she was offended. Even had it come to a little outbreak of passion and tears, she would not, perhaps, have very much minded. But all she did now was to turn away her face. Turning round and gazing very fixedly out of a window after a short interval of very lively and friendly conversation, is a sufficiently marked sign that something is wrong. But Nelly did not utter any reproach. He had faced her, and intimated to her, almost in so many words, that it was a matter she had nothing to do with; and she accepted the intimation. But she did not think it necessary to put an amiable face upon it, as so many girls would have done. She had turned almost her back upon him before they got to Slowley, where the gorgeous carriage of the Riches,—much the most splendid in the county, with a coat-of-arms as big as a soup-plate upon the panel,—was waiting for them. And when Frank got out and gave her his hand to alight, Nelly sprang past him without taking any notice. 'Good-bye, Mr. Renton; I suppose we shall see you before you go,' she said, without looking at him. Mrs. Rich thought her daughter must be out of her senses when she heard the news, which it cost Nelly an effort to tell with composure. She had lost all her colour, and looked black, and pale, and gleaming, and dangerous, when the Royalborough train glided on; and Mrs. Rich after an affectionate farewell to Frank, leisurely ascended into her carriage. 'Have you quarrelled with Frank Renton, my dear?' she said, with a little alarm.

'Oh, dear no!' said Nelly. 'I told him to come and see us before he went away.'

'Before he went away!' said Mrs. Rich, surprised.

'Yes. He has exchanged into the 200th, and they are going to India,' said Nelly, following the train, as it swept along the curves, with an eye which was far from friendly. And Mrs. Rich's conclusion was that the young man must be mad.

Nor must it be supposed that Frank Renton's thoughts were particularly comfortable as he pursued his way. He was not vain enough to be gratified by Nelly's mortification, and he could not conceal from himself the fact that he had not behaved quite as he ought to have done. He had not gone any great length, but still he had said and done enough to justify these kind people in thinking badly of him. He had made them an ungracious return for their hospitality and kindness. And when they should come to know that he was going to be married before he left, and that it was Alice Severn who was to be his bride, what would they think? Would it not look as if lie had gone to Richmont and pretended to pay court to Nelly for the sake of their visitor? Would it not be supposed that both he and his innocent Alice had been traitors;—his innocent Alice, to whom the very thought of evil was unknown? And then there was Alice's mother,—though she did not like him,—who might be injured by this misconception. Mr. Rich was her patron, he had heard. All this maze of humiliating contingencies made Frank half frantic. He was angry with Mrs. Severn for being a painter,—angry with the Riches for buying her pictures,—angry that there should be any connexion, and that, above all, a connexion as of patron and dependant between the family of the girl he might have married and that of the girl he loved. Thinking it over, his very soul grew sick of the imbroglio. If he could but rush up to town and take his Alice to church, and be off to India the very same day,—seeing nobody, making explanations to nobody,—that was the only way of managing matters which could be in the least degree satisfactory; and that was impossible. Mothers of far higher pretensions than Mrs. Severn would, he knew, have received his suit much less cavalierly. He would have her susceptibilities to *ménager* as well as those of everybody else. There was not a point in the whole business, except Alice herself, upon which he could look with the least satisfaction; and indeed it said a great deal for Frank's love that Alice herself retained his allegiance unbroken through it all.

Next morning Frank hurried over to Renton at an hour so early as to startle himself and everybody concerned. He met his cousin Mary as she made her habitual round of the flower-beds before breakfast. It had always been hard work to get him to be ready for breakfast at all, not to speak of sauntering in the garden. And yet he had come all the way from Royalborough. Mary held out her hand to him with a little cry of surprise.

'Is it you, Frank, or your double?' she asked in her amaze. 'It does not seem possible it can be you.'

'I wish I had a double who would be so obliging as to do half my work for me,' said Frank, dolefully. 'It is me, worse luck! and if you don't stand my friend, Mary, I don't know what I shall do.'

'Of course I will stand your friend. But, Frank, what is it?' cried Mary, gliding her arm within his with sisterly confidence. And he took breath for a few minutes without saying a word, leading her from the front of the house out of sight under the shadow of the trees.

'I may as well tell you at once,' he said, after this pause. 'I could not stand it any longer. I have settled all about my exchange, and I am going to India in three months.'

'To India!' said Mary. But she had a brother in India, and perhaps it was not quite so appalling to her as Frank expected it to be. She made a little pause, however, and then she said, 'Poor godmamma!' with as much feeling as he could desire.

'Well,' said Frank; 'could I help it? It is my father you must blame. How was it to be expected that I could get on in the most expensive regiment in the service after what has happened? It was my duty to do something, and this was the only thing I could do.'

'I am not blaming you, Frank; I only said, "Poor godmamma!" she will feel it so,' said Mary; 'especially after what you gave us to understand last time, that—that there might be another way——'

'That was folly,' said Frank hotly; and then he added with humility, 'But I have not told you half all. You must do more for me yet. Mary, I am going to get married before I go.'

'To get married!' Mary repeated with a start; and then she clasped his arm tight with both her hands, and looked up joyfully in his face. 'Then you must have been fond of her after all,' she cried. 'It was not her money you were thinking of. Oh, Frank! don't be angry. It made me so unhappy to think you were going to marry her for her money.'

'Good heavens! this girl will drive me mad!' cried Frank. 'What nonsense are you thinking of now? Money! She has not a penny, and you never heard of her in your life.'

'It is not Nelly Rich then?' said Mary, faltering and withdrawing the clasping hands from his arm.

'Nelly Rich! that was all your own invention, and my mother's,' said Frank,— 'not mine. I said she would have suited Laurie. If you chose to make up a story, that was not my fault.'

There was a pause after this, for Mary remembered but too distinctly the conversation about Nelly, and could not acknowledge that the story was of her invention. But she could hold her tongue, and did so steadily, making no remark, which Frank felt was as great an injury to him as if she had enlarged on the subject. He went along under the trees, quickening his pace in his agitation, without much thought of Mary, who had to change her steps two or three times to keep up with him.

'I suppose you have no further curiosity?' he said at length; 'you don't want to know who it really is.'

'Yes, Frank,—when you will tell me,' said Mary, holding her ground.

'You are very provoking,' said her cousin;—'if it were not that I had such need of you! You should not aggravate a poor fellow that throws himself as it were on your assistance;—I will tell you who it is whether you care to hear or no. It is Alice Severn,—Mrs. Severn's daughter, who was Laurie's great friend.'

'Laurie again!' said Mary, amazed,—'Mrs. Severn! Are we never to have an end of Laurie's friends? You told me she had no daughters. You said something about a little girl. Ah, Frank! I am afraid it is some widow coquette that first made a victim of Laurie and now has done the same to you. I knew there was something mysterious about his going away.'

'I wish you would talk of things you understand,' said Frank, indignantly. 'Alice is only sixteen. She is, I believe, the purest, simplest creature that ever lived. As for Laurie, she was a child to him;—he treated her like a child.'

'Sixteen! Of course she is only a child,' said Mary; 'and the daughter of Mrs. Severn the painter! Frank, you must be mad.'

'I think I shall be, unless you help me,' said the young soldier. 'Her mother is furious against me, Mary; and so will my own mother be, I suppose. But what does it matter when we are going to India? We shall be able to live on what we have. She has no expensive tastes, nor have I.'

'You,—no expensive tastes?' cried Mary. 'Oh, Frank! do pause and think. I did not care for Nelly Rich, but this is far worse. Nelly Rich was of no family, but she had money; whereas this girl is——'

'The creature I love best in the world,' said Frank, interrupting her hastily, with a sudden glow upon his face. 'It is of no use speaking. If I have to give up mother, and home, and friends, and all I have in the world, I shall still have Alice,—and Alice means everything. It is because you don't know her. But I tell you there never was any one like her. And, Mary, if you don't stand by us, I will throw up everything else I care for in the world.'

'But not her?' asked his cousin, raising her eyes to his face.

'Never her!' cried the young man. 'Give up my Alice! Not for twenty mothers! I don't mind what people choose to say. We are going to India, and it will not matter to us,—nor your objections, nor mamma's objections, nor anything in the world. She shall go with me if I run away with her. You understand me now?'

'Is she the kind of girl to run away with you?' said Mary, still looking earnestly in his face.

'No,' said Frank, with a little outburst of impatience, 'I wish she were. You may think how unpleasant it is to me to put myself at that woman's feet, and plead as if I were a beggar. And she hates me; but Alice stands fast, bless her! And her mother can refuse her nothing,' he added, with a sudden breath of satisfaction. He was flushed and excited with his story. Mary had never seen him look so manful, so bright, and full of energy. He had made up his mind;—that was something gained, at least.

And then there was another pause. Mary did not know how to reply. Frank was in love, and that was a great, the greatest recommendation in his favour. But this Alice, this creature of sixteen, a girl altogether out of his sphere! It was impossible for his cousin, brought up in the prejudices of her class, not to feel that there must have been some 'artfulness,' some design upon the innocent young Guardsman, some triumphant scheme, to lead away so guileless a member of society; and what if it were the same scheme which had wounded Laurie too, and sent him away with, perhaps, a broken heart! Such were Mary's thoughts as she listened. And what could she do? Make herself a party to this artful plan? Countenance the girl, and help Frank to ruin himself? How could she do it? And there were all the speculations about Nelly Rich which had thus fallen to the ground,—and all her godmother's hopes of the money Frank was to marry! Her mind was full of perplexity. 'I do not see what I can do,' she said, faltering. 'I don't understand it at all. There was first Miss Rich, and we had made up our minds to that; and now, all at once, it turns out not to be Miss Rich, but a girl no one ever heard of. I don't know what to make of it, Frank. How can I stand your friend? You are scarcely one-and-twenty. You don't want a wife at all, that I can see; and going to India too! And a girl of sixteen! I think you are quite unreasonable. As for poor godmamma, I don't know how she is to bear it. I see nothing but folly in it myself, and what can I say?'

Frank made no answer. He turned with her towards the house, from which, some time before, they had heard the sound of the breakfast-bell. The old butler stood at the window with his napkin in his hand, looking anxiously about the flower-garden for Miss Mary, and much puzzled to divine whose was the figure which he saw in the distance by her side. Mary had dropped her cousin's arm, and the two walked onward, side by side, like people who have quarrelled, or between whom, at least, some difficulty has arisen. 'My mother does not get up to breakfast?' Frank had said, and Mary had answered 'No,' and they had gone on again without further communication. But yet Frank was not so cast down as he might have been supposed to be. He was sure of Mary, though Mary was so doubtful of him. When they sat down together to breakfast in the sunshiny quiet of the great brown dining-room, they went over and over the subject again, and yet again. Frank was not aware that he had any skill in description, but, all unawares, he placed before his cousin such a picture of Alice and her curls as touched Mary Westbury's heart. 'If my mother once heard her play, she would never ask another question,' Frank said, in his simplicity; and he confided to Mary more of his troubles in respect to Nelly Rich than he had ever thought to tell. 'It is a sneaking sort of thing for a man to say,' Frank admitted, with a flush on his face, 'but it wasn't all my doing. I declare I thought old Rich meant to offer her to me the first hour I was in the house. I should never have thought of it myself. And I met her to-day, Mary, and told her plainly I was going to India.

She is sharp enough. You may be sure a fellow would never need to make long explanations to her.'

'And did she understand this too?' said Mary, from her judicial seat.

'No, by Jove, I could not tell her that,' said Frank. 'That is the worst of it. They will think it was all made up then, and that Alice and I were laughing at them. They are sure to think that, but it is not true. Such an idea had never come into her innocent head; and as for me, I tried never to look at her, never to speak to her, to think of Nelly only,—like a cur,—for her money,' said Frank, with a novel fervour of self-disgust. 'And she's not a bad sort of girl, I can tell you, Mary. I'd like her to know there was no treachery meant.'

'I am glad you have so much feeling, at least,' said Mary, the Mentor, looking at him with more charitable eyes.

'Oh, feeling!' cried Frank, 'I wish you would not speak of feeling. And then there is her mother. She will consent for Alice's sake; but she hates me. And mamma will go out of her senses, I suppose,' said the young man, disconsolately. He looked so discouraged, so anxious, so boyish, amid all the serious complications he had gathered round him, that it was all Mary Westbury could do to restrain a momentary laugh. And yet there were few cases less laughable when you come to think of it. To be sure, there always remained the question,—a question which every sensible person might ask,—Why was it needful that a young man of one-and-twenty and a girl of sixteen should marry at all? Seven years later would be quite time enough. They had set their hearts upon it; but why should they more than other people have the desire of their hearts? Mary, for her own part, had set her heart repeatedly on things that had not come, and were very unlikely to come to her. And why Frank and his Alice should have their will at once out of hand she could not see. But, after all, it might be the best way of cutting the knot. It was better in her opinion that he should marry any how for love, than in the most favourable way for wealth. And before Frank quitted Renton, Mary had undertaken this all but impossible task.

CHAPTER IV.

WHAT IT COSTS TO HAVE ONE'S WAY.

SPACE forbids the historian to attempt any description of the difficulties which Mary had to encounter in her benevolent undertaking. By Frank's urgent desire,—for his courage had altogether failed him,—nothing was said on the subject till he was gone; and the consequence was a very uncomfortable day, in which even Mrs. Renton perceived that there was something more going on than was revealed to her. 'What are you always talking to Frank about?' she said, pettishly. 'I never turn my head but I find you whispering, or telegraphing, or something. If there is anything I ought to know, let me know it.'

'Wait a little,—only wait a little, dear godmamma,' Mary answered, pleading; and then, when the hero was gone, the tale was told.

'Going to India,—going to be married!' said Mrs. Renton, in her bewilderment; 'but why should he go to India if he marries? Of course he will be provided for if he makes up his mind to that. Or why should he marry if he goes to India?—one thing is bad enough. Is he out of his senses? Fifty thousand pounds will give them, at least, two thousand a-year.'

'But, godmamma, you are making a mistake,' said Mary. 'It is not Miss Rich Frank is going to marry. It is a young lady,—whom he met at Richmont.'

'Not Miss Rich!' said Mrs. Renton. 'Another girl! The boy must be mad to go on making acquaintance with such people. And how much has she?' the mother added, with plaintive submission to a hard fate, folding her patient hands.

Mary, thus driven to the last admission of all, grew quite pale, but made a brave stand for her client. 'Oh, godmamma,' she cried, 'you must not be hard upon him. He is so young; and isn't it better he should marry her because he loves her than because she is rich? She has not a penny, he says.'

When this awful revelation was made, Mrs. Renton was excited to the length of positive passion. Words failed her at first. Her eyes, though they were worn-out eyes, retaining little lustre, flashed fire. Her faded cheeks grew red. She was inarticulate in her rage and indignation. It was Mary who received the first brunt of the onslaught, for encouraging a foolish boy in such nonsense, and for taking it upon her to defend him against all who wished him well. You would have thought it was Mary who had inspired him with this mad fancy, put it in his head, encouraged him in it, urged him to commit it, and compromise himself in the face of the strenuous, steady, invariable opposition of 'all who wished him well.' The poor lady made herself quite ill with indignation, and had to be taken to bed, and comforted with more tonics and arrowroot than ever. She lay there moaning all the evening, refusing to allow poor Mary to read to her, or to perform any of her usual ministrations. If it had not been that Frank had left his boat, having himself returned to Royalborough by the railroad, and thus afforded Mary the opportunity of getting easily across the river, and running all the way to the Cottage to be comforted by her mother for half-an-hour before returning to her charge, I don't know what would have become of her. Mrs. Westbury did not look the sort of woman to seek comfort from, but she was Mary's mother, which makes all the difference, and she had never got over her compunction about her nephews. This trial they were all going through was her doing, and though she sympathised much more with her sister-in-law than with Frank in the present case, she was not without a certain pity for the boy. 'He must be mad,' she said; 'but if it can't be put a stop to, it must be put up with; and your aunt will have got a little used to it by to-morrow.' Thus comforted Mary went back, not without a little wondering comparison in her own mind between the people who could do rash things and have their will, and those who had 'to put up with' everything that might chance to come in their way, and never had it in their power to please themselves. She was a very good girl, full of womanly kindness and charity; but it is not to be supposed that close attendance upon a weariful invalid like her aunt, not ill enough to move any depth of sympathy, but requiring perpetual *pettis soins*, and endless consideration in every detail of life, was a kind of existence to be chosen by a lively girl of twenty. Poor Mary was the scapegoat and ransom for the sins of her family. The three 'Renton boys' were all going away on their own courses, comforting themselves about their mother,—when they thought of her at all,—by the reflection that Mary was with her. They could go away, but Mary could not budge. It was rather hard, when you came to think of it. And that Frank, not three months older than herself, should marry and set out in life, and go blithely off to all the novelty and all the brightness, and no one have any power to stop him; while she stayed at home, making excuses for him, and doing duty for all three! Mary was a comfortable kind of young woman, and went into no hysterics over her fate; neither did she rave to herself about the awful blank of routine and the want of excitement in her life. But she did feel a little envy of Frank, and pity for herself, as she glided across the silvery river in the summer twilight. Doing must be a pleasanter thing than 'putting up with,' even to a philosophical mind.

The next day Mrs. Renton had got a little used to it. She exerted herself to the unusual extent of writing Frank a letter, conjuring him by all his gods to repent ere it was too late, and to return to the paths of common sense and discretion; and when she had done this, she called Mary to her, and asked a hundred questions about 'the girl.' 'Her mother was one of Laurie's great friends,' Mary said, trying to make the best of it.

'All the doubtful people one knows of seem to be Laurie's friends,' said his mother, pathetically. And thus the crisis was over at Renton, for the moment at least.

At Richmont, however, affairs took a much more serious turn when the whole truth was known. Nelly's intimation that Frank was going to India had not very much affected that sanguine household. 'It will bring things to a point,' Mrs. Rich had said to her husband. 'He has done it in some little spirit of independence, not to be obliged to his wife, you know; but if he comes to an understanding with Nelly, we'll make him exchange again.'

'Ah! if he comes to an understanding with Nelly. But she shall never go to India with him,' said the father. 'No young fellow shall blow hot and cold with my daughter. I'd have done with him at once.'

'Nonsense! It has been some little tiff between them,' said the more genial woman. And even Nelly got by degrees to believe that it was not yet finally over. But when the whole truth was whispered at Richmont,—as it soon was by one of the officers who had learned the fact, no one knew how,—the family in general became frantic. Nelly kept her temper outwardly at least, and held her tongue, having some regard for her own dignity; but the father and mother were wild with rage. People whom they had patronised so liberally!—a woman to whom they had just given such a commission! When this thought occurred to them, they exchanged glances. Next day, without saying a word to any one, Mr. and Mrs. Rich went up to town. They bore no external signs of passion to the ordinary eye, but in their hearts they were breathing fire and flame against every Renton, every Severn, every creature even distantly connected with either. There was very little conversation between the two indignant parents as they made their way solemnly to Fitzroy Square. A certain judicial silence, and stern restraint of all the lighter manifestations of feeling, alone marked the importance of their mission. They were shown up to Mrs. Severn's studio by their own request,—having peremptorily refused any such half-way ground as the drawing-room, as if they had come to treat with their equals. The workshop of the woman who was, as it were, in their employment, working to their order, was the more appropriate place.

They found the padrona standing at her work with looks very different from her usual aspect. Something spiritless and worn was in the very attitude of her arm, in the fall of her gown, and dressing of her hair. It was not that she was less neat, less carefully dressed, less busy. But the woman was in such unity with herself, that her unusual despondency communicated itself to every detail about her. She had no heart for Cinderella,—the little loving figure triumphing in its new life,—the sour, elder women standing by who were grudging,—what were they grudging? The child's happiness, or her triumph, or the loss of her? She had not even heart enough to rouse her to the heights of artist-passion, and to work in her own heart into the picture, as doubtless she would yet do, some time when all was over. She stood with her sketches hung round the walls, and the whole room full of this commission of her rich patron,—the commission which made her living quite secure and above the reach of chance, and her mind easy for the year,— but listless, spiritless, mechanical, her heart gone out of her life.

Mrs. Severn was so much pre-occupied that she did not even notice, what at another time she would have been so ready to notice,—the changed tone of the Riches as they came in. Luckily for her own comfort, she had never heard that there was 'anything between' Nelly Rich and Frank Renton. Such a reason for having nothing to say to him would have been very welcome to the padrona. But she could not refuse to have anything to say to him without breaking her child's heart; and, accordingly what did it matter? It was to Alice, not to him, that she had yielded. Therefore, she received very much as a matter of course Mrs. Rich's pretended congratulations. 'We hear that great things have been happening with you,' she said. 'I am sure I had no idea, when Alice was at Richmont, that she was such an advanced young lady. I suppose it was going on then, though we knew nothing about it.'

'I don't know,' said the padrona. 'I cannot give you any information. It is not a pleasant subject to me; but I don't suppose it was going on then.'

'Not a pleasant subject!' cried Mrs. Rich, with not unjustifiable virulence. 'Oh, my dear Mrs. Severn, you must not tell me that. We all know what a mother feels when she has succeeded in securing a charming *parti* like Mr. Frank Renton for her favourite child.'

'Is he so?' said the padrona. 'Indeed, I should not have thought it. But I am not in charity with Mr. Frank Renton. I wish we had never seen him. I am like Cinderella's sisters,' she said, with an attempt at a smile;—'I am spiteful;' and there was a something in the droop and languor of her aspect which began to melt the hearts of the avengers. She looked so unlike herself.

'Nay, nay,' said Mrs. Severn's patron. 'Of course it is a fine thing for you to have your daughter settled so soon. And a fine thing for her too,—a girl without any fortune. Not many men, I can tell you, would have been so rash.'

'Then I wish Mr. Frank Renton had not been so rash,' cried the padrona, with rising spirit. 'I would have thanked him on my knees had he kept away from this house. I cannot see any good in it. Forgive me! I have no right to trouble you with my vexations. I will show you my sketches, which are more to the purpose.'

'Yes,' said Mr. Rich, with hesitation. 'It was principally about them,—we came to speak.'

The padrona, in her unsuspiciousness, became half apologetic. 'I should have written to ask you to come and see them,' she said; 'but this business has put everything else out of my mind;' and she began to collect her drawings in their different stages, and to rouse herself up, and show her work, as became her. The avengers, meanwhile, looked at each other, recruiting their failing courage from each other's eyes.

'Pray don't give yourself any trouble,' said Mr. Rich. 'The fact is, Mrs. Severn,—I am very sorry,—my wife and I have been talking things over, and she,—I,—I mean we,—are not quite sure———. What I would say is, that if you could make a better bargain with any one,—a dealer, perhaps, or any of your private friends,—for these pictures,—why, you know I would not stand in your way.'

'A better bargain!' said the padrona in amaze, not perceiving in the least what he meant; 'but I never should dream of a better bargain. I am painting the pictures for you.'

'Yes; I know there was some understanding of that kind,' said the uneasy millionnaire. 'Some sort of arrangement was proposed,—but, you know, circumstances alter cases. I,—I don't see,—and neither does my wife,—that we can go on with that arrangement now.'

The padrona had been standing by her great portfolio, taking some drawings out of it. She stood there still, motionless, as if she were paralysed. Every tinge of colour left her face; her eyes gazed out at them for one moment blankly, with a sudden pang which made itself somehow dimly apparent, though she did not say a word. It was a cruel blow to her. For a moment she could not speak, or even move, in the extremity of her astonishment. Before the echo of these extraordinary words had died in her ear, Mrs. Severn's rapid mind had run over in a moment all there would be to do in the dreadful year which was coming,—Alice's outfit, and the marriage which was such pain to think of, but which, nevertheless, must be planned and provided for, so that her child should have all due honour. As she stood and gazed at the two faces which were looking at her, it was all she could do to keep down two bitter tears that came to her eyes.

'I thought it was more than an arrangement,' she said; 'perhaps because it was of more importance to me than it was to you. I thought it was a bargain. The price was settled, you know, and everything.'

'Yes, oh yes,' said both together. 'I know there was a great deal said.' 'Mr. Rich was in a buying humour that day,' said the wife. 'But circumstances alter cases,' said the husband. They had done their work more completely than they meant to do it; but yet they were not going to give in.

Mrs. Severn bowed her head. She could not speak. It was the cruellest aggravation of all her other troubles! 'If that is the case,' she said, after a long pause, 'of course I must arrange otherwise;' and then she came to a dead stop, turning over the drawings unconsciously with her agitated hands.

'Oh, you will find no difficulty about it,' said Mr. Rich, rubbing his hands; 'you are so well known. There is Lambert will take as many of your pictures as you can give him, and there is that man in Manchester——'

'Thanks,' said the padrona. 'I shall find a purchaser, I hope.' And then there was a dead silence; and the two avengers felt inclined to drop through the floor and hide themselves. They were not cruel. They had taken no thought of what they were doing, and when they perceived the reality of it, could have bitten out their tongues for saying such words. And yet what were they to do? They could not unsay what they had that moment said.

As for Mrs. Severn, she was too much occupied with her own thoughts to exert herself to set at their ease the dealers of so cruel a blow. But yet, after a while, the instinct of courtesy, which is so strong in some natures, came to the surface. Those two tears which had wanted to come had been reabsorbed somehow, and she gave herself a little shake; and, with a curious smile about her mouth, went forward to the two embarrassed, uncomfortable people. 'Perhaps you will look at the picture all the same, and tell me if you like it,' she said. And then the startled pair, feeling very small and very angry with her for her magnanimity, made a few steps forward, huddled together for mutual support, and gazed in grave silence at Cinderella. She set it in the best light for them, and showed them how much was complete, and how much was still to do. The arrow they had sent at her was still sticking, quivering, in her heart. And she had not time to pluck it out, but she had time to be very civil, and smile upon the discomfited pair. Perhaps she overdid it just a little; but to such a brave spirit, confronting all the world, as it were, and standing alone in the fight, it is difficult to keep a certain glimmer of contempt out of the lofty forgiveness which it awards to its enemies. There was a touch of scorn in the padrona's smile. But when Mr. and Mrs. Rich had crept down-stairs to their carriage, it is impossible to describe the state of downfall in which they found themselves. 'She did not feel it a bit,' said Mrs. Rich, trying to console herself. 'And she has many friends among the dealers,' said the millionnaire, a little ruefully. 'I shouldn't wonder if some fool gave a hundred or two more for the series,—and my idea!' he added, with a certain indignation. And they went home very uncomfortable. He might be free to withdraw from his bargain, according to the letter of the law, but he could not charge his fee-rent for the idea, having rejected the pictures in which it was to be carried out.

When she had seen them safely out, the padrona dropped softly into her big chair, and hid her face in her hands. Alice's outfit, and the wedding, and all the year's expenses, which she had thought safely provided for, and her little triumph in being free of the dealers for once,—they were all gone! It was not such a moving spectacle, perhaps, as if she had been a young girl weeping for her lover. But those two tears that forced themselves out, womanish, against her clasped hands, what concentrated pain was in them! They were more bitter than many a summer torrent out of younger eyes. And then she sprang to her feet, and snatched at her palette, and went to work with flaming cheeks and a headache, and all her old fire in her eyes. She had been listless enough before, but she was not listless now.

When Nelly Rich, however, heard of this wonderful proceeding, their grand house became too hot to hold the unhappy pair. 'Withdraw your commission! for what reason, in heaven's name?' cried Nelly, blazing at them in thunder and lightning. The girl was half crazy with shame and disgust. She brought her father almost to his knees before the day was over, and flew to London, post haste, by herself, in spite of everybody's remonstrances, to make up the matter. 'Papa had gone out of his senses, I suppose,' she said, dissembling her fury, to Mrs. Severn. 'Padrona mia, for the sake of old times, you will not mind? He is so sorry. They were both mad, I suppose.' If Mrs. Severn had followed her first impulse, she would have held by the dealers, who were not liable to such madness; but she was her children's mother, and had the bread and butter to think of, and was not able to afford such luxuries as revenge or pride. So that nobody was the worse for the patron's ill-temper except himself; and two people were the better,—to wit, Nelly and Cinderella, the latter of whom had been undoubtedly languishing under the weight of Mrs. Severn's heavy heart, until this violent pinch of apparent evil fortune came to sting her into life.

As for Nelly, setting her foot into the studio did her good. The smell of the pigments, and the sight of the rubbish about,—all the sketches, and unused bits of canvas, and bursting portfolios, were balm to the impetuous but not ungenerous girl. 'I don't want to see Alice,' she said; 'it was sly of her not to tell me. No, I don't want to see her; but she is very happy, I suppose;' and it was not possible that this could be said without a certain bitterness, considering all that had come and gone.

'Nelly dear, don't speak of it,' said the padrona, who was ignorant of all the complications; and she went and gave the little messenger of consolation a kiss, and suffered herself to shed a tear or two out of her full heart. 'I thought it would have killed me at first,' she said, going back to her work with trembling hands. And the hand that shook so made a dreadful business of Cinderella's white dress, and then the mother put away her tools, and sat down and cried. Nelly had been poor Severn's pupil in the old, old days, and the sight of her brought nothing but softening thoughts to the padrona's mind; and the fountain was opened that she kept so bravely shut. As for Nelly herself, every moment in that room was good for her. She cried too, and washed all her bitterness away in those tears, and turned Frank Renton and all his misdoings courageously out of her imagination. I doubt whether he had ever got so far as her heart.

'I only want you to tell me one thing,' she said, somewhat fiercely, to Alice, who came in, all unconscious, after the tears were dried, glad and wondering. 'Was it going on when you were at Richmont?'

'It?—what?' said simple Alice, and then the child's ready blush covered her face. 'Oh, no, no! It never came on at all; it came into our minds in a moment, when we knew he was going away.'

And Nelly Rich was so magnanimous as to kiss Alice too.

'Tell him I did it,—and that I bear no malice,' she said, with a laugh; and then went away with Miss Hadley, who saw her safely to the railway station, and made the story still more plain to her. The governess thought it strange of Mrs. Rich to permit her daughter to run about alone in this way, but reflected that it might be one of the strange customs of 'those sort of people,' and did her duty by the young lady, putting her under the care of the guard, and keeping an eye on the carriage till the train started. The journey might be slightly indecorous, but it did more good than any tonic in the world.

And so it came about that in September Frank Renton sailed from Southampton to join his regiment, with his young wife,—the only one of the brothers who made anything like a practical conclusion to the little romance of their beginning. Though he had hesitated for some time as to whether he should follow interest or inclination, Frank was not the sort of man, when his choice was made, to care very much what he might tread upon in his way. He would have given no one pain willingly, but to have his way was the most important matter, and he had it accordingly. They were a couple of babies to set forth thus together, to face the world,—one-and-twenty and sixteen! but their very youth kept them from any consciousness of the gravity of the undertaking. They went forth with the daring ignorance of two children, hand in hand. There were several hearts that ached over the parting, and one had almost broke in the effort. And the bride shed a few soft tears, and the bridegroom kissed his hand to the people who stayed behind; and thus the last of the three Rentons carried out his father's will, and launched himself upon the world.

CHAPTER V.

THE FALLING OF THE WATERS.

THE readers of this history must be prepared to pass over an interval of something less than seven years from the end of the last chapter. I allow that it is a most undesirable break, but yet it has been involved from the beginning as a necessity of the narrative.

Nearly seven years had elapsed since Mr. Renton's death at the moment when we again approach Renton Manor. He died in September, and it was the beginning of August when Mrs. Renton received a note from Mr. Ponsonby, the lawyer, announcing his intention of arriving at the Manor the next day. Mrs. Renton had not improved much in health, but she had laid aside her mourning, and wore grey and violet, and pretty caps, once more. Her existence had known very little change during all these years. Now and then the tonics had been changed, and she had substituted for a whole year the Revalenta Arabica for the arrowroot; but the difference was scarcely perceptible except to the maid and the cook, and I believe, on the whole, the arrowroot was found to agree with her best. She had taken her drive almost every day with a feeling that she was doing her duty. 'My dear husband always made such a point of my drive,' she said, plaintively, though for her own part she would have preferred her sofa; and so had lived on, very punctual in taking her medicine, a woman humbly conscious of fulfilling all the duties of her life. Mary Westbury had been generally her companion in these drives; and as she was younger and not so settled in mind, had sometimes, it must be allowed, felt as if life was no better than a leisurely promenade between two rows of hedgerows, sometimes green and sometimes brown. The carriage was very comfortable and the horses were very fat, and there were a great many charming points of view within a radius of fifteen miles round Renton; but still there were moments in which Mary was such an infidel as to wish herself jogging to market in the passing cart, or carrying a basket along the road, or anywhere rather than in that luxurious corner. If anything had happened to make Mrs. Renton 'put down,' as people say, her carriage, she would have regarded it as a calamity altogether immeasurable; but I think that both she and her niece would have felt a burden taken off their minds. She would have been left at peace on her sofa, and Mary could have taken needful exercise in her own way. But such a blessing in disguise was beyond praying for. Mr. Renton, though he had been so hard upon his sons, had provided very tenderly for his wife's comfort.

Renton had been hers for these seven years, and had been kept precisely as it was when it was the home of the whole family,—not a servant dismissed nor a change made; and thus the height of comfort had been secured. Mary, too, was very comfortable,—no young woman could be more so. She had a maid of her own, which would have been an impossible luxury at home, and a liberal allowance for her dress, and a fire in her room, if she chose, from October to May, or indeed all the year through, if such was her pleasure; and the freedom of various libraries, and an excellent piano, and any amount of worsted work she chose. And then the drive every afternoon, wet and dry, 'so that she has the air and the change, when we poor people, who have no carriage, must stay indoors,' Mrs. Westbury said when she described her daughter's happiness. And this felicity had gone on for nearly seven years.

'I wonder what Mr. Ponsonby wants,' said Mrs. Renton. 'He might have come without any intimation. I am sure he generally does. Why he should send word like this, as if he had some news to bring, I cannot conceive. I do hope it is nothing about the boys.'

'It cannot be anything about them,' said Mary. 'Consider, godmamma, you had a letter from Ben just the other day, and Frank and Alice wrote by the last mail.'

'That is all very true,' said Mrs. Renton; 'but how can I tell that they may not have telegraphed or something? And then there is Laurie always wandering all over the world. He may have gone off, as he did the first time, without letting any one know.'

'But he would never have dreamed of sending Mr. Ponsonby to tell you,' said Mary; 'he would have written direct. Laurie is the best correspondent of them all.'

'Or he may be going to be married,' said Mrs. Renton,—'he or Ben. By the way, he says something about Ben; but all those business people write such bad hands. Perhaps you can make it out. I am sure it is too much for me.'

After this little introduction, Mary took the lawyer's letter with some slight tremulousness. She was nearly seven-and-twenty by this time, and ought, she said to herself, to have been quite steady about such matters. Of course some day Ben would marry, and so long as it was any one who would make him happy she could only be glad. Many a wandering thought about Millicent Tracy had come into her mind. Had she been faithful to him? Had there been any intercourse between them? Had he kept steadfast to his imagination of her for all these years? For it was only an imagination, as Mary felt sure. Every letter that came from Ben had caused her a certain tremor,—not, as she said to herself, that it would make any difference to her; but if he were to bind himself to a woman unworthy of him! And now that he was coming back so soon, it was with a thrill of more intense expectation than usual that she took Mr. Ponsonby's letter in her hand. But there was nothing about marrying or giving in marriage in that sober epistle. It intimated to Mrs. Renton, in the first place, that the time specified in her husband's will had nearly expired; that he had received a letter from her son Ben, informing him that he intended to meet him at the Manor, along with the other members of the family, on the 15th of September; and that, accordingly, Mr. Ponsonby was coming to Renton next day to go over the property with the bailiff, and see with his own eyes the condition in which everything was, that there might be no delay, when the time came, in making everything over to the heir. All that Mrs. Renton had made of this very distinct letter was the fact that the lawyer was to pay her a visit, and that there was something about Ben. But indeed Mr. Ponsonby did not write a legible hand.

'Then it is just what Ben told us about coming home,' said Mrs. Renton, 'though he was not so particular to me in naming the day. He said the beginning of September, if you recollect, Mary; and Frank and his wife are coming by the next mail. I am afraid the children will make a dreadful commotion in the house, and altogether it will be so odd to see Renton full of people again. Of course, Laurie is coming, too. I don't know what I shall do with them all. They can't expect me to have parties and that sort of thing for them, Mary, in my state of health?'

'No, dear godmamma,' said Mary, soothingly, 'they will not expect anything of the kind; and you will never think of the trouble when you have all the boys at home. Fancy Frank having boys of his own!' she cried, with a little laugh. The choice lay between laughing and crying, and the first was certainly the best.

'I hope his wife has kept up her practice,' said Mrs. Renton, still with a cloud on her brow, 'since that was what he married her for.'

'Godmamma!' cried Mary, with consternation.

'Well, my dear, I don't know what else she had to recommend her. No family, nor connexions; not a penny,—not even expectations! If it was not for her music, what was it for? And so many women give up practice when they marry. I always forget,—is it three or four children they have?'

'Two, godmamma,' said Mary, gently; 'don't you remember the poor, dear, little baby died?'

'Well, it is quite enough,' said Mrs. Renton; 'with nothing but their pay to depend upon. And there will be a black nurse, you may be sure, driving the servants out of their senses. But if she has kept up her practice, it will be an amusement for the boys. And things might have been worse. There might have been three families instead of one, you know, Mary; and then I think I should certainly have run away.'

'Yes,—perhaps it is selfish,' said Mary; 'but I am glad, too, that they are not all married. It will be more like old times.'

'Selfish!' said Mrs. Renton. 'I can't see how it can be selfish. Of course Ben will have to marry some time or other, for the sake of the property. But I never can make out why young men marry, for my part. Haven't they everything that heart can desire? and no care, and much more petted and taken notice of in society than if they were dragging a wife about with them everywhere? A girl is quite different. She has everything to gain, you see. I often wondered whether I have been doing my duty by you, Mary, keeping you out of the way of a good establishment in life.'

'Pray don't speak so, godmamma,' said Mary, with a blush of indignation; 'not to me at least.'

'But I do, my dear. And I am sure no one ever deserved to be comfortably settled better than you do. However, I have always found, in my experience,' said Mrs. Renton, with a profound look of wisdom, 'that when these things are coming they come, however quietly you may be living; and, if they are not to come, they don't, however much you may go into society. Look at Jane Sutton, who never was seen out of her father's house, and now she's Lady Egmont! I suppose we must expect Mr. Ponsonby to lunch.'

'I should think he would come early,' said Mary, with a smile; and, as it was Mrs. Renton's hour for taking something, she went away to tell the housekeeper of the guest. And then she made a little tour of the house; peeping into the rooms, in some of which preparations had already begun. The west wing, in which the 'boys' rooms' were, was all in commotion,— carpets taken up, women with pails and brooms in every corner. The only one as yet untouched was the little sitting-room, or dressing-room, attached to Ben's chamber, where his old treasures were still hanging about,—his books and his pictures, and all his knicknacks. Into this oasis Mary strayed, with a strange thrill of expectation creeping over her. Seven years! what a slice it was out of a life; and how much had happened to the others and how little to herself! Mary felt as if she had done nothing but drive all these years in that most comfortable of family coaches, with her aunt by her side, and a bottle of medicine in the pocket of the carriage. And now they were all coming back! To what? What change should she find in them? and ah! what changes would they find in her? Ben must be thirty-two by this time; and Mary was seven-and-twenty, which, for a woman, is about twenty years older, as all the world knows!

As for 'the Frank Rentons,' they were not to be placed in the west wing at all, but in a suite of rooms over the great doorway, the guest-chambers of the house, as became their dignity as married people with children and nurses to be accommodated. How funny that was! Frank, who had always been the youngest in every way, whom they all,—even Mary herself in a manner,— had bullied and domineered over,—and here had he attained a point of social dignity to which none of the others had yet approached! Mary laughed to herself, and then she dried her eyes. It was an agitating crisis altogether, to which she looked forward with the strangest mixture of feelings. Laurie, it was true, had come home long since; and came to the Manor now and then, and had not drifted out of knowledge. But, then, one always knew exactly how Laurie would be, and it did not matter if he were in London or at the end of the world, so far as that went; but Ben—— And to think everything was going to be settled, and they were all coming home!

Mr. Ponsonby arrived next day; not, as they expected, to luncheon, but in the evening. He was an old friend of the family, and Mr. Renton, as people say, had no secrets from him. But that was a figure of speech, for the Ponsonbys had managed the Rentons' affairs for generations, and there were no secrets to keep. 'I shall want the whole day for what I have to do,' he told Mary when he arrived; 'so I thought it best to come overnight.' And he dined with the two ladies, and did his best to make himself agreeable. His coming and his talk were the most tangible sign that they had yet had that their long vigil was over, and that the tide of life was about to flow back to them. He spoke in a very guarded way, betraying nothing of the secret he had kept those seven years; but when Mrs. Renton spoke of one thing and another which she wanted to have done, Mr. Ponsonby made answers which infinitely piqued Mary's curiosity. 'We must see what the will says about it,' said the lawyer. 'It is not worth while doing anything now till he is here to decide for himself. All that is the heir's business, not mine.'

'Do you mean Ben?' said Mrs. Renton; for even she was moved to a little surprise.

'I cannot tell whom I mean until the will is read,' he said; 'but, of course, whoever is the heir will be but too happy to do what you wish, my dear Mrs. Renton. It must be a great pleasure to you to have all your boys at home.'

'Ye-es,' said Mrs. Renton; 'but when one does not know whether they are coming to disappointment or to satisfaction! If they should have had to travel all this way for nothing, what a thing it would be,—if it were only for the expense!'

'But I trust it will be satisfaction this time, and not disappointment,' said the lawyer. 'I am heartily glad, for my part, that the seven years are over. I hear the boys have all done so well, which is immensely to their credit, and, of course, is just what their excellent father meant.'

'I never could think what he meant,' said Mrs. Renton. 'Lydia always says it was her fault; but he was not a man to follow anybody's opinion but his own. As for doing well, I am not so sure about that. Ben has become a railway man;—think of that, Mr. Ponsonby! I never even approved of the railroad myself. I don't see what use there is for so much hurry. I am sure I went a great deal oftener to town when we used to drive our own horses than now that there is a railway close to the gates. But he has pleased himself, which is always something. And Laurie has pleased himself, too. He paints very pretty pictures sometimes; but I don't believe he will ever earn enough to keep him in gloves. And as for Frank,—a poor soldier with nothing but his pay and a family of little children! It is very different from what I had once hoped.'

'But probably this is all over now,' said Mr. Ponsonby,—'or at least, we have every reason to believe so; and in the meantime they have had their struggles, and know what they are capable of. Let us hope, my dear madam, that everything will prove to have been for the best.'

'I don't doubt that everything is for the best,' Mrs. Renton answered in plaintive tones. And then Mr. Ponsonby was left to his wine in the great old dining-room, which he had not been in since that dismal day when he read the will,—or rather the preface of the will,—to the startled family. It was a bright room enough in the morning when the sunshine came in, or on winter nights when the fire sparkled and glimmered in the wainscot; but it was very sombre in the dimness of a summer night, with one lamp on the table and the windows open, admitting the night with all its ghosts of sound and profound soft glooms. The family solicitor was not an imaginative man, and yet he could not help feeling that his old friend might come in any moment through the curtains, which hung half over the open window, and dictate to him some new condition in the will which had already wrought so much mischief. 'Not a word more,' Mr. Ponsonby caught himself saying; and then he roused up and went to Mary in the drawing-room, where she was seated alone in much the same magical half-darkness as that he had left.

'I suppose it is the instinct of a Londoner,' he said; 'but I declare I don't think this is safe. Sitting with windows open to the lawn, all alone at this hour! Suppose some one should walk in upon you before you had time to give an alarm?'

'Who could walk in upon me?' said Mary, laughing. 'We are at Renton, you know, and not in Harley Street.'

'Sure enough,' said the townsman. 'No, thanks; I prefer to face that window. Let me not be approached from behind; let me see what is coming, at least.'

'How odd to think of such a thing!' said Mary. 'I sit here every evening after godmamma has gone to bed, and one cannot live unless all the windows are open. But oh, Mr. Ponsonby, do talk to me a little! Do you think,—do you really think,—that now, at last, things will be comfortable for the boys?'

'Let us hope so,' said the man of law, arranging himself comfortably in an easy-chair. 'I suppose Mrs. Renton has gone to bed. Let us hope so, at least.'

'Hope!' cried eager Mary,—'of course we all hope; but what do you think?'

'My dear, I can't tell you what I don't know, and I must not tell you what I do know,' said Mr. Ponsonby. 'Do you never have any change from Renton? It is very fine air; but I don't think it is exhilarating for young people. Do you ever go out?'

'We drive every day,' said Mary, with the faintest little grimace; and then she looked at her old friend, and permitted herself the relief of a laugh. 'It is dismal sometimes,' she said; 'but when the boys are back I shall be free again, and go home.'

Mr. Ponsonby looked at her in silence as she spoke. 'Home' was a cottage, instead of a great house; but otherwise, in the eyes of the man accustomed to the world, there was not much difference between the one widow's house and the other. 'How do these women live?' he said to himself. When the boys came home there might be a little movement, perhaps, and feeling of life about the old place,—and then she would go home! 'That is just the time you ought to stay, I think, and see if they cannot make it a little more amusing for you,' he said. 'Do you never ride now?'

'I have no one to ride with me. I could not go out alone, you know,' Mary answered, without raising her eyes.

'Well, I am not much of a man to ride with a young lady, but you shall come out with me to-morrow and go over the estate,—if there is anything you can ride in the stables. It will do you good. I must see that everything is in order for the heir. And you will not mind giving up the drive,—not for one day,— for the sake of an old friend?' said the lawyer. 'Good Lord! there's a fellow coming in at the window, as I said. Ring the bell, my dear! Quick, and leave the rest to me!'

'Why, it is Laurie!' cried Mary, springing up, as Mr. Ponsonby seized the gilded stick which supported a little screen, and brandished it in the face of the new-comer. 'That is just his way, frightening people out of their wits. Come in quickly, Laurie, if it is you, and not your ghost.'

'It is not my ghost,' said the figure at the window, advancing to shake hands with Mr. Ponsonby, who was still a little excited. 'A ghost was never so dusty nor so thirsty. I have walked down from town all the way, to get a breath of air, and very much mystified I was to see a man in the dining-room from the end of the avenue as I came along. I thought at first it must be Ben.'

'So there was some one about!' said Mr. Ponsonby; 'that explains my sensation. I had just been giving your cousin a lecture upon sitting alone with the windows open. Yes, Laurie, my boy, here I am, come to look over the ground for the last time, before it is given up to the heir.'

'Ben will not be hard upon you,' said Laurie, with a laugh; but as he spoke he looked fixedly at the solicitor, hoping,—which was like Laurie,—to beguile that astute practitioner into self-betrayal.

'I don't know any thing about Ben,' he answered, smiling at the simple artifice; 'but I know I must set my affairs in order, and be prepared to give up my trust. I want Mary to go with me over the estate. She is moping and pale, and a brisk canter will do her good. Will you see if there is anything she can ride?'

And then there ensued a little consultation as to whether Fairy was up to it. Fairy was a pet pony, as old as the hills, who had been eating herself into a plethoric condition for years; but Mary, who was not a very bold horsewoman, believed in the venerable animal, as did every soul about Renton. 'She's hold in years, but she's young at 'art, Miss; she'll carry you like a bird,' was the coachman's opinion when he was called into the consultation. And then Laurie had a vast tankard brought to him, and refreshed himself after his long walk. When Mr. Ponsonby retired, the cousins stepped out again on to the lawn, and Mary looked on and talked while Laurie had his cigar. The moon, which was half over and late of rising, began to lighten slowly upwards, shining upon the river far below, while they were still left in darkness on the higher bank. 'It is so strange to think we are all on the brink of a new life,' Mary said, as she gazed down through an opening in the trees upon that silvery gleam, which was framed in by the dark, rustling branches. 'Are we?' said Laurie, with a kind of echo in his voice. Somehow he had taken his life awry, by the wrong corner, and there did not seem vigour enough left in him to care for a new beginning,—at least for himself.

'Laurie,' she said, encouraged by the darkness. He had thrown himself down in a garden-chair, and was visible only as a shadow, with a red point of cigar indicating his face; while she stood leaning on one of the lower branches of the lime-tree which framed in that glimpse of the light below. Their voices had the softened, mysterious sound which such a moment gives, and as neither of them was happy enough to draw new delight out of the influence of the night, both of them, by natural necessity, grew a little sad. 'Laurie,' Mary said, and faltered. 'Sometimes I think I should like to know a little about you. I do know something about the others,—even Ben,—but you have always been a mystery to me since you first went away.'

'I don't think I am much of a mystery,' said Laurie, not moving from his chair.

'But you are a mystery,' Mary repeated, with a little eagerness. 'I don't know what has come to you,—whether it is love, or whether it is loss,—don't be angry, Laurie.'

'It might be love and loss too,' he said, with a little laugh, which was not cheerful, and then he rose and tossed away his cigar. 'What if I were to say you were a mystery, too?' he continued, not knowing how Mary's cheeks burned in the darkness. 'We all are, I suppose; and my poor old father that meant to do so well for us, and tossed us all abroad to scramble anyhow for life,—what do you say to that for a mystery, Mary? and here is the moment coming to prove which of us is preferred and which condemned. I am the poor fellow with one talent, who laid it up in the napkin. If he had not been so mean as to abuse his master, I think I should have sympathised with that poor wretch.'

'I cannot say I sympathise with him,' cried Mary, woman-like. 'To be able to do, and not to do, that is what I cannot understand. But you have not hid your talent in a napkin, Laurie. I wish you had a better opinion of yourself.'

Upon which Laurie laughed, and drew her hand through his arm, and the two strayed together, silent, down under the shadow of the trees towards the opening which looked on the river. The moon creeping higher every moment, began to thread through the bewildering maze of branches with lines and links of silver; and there was always that one brilliant spot in the midst of the river, far below them, shining like burnished silver, scarcely dimpling under the moonbeams, which seemed to swell as well as glorify the rather scanty water. Their hearts were full of wistfulness and dreams. The world lay all as dark before them as those rustling, breathing woods, with, for one, a brightness in the future which might or might not,—most probably should not,—ever be attained; and for the other, only some fanciful, silvery thread twining through the sombre life. They paused, arm-in-arm, by that beech-tree at the corner where Ben and Mary had paused when he was last at home, and where he had shot that arrow at her,—as she said to herself,— of which she could still feel the point. But Laurie was very different from Ben. No spark of emotion went from one soul to the other as they stood so close and so kindly together. They were the parallel lines that never meet,— each thinking their own thoughts, each with a sigh that was not all pain, contemplating the well-known road behind them, the invisible path before;—and all the world around lying dark and light, stirring softly, breathing softly, in the long speechless vigil which we call night.

Next day Mr. Ponsonby went over the home-farm, and all the neighbouring land, inspecting everything, looking to farms, farm-buildings, drainage, timber,—all the necessities of the estate. Mary rode by his side on Fairy, who verified the coachman's verdict, and carried her mistress like a bird,—at least as nearly like a bird as Mary wished. Laurie had gone back to town that morning by the train. When his cousin returned to luncheon, freshed and roused by her ride, it seemed to her almost as if the new life had already begun. The work-people who had been sent for from town had arrived with a van full of upholstery,—bales of fresh, pretty chintz for 'the boys' rooms,' and new furniture for the extempore nursery. An air of movement was diffused about the whole house. The flood which had swept over Renton, almost engulfing the peace of the family, was almost over,—the waters were going down,—the household ark standing fast, and the saved ones beginning to appear at the long-closed windows. Such were Mary's feelings as she went with her aunt for that inevitable drive. To-day the hedgerows were not so monotonous, the dust less stifling; and when they met Mr. Ponsonby on his cob, with the bailiff in attendance, the returning life rose into a sparkle and glow in Mary's face. 'Her ride has done her no end of good,' Mr. Ponsonby cried, waving his hand as he rode past. 'Good?' said Mrs. Renton: 'was there anything the matter with you, Mary? I am sure, if there is any good in riding, I wonder Dr. Mixton has never recommended it to me.' And then the two drove on, as they had been driving, Mary thought, all these seven long years.

CHAPTER VI.

THE RAVEN.

SOME days after Mr. Ponsonby's visit, Mary Westbury saw from her room, where she happened to be sitting, a carriage drive up the avenue. It was only about twelve o'clock, an unusual hour for visitors; and the carriage was of the order known as a fly, with just such a white horse, and coachman in white cotton gloves, as had made an important feature in the landscape to Ben Renton seven years before in Guildford Street, Manchester Square; but there was not, of course, any connexion in Mary's mind between such a vehicle and her cousin's brief romance. She watched it, with a little surprise, as it came up. Who could it be? There was somehow, a greater than ordinary attempt to look like a private carriage about this particular vehicle, with, as might have been expected, a failure still more marked. And flys of any description were not well known at Renton. The lodge-keeper had looked at it disdainfully when she opened the gate; and the butler, who was standing at the door, received the card of the visitors with a certain mixture of condescension and contempt. 'For Miss Westbury,' he said, giving it to a passing maid to carry up-stairs, and only deigning, after an interval, to show the visitors into the drawing-room. The card which was brought to Mary had a very deep black border, and the name of Mrs. Henry Rich printed in the little square of white. Who was Mrs. Henry Rich? There had been very little intercourse between the Riches and the Rentons since Frank's marriage; but Mary recollected with an effort, when she turned her mind that way, that one of the sons had died some time before, and that he turned out to have been married, and to have left an unknown widow to be provided for after he died. These facts came quite dimly to her mind as she pondered the name. But she had never heard who the widow was, and could not think what a stranger in such circumstances could want with her. 'I don't know them well enough to do her any good,' Mary said to herself. The border was so black, and the fly had impressed her with such a feeling of poverty,—wrongly, to be sure, for of course had Mrs. Henry Rich possessed a dozen carriages she could scarcely have brought them with her to Cookesley,—that the idea of a weeping widow seeking something very like charity, was suggested to Mary by the name, and the deep mourning, and the hour of the visit. Civility demanded of her that she should see this unexpected visitor. 'But I must tell her we see very little of them, and that I can do nothing,' Mary said to herself as she went down-stairs. She was dressed in one of her fresh, pretty muslins, pink and white, with all the pretty, crisp bits of lace and bows of ribbon that makes up that toilette *fraîche et simple*, which is one of the greatest triumphs of millinery, and next to impossible to any but the rich. And a pleasant figure to behold was

Mary amid the sunshine, in the calm of the stately, silent house which was so familiar to her, and in which her movements were never without a certain grace. The most awkward being in the world has an advantage in her own house over any new-comer. And Mary was never awkward. The worst that could be said of her was that she was in no way remarkable. You could not specially distinguish her among a crowd as 'that girl with the bright eyes,' or 'with that lovely complexion,' or 'with the fine figure.' Her eyes were very nice, and so was her colour, and so was her form; but, as she herself said, her hair was the same colour as everybody else's; she was just the same height as other people; her hands and feet the same size; her waist the same measure round. 'I have never any difficulty about my things,' Mary would say, half laughing, half annoyed; 'everybody's things fit me;' and though she had preserved a great deal of the first fresh bloom of youth, still it was a fact quite known and acknowledged by her that the early morning and the dews were over with her. Such was the pleasant household figure, full of everything that makes a woman sweet to her own people, and yet not beautiful, which went softly into the great Renton drawing-room, in the morning sunshine, to see her visitor, not having the least fear of the stranger, or anything but pity, and a regretful certainty that her own ministrations, which she supposed were going to be appealed to, could be of no use.

Mary went in so softly that she surprised the ladies,—for there were two of them,—in an investigation into some handsome cabinets which were in the room, and which, indeed, were perfectly legitimate objects of curiosity. But to be discovered in the midst of their researches discomposed the strangers. They stood still for a moment between her and the window,—two tall, sombre, black figures,—draped from head to foot in the heaviest mourning. They had their backs to the light, and Mary could not for the moment distinguish their faces. She went forward with her soft smile and bow; and then she made a bewildered, involuntary pause. It was many, many years since she had seen that face, and she could not remember whose it was; but yet it struck her, even in her ignorance, a curious paralysing blow. It was the kind of blow said to be given by that mysterious monster of the seas, which the great French novelist has introduced into literature. It jarred her all over, and yet seemed to numb and take all power from her. 'Mrs. Rich?' she faltered, with a wonderful mingling of recollection and ignorance; and then stood still, too much startled to say more.

'Dearest Mary, have you forgotten me altogether?' said the youngest of the two ladies, coming up to her with both hands outstretched. Still Mary did not remember whose face it was, and yet she grew faint and sick. The tall figure towered over her middle-sized head; the lovely blue eyes looked appealing into her heart. 'Don't you remember Millicent?' said the sweet voice; and then her reluctant hand was taken, and those softest rose-lips touched her cheek. Mary was glad to point to a chair, and shelter her own weakness upon one beside it. 'It is so unexpected,' she said, making a feeble apology for her consternation; and then Mrs. Tracy came and shook hands with her, and they all sat down in a little circle, poor Mary feeling the room go round and round with her, and all her courage fail.

'You did not know me under my changed name,' said Millicent; 'and I am so changed, dear Mary, and you are exactly as you were,—you are not a day older;—that is the difference between living such a quiet life and being out in the world.'

'I should have known you anywhere, my dear,' said Mrs. Tracy, coming a little closer to Mary's chair.

'That is very strange,' said Mary, recovering herself, 'for I think I only saw you once. But I am very much surprised. Millicent, was it you that married Mr. Henry Rich?'

'Who else could it be?' said Millicent, slowly shaking her head with a soft pity for herself, and then she pressed her handkerchief lightly to her eyes. She was dressed in profound black, in what it is common to call the most hideous of garbs—a widow's mourning dress. Her bonnet was of crape, with a veil attached to it, which was thrown back, showing the lovely face, just surrounded by a single rim of white. Though it goes against all ordinary canons of taste to say so, I am obliged to add that her melancholy robes were very becoming to Millicent, as indeed they are to most women. Her dazzling whiteness of complexion, the soft rose-flush that went and came, the heavenly blue of her eyes, came forth with double force from the sombre background. Poor Mary was overwhelmed by her beauty, her quiet consciousness of it, her patronage, and tone of kindness. And to come here now, at such a moment, when the world was about to begin again! It was so much her natural instinct to be courteous, that she could not make any demonstration to the contrary, but her manner, in spite of herself, grew colder and colder. The only comfort in the whole matter was that Mrs. Renton had not yet come down-stairs.

'Her happiness lasted but a very short time,' said Mrs. Tracy, taking up her parable; 'such a young man, too! But my poor dear child has been very badly used. It was not only that; he died just when he ought to have been making some provision for her.'

'Oh, mamma dear, that was not poor Harry's fault!'

'But we found out afterwards,' continued Mrs. Tracy, 'that he had not anything like what he had given himself out to have. He had squandered his money in speculation,—that was the truth; and now his family, instead of appreciating the position of a poor young creature thus deprived of her natural protector——'

'Oh, please,' said Mary, interrupting her; 'I know the Riches a little, and I'd rather not hear anything about their affairs.'

'I am speaking of our affairs, my dear,' said Mrs. Tracy, solemnly; 'of Millicent's affairs; for, alas! I can scarcely say I have any of my own. Since my poor boy died, seven years ago, I have not cared much what happened,—to myself.'

'Poor mamma worries about me more than she ought,' said Millicent. 'But we do not come to trouble you about that, dear Mary. How nice you look in your pretty muslin! I wonder if I shall ever wear anything pretty again. I feel such an old woman in those hideous caps. Don't I look like a perfect ghost?'

'I think you look more beautiful than usual,' said Mary, with a certain spitefulness. She intended no compliment. It was rather a reproach she meant, as if she had said, 'You have no right to be beautiful. Why shouldn't you look a perfect ghost like other people?' It was sharply said, not without a touch of bitterness, though it sounded pleasantly enough; and Millicent shook back her veil a little further, and laid her fingers caressingly upon Mary's hand.

'Ah, it is you who are partial!' she said, while Mary boiled with secret wrath. 'But tell me about Thornycroft, and if it is still kept up; and our old Gorgon, you know, and all the people. There was that poor Mr. Thorny, too,' said Millicent, with a little laugh; 'tell me about them all.'

'Mr. Thorny died,—as you must have heard,' said Mary; 'and it was your doing, everybody said; and then poor Miss Thorny gave up. I wonder you like to think of it. It might have been going on like old times but for you——'

'Could I help it?' said Millicent, with a little shrug of her shoulders. 'If a man is a fool, is it my fault? You must know by this time, Mary, as well as I do, what fools they will make of themselves; but it is too bad to call it our fault.'

'I don't know anything about it,' said Mary, fiercely, and then there was a pause.

'This is such a lovely place,' said Mrs. Tracy; 'we have heard so much about it. We used to know your cousin, Mr. Benedict Renton, Miss Westbury,—at one time. I suppose he is still abroad?'

'Yes, he is still abroad.'

'What a sad thing for him, with his prospects! It must have upset all your calculations. But the time is up now, is it not?' Mrs. Tracy said, with her most ingratiating smile.

Mary perceived in a moment what was their object, and hoping it might be but a voyage of inquiry, shut up all avenues of intelligence in her, and faced the inquisitor with a countenance blank of all meaning—or so at least she thought. 'What time is up?' she said.

'Oh, the time,' cried Millicent, breaking in impatiently,—'the time, you know, for the will. As if you did not know all about it! Oh, you need not be afraid to trust us. Ben Renton was not so careful; he told me everything about it. I must tell you that we saw a great deal of Ben at one time,' Millicent added, with one of her vain looks. Mary says it might have been called an arch look by a more favourable critic. 'He was, in short, you know, a little mad—but you will say that was my fault.'

'I have no more to do with my cousin's private affairs than I have with Mr. Rich's,' said Mary; 'indeed, I wish you would not tell me. My cousin is not a man to like to have his affairs talked about. I would rather not hear any more.'

'Miss Westbury is quite right, Millicent,' said Mrs. Tracy, 'and shows a great deal of delicacy. She is always such a thoughtless child, my dear. She never stops to think what she is going to say. The harm it has done her, too, if she could only see it! Millicent, my darling, if you would but learn some of Miss Westbury's discretion! But it will be pleasant for you to have your cousins home again, I am sure.'

To this artful question Mary gave no answer at all. Indignation began to strengthen her. She sat still, with an air which any well-bred woman knows how to assume when necessary,—an air of polite submission to whatever an unwelcome visitor may choose to say. It neither implies assent nor approbation, but,—it is not worth while to contradict you. Such was the expression on Mary's face.

'Ah, mamma, Mary has not such a warm heart for old friends as I have,' said Millicent at last. 'I have been raving about coming to see her for weeks back, but she does not care to see me. She is indifferent to her old friends.'

'Were we ever old friends?' said Mary. 'I don't remember. You were older than I was. I thought you were very pretty, as everybody did, but——'

'But you did not like me. Oh, I am used to that from women,' said Millicent, with a mocking laugh; and she actually rose to her feet to go away.

And the colour rushed into Mary's face. Used to that from women! because of her beauty, which transcended theirs! The ordinary reader will think it was a self-evident proposition, but Mary was of a different opinion, being thus directly and personally accused.

'I don't know about women,' she said, indignantly; 'but I have never had any occasion,—to be jealous of you.' This was said with a fierceness which Mary never could have attained to had it been simply true. 'I admire you very much,' she added, with a little vehemence. 'I did so at school; but that does not alter the truth. We were never great friends.'

'Well, it is kind of you to put me in mind of that,' said Millicent. 'Mamma, come. You see it is as I told you. We shall find no nice neighbours at Renton. It is best to go away.'

The word 'neighbours' made Mary start, and she had not time to realise that she was about to get rid of them, when the door was suddenly pushed open, and Mrs. Renton's maid appeared with her shawls, and her cushions, and her knitting. 'Mrs. Renton is coming down immediately,' said the woman; and on this, to Mary's bewilderment, her visitors sat down again. She was driven to her wits' end. To leave them to encounter poor Mrs. Renton was like bringing the lamb to an interview with the wolf.

'May I ask you to come to the library?' she said, hurriedly. 'My aunt is a great invalid, and sees no visitors. Pray forgive me for asking you;—this way,' and rushed to the door before them. But the fates were against poor Mary on that unfortunate day.

'We have made quite a visitation already,' said Mrs. Tracy, and got up again to shake hands. As for Millicent, though she had been so angry, she took Mary's two hands again; and, stooping over her, gave her another kiss. And all these operations took time, and, before they had made any progress towards their departure, Mrs. Renton came in, and received with some astonishment the curtsies and salutations of the unknown guests.

'Pray don't hurry away because I have come. I am always so glad when Mary has her friends to see her,' Mrs. Renton said, with the sweetest amiability; 'do sit down, pray.' The mother and daughter waited for no second invitation. They put themselves on either side of Mrs. Renton, as they had done off Mary; and thus a kind of introduction had to be performed most unwillingly by the victim, who felt that her cause was lost.

'Mrs. Rich!' said the lady of the house, gathering up her wools,—'that must be a relation of the Riches of Richmont. Oh, yes; we know them very well,— that is, they are very good sort of people, I am sure. When my son Frank was at Royalborough, he used to go to see them. All the officers do, I believe; and he made me call. Oh, yes, of course, I understand,—the son who died. Poor thing! your daughter is a very young widow.' This was aside to Mrs. Tracy, who had already volunteered to arrange the cushions in Mrs. Renton's chair.

'Not much more than a child,' said that astute mother; 'and left so poorly off, after all! You may suppose, Mrs. Renton, if I had not thought it would be a very good marriage in point of money, I should never have sacrificed my child to the son of a man in the City. I would rather have starved. And then it turned out he had not half what he was supposed to have. People that do those sort of things should be punished,' Mrs. Tracy said, with fire in her eye.

'Indeed, that is my opinion,' said Mrs. Renton; 'but I always thought the Riches were rolling in money.' And then she made a little internal reflection that, perhaps, on the whole, Frank had not done so very much amiss.

'So we thought,' said Mrs. Tracy, confidentially; 'or rather, so I thought, for my poor child is as innocent as a baby. But poor Harry had speculated, I believe, or done something with his money; and his father is as hard,—oh, as hard—— If I could but see justice done to my Millicent, I care for nothing more.'

'And, dear me, we had thought they were such liberal kind of people!' said Mrs. Renton, thinking more and more that Frank, on the whole—— 'And your daughter is so very prepossessing,' she added, in a lower tone. 'Of course they knew all about it,—before——'

'That is just it,' said Mrs. Tracy; 'the marriage took place abroad, and we were both so ignorant of business, and I fear the settlements were not quite *en règle*; I am so foolish about business; all I trust to is the heart.'

'Dear, dear, what a sad thing! But I should always have looked over the settlements,' said Mrs. Renton, who knew as much about it as her lap-dog, shaking her head and looking very wise. Millicent had pretended to talk to Mary while this was going on, but principally had employed herself in gazing round the room, noting all its special features. Furnished all anew, in amber satin, it would look very well, she thought; and, oh, what a comfort to have such a home, after all the wanderings of her life! And then she wondered what the house was like in Berkeley Square. Poor, dear Ben! what a surprise it would be to him to find that she was established at the Willows! She wondered whether he would be very angry about her marriage, or whether he would think, as a great many men did, that a young widow was very interesting; and how long a time it would be before they had made up their quarrels and he was at her feet again! These questions were so full of interest that Mary's taciturn manner did not trouble her. 'I daresay she would like to have him herself,' Millicent said; and the desire seemed so natural that her respect for Mary rather increased than otherwise. If she had let such a prize slip through her hands without so much as an attempt to secure it, then Millicent would have thought her contemptible indeed.

At length there came a moment when it seemed expedient that she too should strike in to the conversation with Mrs. Renton. There was an audible pause. Millicent was not so clever as her mother; but in such a crisis as the present she was put upon her mettle. So long as there were only men to deal with there was no need for much exertion. Nature had provided her with the necessary weapons to use against such simpletons,—her eyes, the turn of her head, her smile, a soft modulation of her voice; but with a feminine audience it was a different matter. There, wit was more needful to her than beauty,— mother wit,—adroitness,—the faculty of adapting herself to her part and her listeners. Mrs. Tracy looked at her with an anxiety which she could not disguise. A statesman looking on while his son made his first speech in Parliament, could scarcely have experienced a graver solicitude. As it was, Millicent addressed herself to her mother with the softest of voices. 'Mamma,' she said, 'does it not seem strange to find yourself here, after all Mr. Ben Renton used to tell us? How fond he was of his beautiful home!'

And then came the expected question from his mother,—'Ben? my son Ben? Did you meet him abroad? Is it long since you saw him? Dear, dear, why I am looking for my boy home every day. They are all coming home about,— about——' Here Mrs. Renton caught Mary's warning eye, and paused, but immediately resumed again. 'Why, of course, everybody knows! Why should not I say what it is about? It was an arrangement of my poor dear husband's. They are coming to read the will. We don't know how we are left, none of us, for it was a very odd arrangement; but I am sure he meant it for the best. We shall be together next month, and I am sure Ben will be charmed to resume his acquaintance with you. What a nice thing you should be in the neighbourhood! The only thing is, that I am afraid you will find The Willows damp.'

'But what a pleasure for you to have all your family with you!' said Millicent; 'and oh! what a delight to your sons to return to you!'

'Yes,' said Mrs. Renton. 'Of course I shall be very glad to see them. And then, to be sure, shooting will have begun, and they will be able to amuse themselves. I am such an invalid, I tremble at the thought of any exertion.'

And when Mrs. Renton said this, Millicent rose, and declared she knew that she could put one of those cushions more comfortably in the chair.

It was quite late in the afternoon when they left the Manor at last, for Mrs. Renton insisted that they should stay to luncheon. She was distressed beyond measure when she heard of the fly which had been waiting for so long. 'It will cost you a fortune,' she cried; 'and we could have set you down when we went for our drive.'

'We are not very rich,' Mrs. Tracy said in reply; 'but to have made acquaintance with you is such a pleasure. And it is not often we indulge ourselves.'

Mrs. Renton declared, when they were gone, that it was years since she had seen any one who pleased her so much. 'As for the daughter, she is perfectly beautiful!' she cried, in rapture; 'and to think that such a lovely creature should have married Harry Rich!'

'But we don't know anything about Harry Rich,' said Mary, who was disposed to be misanthropical; 'perhaps he was a lovely creature too.'

'I don't understand what has come to you, Mary,' said her aunt. 'Why should you be so disagreeable? Such a nice, pretty creature; one would have thought she was just the very companion you want. And your own old schoolfellow, too! I never like to give in to what people say of girls being jealous of each other, but it really looks more like that than anything else.'

'Yes; I suppose I must be jealous of her,' said Mary; and Mrs. Renton took the admission for irony, and read her a long lecture when they went for their drive. It is hard upon a young woman to be lectured when she is out driving, and can neither run away nor occupy herself with anything that may make a diversion. Poor Mary had to listen to a great many remarks about the evils of envy and self-estimation, and the curious want of sympathy she showed.

'Poor thing!—a widow at such an early age, and badly left, and with such very sweet manners. And the mother such a very judicious person,' said Mrs. Renton. 'I am so glad they are at The Willows. It will be quite a resource to the boys.'

Then indeed something very like bitterness rankled in Mary Westbury's heart. Envy, and hatred, and malice, and all uncharitableness. Yes, very likely it would be a resource for the boys. In all her own long and tedious fulfilment of their duties, Mary had never once proposed to herself any reward 'when the boys came home,' and yet, perhaps, there had been in her heart some hope of appreciation,—some idea that they would understand what abnegation of herself it had been. They would know that this long, monotonous stretch of duty,—which was not, after all, her first natural duty,—was not less, but perhaps more hard, than their own wanderings and labour. And now all at once a cloud had fallen over this prospect. One soweth and another reapeth. Mary had laboured and denied herself for their sakes; but it was this stranger who would be the great resource for the boys. And Ben! Mary's heart contracted with a secret, silent pang as she thought of Ben coming defenceless, unprepared, to find the syren who had,—she did not doubt,—bewitched and betrayed him, seated at his very gates. Her last conversation with him rose up before her as clear as if it had but just occurred. Ben, too, had ventured to suggest that she,—that all women,—would be envious of Millicent. Her heart rose with an indignant swell and throb. Was there nothing then in the world better than blue eyes and lips like rose-leaves, and the syren's voice and smile? If that was all a man cared for, was he worth thinking of? She had gone and married Henry Rich when Ben was poor. And now that the man whose name she bore had opportunely vanished from her path, she had returned now Ben was about to regain his fortune, to lie in wait for him, with a miserable pretence of old friendship and tender regard for his cousin, who was to be the victim, and scapegoat, and sacrifice for all! Perhaps it was not much wonder that Mary was bitter. And she had all a woman's natural distrust in the man's powers of resistance. It never occurred to her that the syren of his youth might now have no attraction for him. 'They are like that,' she said to herself, with a true woman's feeling of half-impatient tolerance, and pity, and something like contempt,—not blame, as if he were a free agent. It was not he, but she, upon whom it was natural to lay the blame.

CHAPTER VII.

THE DOVE.

ABOUT a week after the arrival of the visitors from The Willows, an arrival of a very different kind happened at Renton;—and yet it could not be called an arrival. There had been no further news, and the Manor was still in the same state of pleasant confusion and preparation,—the maids sitting and chatting over their work in the west wing, and a roomful of seamstresses working at the new carpets and curtains for 'the boys' rooms,'—when one morning Mary was mysteriously called out from Mrs. Renton's room, where she was reading the newspaper, her usual morning occupation. 'It was a lady who wanted to see her,' the maid said; and was stolid, and refused all further particulars. 'A lady,—any one who has been here lately?' Mary asked, stiffening into sudden offence. It could be nobody but Millicent, she thought, though Millicent had been at the house repeatedly since her first visit, and was already known. 'I never saw her before, miss,—not at Renton,' was the reply; and Mary, annoyed, went to see for herself who the unknown visitor was. She had been set on edge by the events of the last few days. 'Wheresoever the carrion is, there will the eagles be gathered together,' she said to herself, with a kind of spiteful misery. So long as nothing was going to happen in the family, no mysterious visitors, neither men nor women, came near Renton; and now here was the second in a week! Perhaps some other syren to put herself in Ben's way; perhaps somebody who possessed Laurie's secret, whatever that might be. As for Frank, he was a married man, and had his wife to take care of him, and, heaven be praised! could have no secrets,—at least, none in which Mary could be compelled to interfere.

She went to the drawing-room door discontented, with no comfortable expectation. But when she had opened it, the most unexpected scene burst upon her eyes. The first thing she saw was a Hindoo ayah holding in her arms one of those milk-white, blue-veined children whose delicacy of tint contrasts so strangely with the dusky arms that carry them,—the kind of child of which one says involuntarily that it is an Indian child. Her first glance was at that pearly, blue-eyed creature, and then she turned round with a start and cry of joy upon a lady who stood by smiling.

'Is it Alice?' she cried. The comfort it was to her, the relief and satisfaction and sense of strength it gave her, would be difficult to describe. Mary was not given to enthusiasm, but she clasped her arms about the new-comer with a warmth which brought tears to her eyes. 'I thought it was some one disagreeable, and it is you!' she cried in her delight. She had been looking for an enemy, and here was a natural assistant and ally.

And then ensued a flutter of explanation and welcome, as was natural. It was Alice who had thus come unaccompanied and unexpected,—or, rather, it was Mrs. Frank Renton, a young matron of six years' standing, with one wistful, bright-eyed, wondering little girl by her side, and the child on the nurse's knee.

'We came to give mamma a surprise,' said Alice; 'not to keep her anxious till the last moment, thinking everything impossible must have happened to us. I know how she watches every day and thinks. And this was such a good opportunity for coming! We came when she had not the least expectation of us, and saved her all that. It was Frank's idea,' said the young wife, with a happy smile.

'And where is Frank?'

'Coming next mail. Yes, that is the worst of it; but, as he said, we could not have everything; and I came with Lady Sinclair, the Governor-General's wife, you know. Think what an honour it is! And she was so kind to us. She has quite taken a fancy to us, which is odd. I don't mean it is odd that they should all be fond of Frank, for everybody is. Don't you think baby is like him? Come and look at baby. I am sure you have not had a good look at him yet. Mamma has done nothing but carry him about in her arms. It is so funny to see my baby in mamma's arms,' cried Alice, with a sudden gush of bright tears; 'and, oh! so nice! I love him the more for it. She thinks he is rather pale. Well, perhaps he is a little pale. I suppose Indian babies generally are,—and then the journey, you know. Renton is not a bit changed. I stood just now, when you came in, on the very same pattern of the carpet that I stood on when Frank brought me here first; and I was so dreadfully frightened; and then you came and put your arms round my neck——'

'You were such a child,' said Mary; and the two kissed each other once more.

'It was so good of you to put your arms round my neck. Not just a regulation kiss, as Frank says. I put myself on the very same square this time to see what you would do.'

'Why you are a child still!' said Mary, looking at her with that curious mixture of amusement and wonder and respect with which an unmarried woman looks upon the matron who is younger than herself. How many experiences Alice had gone through of which the home-dwelling girl knew nothing! And yet she was a child still!

'So mamma says,' said Alice. 'But, oh! how nice and fresh and bright you look! Is that how dresses are made now? Am I a dreadful fright in my old things? For money does not go so far in India as one thinks; and what with the children and everything, I have had to be very economical. Mamma says I am about fifty years behind other people; and they all laugh so at poor baby's things. But he has got on his new pelisse to-day, and I think he looks very nice. Is grandmamma up yet? Do you think she would like the children to go and see her in her room?'

'I must let her know first,' said Mary.

But she lingered, and this babble ran on, which was so pleasant; and the children's hats were taken off, and Alice exhibited little Mary's hair, which was pale gold, of the softest, silkiest kind; but would not *crêper*, nor stand out, as 'the fashion' was, to her despair.

'You would not think she had half so much as she has,' the mother said; 'it is so soft. Look here, how thick it is! but it will not hang as it ought. Should I take her to Truefitt, or somebody? Frank thinks it is pretty as it is, but then he did not know what was the fashion; and he is silly,—he likes curls.'

'And, by-the-bye, where are your curls?' said Mary.

Alice laughed and shook her head with the pretty movement that these same curls had made habitual to her.

'I put them up to come out,' she said. 'Fancy coming out with the children, and without Frank, with those things bobbing about my shoulders like a baby! I wish you would speak to him about it, Mary. Mamma agrees with me that I ought to put them up when I go out; but he is such an old goose. Don't you think we ought to go to grandmamma? She may think that it is unnatural of us not to go to her at once.'

'It will do by-and-by,' said Mary. 'You know what an invalid she is. How good the children are, Alice! I am sure she will be delighted with them, after all.'

'After all?' cried Alice, amazed. 'But you must not think they are always good; you should see mamma with them. Mamma looks as if it was natural to her to have a baby in her arms. Wasn't it good of Frank to make up the plan for me to come over and save her all the anxiety? I did not want to come till he was ready myself. It was all his consideration. And then Lady Sinclair wanted me so much to travel with her. Of course it was more comfortable. And as I am not a great lady myself, nor anybody particular, it was nice to have Lady Sinclair to take me up, you know, for Frank's sake.'

'Why, you are quite a little woman of the world!'

'That is what mamma says; but so would you, if you were asked about your people, and all sorts of questions put to you. I always used to feel so ashamed, when the colonel's wife began to talk to me, that I had not an uncle an earl, or even a baronet. That would have been better than nothing, for Frank's sake. I do think he felt it sometimes, and was angry that his wife was a nobody; but then when Lady Sinclair took me up,' Alice said, with a sparkle in her eyes,—'and the Governor-General is baby's godfather,—that made all the difference. It was quite absurd the difference it made.'

'And I hope you have kept up your music,' said Mary, thinking of Mrs. Renton. But to Alice the question had another meaning, and covered her soft face with a sudden blush.

'I am so glad! Lady Sinclair does not care for music,' she cried; 'not one bit! She does not know Beethoven from Verdi. It was me she liked, and not my playing. Oh, if you knew how impertinent they used to be! saying I must have been professional, and such cruel things;—not that there would have been any harm in being professional,—but only you know men have such prejudices, and it made Frank furious. But it was me Lady Sinclair liked, though I dare say you are surprised,' Alice added, with a laugh of pleasant girlish vanity. Her heart was thrown wide open by the excitement of the home-coming; all its envelopes of shyness and strangeness having been forgotten for the moment. Except with 'mamma,' she had never chattered so freely to any one in her life.

'Very much surprised,' Mary said, kissing the bright face which had come upon her like a revelation. They had jumped all at once into the tenderest intimacy. Frank's bride had been a timid little stranger the last time she was at Renton, afraid to speak, carrying herself very gingerly among her unknown relations; but she was flushed by the delight of being among her own people this time, and confident of everybody's regard.

'I think really I ought to go to grandmamma now,' she added, after that pleasant laugh. And Mary hastened to her godmother to prepare the way. Mrs. Renton had just finished dressing, and was lying on her sofa, to recover from the exertion, sipping her cup of arrowroot. She was in a pale grey dress, which, she flattered herself, was slightly mourning, but had some pretty pink ribbons in her cap, to which that description could scarcely be applied. They were not perhaps very suitable to her widowhood, but then they were very becoming; and when the sun is shining brightly, even an invalid lady upon a sofa is apt to feel an inclination towards such innocent vanities.

'My mistress has taken a biscuit with her arrowroot this morning,' said the maid, in a tone of exultation. 'I always said as a little bit of company was the thing that would do her most good.'

Mrs. Renton gave a soft smile in acknowledgment of this commendation. She was aware that it was good of her to eat that biscuit, and a gentle self-approval filled her heart. 'I quite enjoyed it,' she said; and Mary had to pause and hear an account of what kind of biscuit it was, and to express her delight at the feat. 'And I have something else to tell you, dear godmamma,' she said; 'if you are quite sure you will not be upset by the surprise. Some one has just arrived,—Alice and the children! She had an opportunity to come by this last mail, with Lady Sinclair, the Governor-General's wife, who has taken a great fancy to her. Frank would not let her miss the opportunity. She arrived the day before yesterday, and she is with the children, looking so nice! I am sure you will be delighted to see them. Shall I bring them up here?'

Mary's nervousness betrayed itself in the haste with which she delivered this long explanation, never pausing to take breath. And Mrs. Renton put down her arrowroot and sat upright on the sofa. 'Bring them here!—Alice and the children! Good heavens, Mary! are you out of your senses?' said the invalid, 'when I have just this moment got out of bed!'

'But she will wait as long as you please,' said Mary, anxiously.

'And you know I hate surprises,' said Mrs. Renton. 'It may be all very well for you robust people who are never ill; but such a thing upsets my nerves altogether; and nothing is ready, you know; and why did Frank not come with her? But it just shows how dreadful it is to have to do with people who are out of society!' cried Mrs. Renton, putting one foot to the ground. 'I suppose I must go and see to things myself.'

'Missis will make herself quite ill!' cried the maid, in alarm. 'Oh, please, ma'am,—if you would be so good, ma'am,—Dr. Mixton would never forgive me if you went and walked about after you've took your arrowroot.'

'Don't worry me, Davison!' cried Mrs. Renton, ready to cry; 'as if I had not enough to worry me! Couldn't she write? or keep to her proper time? I don't understand how you can countenance such a thing, Mary! As for walking about, I can't do it. If all the house goes to sixes and sevens,—and there is no place for anybody to sleep in,—I can't help it; I cannot do it. I have my duty to my children to think of, and I am not going to kill myself.'

At this moment Alice, who had become impatient, knocked at the door. Nobody conceived that such an invasion was possible, and therefore Davison opened the door, cautious, but unsuspecting, while Mrs. Renton put up her foot again, and lay back, the image of exhaustion, on the sofa. Davison gave a little cry of mingled horror and delight, if such a mixture may be. Alice stood in the doorway with a child in each hand. They were all lightly clad in white summer dresses, the young mother and the two children. Little Laurence tottered forward a step or two, holding by his mother's hand, and Mary held back, gazing, with wistful blue eyes, at the strange scene. Mrs. Renton, as long as she was by herself, was an invalid given up to all sorts of indulgences; but when she was brought face to face with the outside world she was a lady, and knew how to adopt that gracious *rôle*. Before Mary Westbury could recover from her astonishment and consternation, the mistress of the house held out her hands to her daughter-in-law. 'Ah, Alice, come in,' she said; 'bring them to me. I am not able, my dear, to go to you.'

And in five minutes more, the chatter and the laughter, the tumult of pleasant explanations and questions, and all the talk that belongs to an arrival, was in full course by the side of Mrs. Renton's sofa. As for Alice, it had never occurred to her to be afraid of her mother-in-law. She was afraid of nobody in the present felicitous state of her affairs. She had forgotten altogether how little she had been at Renton, how small her personal knowledge was of the household there. Somehow, through those six years of correspondence, the Manor and the Square had got jumbled together in the mind of Mrs. Frank Renton. Had she come with any doubt of her reception, the chances were that things would not have gone so pleasantly. But she had not the least doubt of her reception. She could not be kept away even so long as was necessary to get grandmamma's reply. She took it for granted that her husband's mother belonged to her almost as much as her own. Who should go and ask admission for Frank's children into the room their father was born in, but she? And this fearlessness vanquished the invalid, who felt all her tremors of anticipation quieted in a moment. The children did not scream, but only gazed at her in silence, with big, wide-open eyes,—and baby was like his father. And Mrs. Renton, though she had been so long accustomed to think of herself first, and watch over her own peace and comfort, was still Frank's mother. After awhile old recollections came over her, and she cried a little over Frank's boy. 'I remember when his father was just like him,' she began to tell Alice, and ran into a hundred little nursery stories, which roused her heart within her. 'I might have talked to her for a hundred years before she would have thought of telling them to me,' said Mary, with again an unmarried young woman's admiration, and soft half-envy of the young mother's privileges. Alice drew a low chair to the side of the sofa, and put the baby—most daring proceeding of all—on the very couch itself, that grandmamma might give her opinion of his little dimpled arms and legs, and say if she did not think he was stout enough, though perhaps not so fat as an English baby ought to be. 'But mamma says she does not care for those very fat babies,' Alice said, with eyes intent upon the face of the critic. 'And neither do I,' Mrs. Renton said with solemnity, holding her grandson's little pink foot in her hand. 'If I had done it, poor godmamma would have been quite ill all day,' Mary said afterwards, describing the meeting to her mother. And for an hour or two there was nothing to be heard but that soft feminine talk, all full of bits of private history, and interspersed with every kind of digression, which women love. Alice gave them no narrative of her six years' absence; but *apropos* of everything and nothing, there would come a little chapter out of the heart of it. 'It was that time when I was rather ill—that Frank wrote to you about. He took me up to the hills, and we had to leave little Mary at the station. We went along with the General and his wife, and they were so friendly; and it was he, you remember, who recommended Frank for that appointment he has held ever since. To tell the truth, we had got into debt,' said Alice, with a blush; 'it was that that made me ill, as much as anything. We were determined not to tell you, but struggle out of it as best we could, and you can't think how glad we were of that appointment. I thought you would all think me such a wretched little creature to have brought Frank nothing, and yet have let him get into debt. It was there I first saw a lady with a chignon. I could not tell what to make of it at first, and Frank thought it hideous; but then it was too big—it was as big as her head.'

'Depend upon it, my dear, it was false hair; they say everybody wears false hair now-a-days,' said Mrs. Renton, who was still holding in her hand the baby's little dimpled foot.

'But I don't believe that,' said Alice. 'I like you in the chignon, Mary; it suits you much better than the other fashion; and what a comfort it must be not to have any curls to do when you are sleepy! Grandmamma dear, I wish you would tell me what to do with little Mary's hair. It is so soft it will not *crêper*, nor anything. Lady Sinclair's niece's little girl looks to have a perfect bush of hair, and Mary has just as much, but it will not stand out.'

'It must be plaited every night before she goes to bed,' said Mrs. Renton, 'and just damped a little before it is plaited. Have you an English nurse? Of course your ayah must be sent back. And, Alice, I hope you are quite sure about that debt.'

'It was all paid, every penny! Don't be afraid. I could never have come home and looked you in the face if it had not been paid. And I have taken such care ever since! Frank is,—too generous, you know. He asks people, and does not think. And then everybody that pleases comes and stays with you. India is such a funny place for that. When we were at Goine Ghurla, the Fentons lived with us for six weeks; they could not get a house to suit them, and we had a larger one than we wanted, and of course they came to us as if it were the most natural thing in the world. It is very nice, but it is rather expensive. Of course we could have gone to them in return had we wanted to go, but we never did. How nice it is to see you in your pink ribbons, grandmamma, after that dreadful widow's cap!'

'My dear, I am only in my own room; it is only something Davison made up for me,' said Mrs. Renton, confused. 'I never wear colours down-stairs. Indeed, my spirits will never be equal to it again.'

'But they are so becoming to you,' said Alice. And thus the talk ran on. And the children, awed by the novelty of everything, behaved themselves like little angels, not uttering a cry, nor shedding a tear. When the time of the afternoon drive came, little Mary, inspired by her good genius, made a petition to go in the carriage with grandmamma. And that day the marvellous sight might have been seen of Mrs. Renton with the ayah and the baby seated opposite her, and little Mary, in great state, by her side, perambulating the lanes. Mrs. Renton made the coachman stop when they passed the rector's pony carriage, and explained, 'My son Frank's children, just come from India,' with such pride as she had scarcely felt since Frank had been the baby. Already these sweet *avant-couriers* of return and restoration had loosened the prison bonds for the invalid in her unconscious selfishness. She forgot all about her medicine, and even her cup of tea, when she went in, and demanded to know instead if her favourite biscuits had been provided for the children. On the whole, it was pleasanter thus taking thought for others than thinking only of herself.

When they were left alone, Mary and Alice went out together to stray about the lawn and down the favourite haunt of the Rentons,—the path to the river. And they had a great deal of talk and consultation, confidential and serious, which was comforting to both. 'Don't you know in the very least how things are to be?' Alice asked, with a certain wistfulness. 'I don't care about money, indeed; but, oh, it would be so nice to stay at home!'

'Nobody knows,' said Mary; 'not even Mr. Ponsonby, I believe. It makes one very anxious when one thinks of it. If poor, dear uncle's mind was touched, as some people think, he may have made some other stipulation. I don't know,—but Renton ought to come to Ben.'

'I have heard Frank say often that if the will did not do that, Laurie and he had both agreed to settle it so,' said Alice. 'Of course they could not take it. But if it is not wrong to say so,—and as poor Mr. Renton is dead I don't think it can be wrong,—I should like if there was some money for us.'

'There must be some money for you,' said Mary; and thus speaking they moved down the bank, and, coming to the beech-tree at the corner, which was associated in Mary's mind with so many tangles of the tale, stopped short to contemplate the view. A little to one side from that famous point of vision a peep could be obtained, through some branches, of a house close by the water's edge,—a little house, with its trees dipping into the stream, lying under the shadow of a high, wooded bank. Mary's mind was full of her special griefs and apprehensions, and she could not keep her eyes from that peaceful little place, which lay full in the afternoon sunshine. 'That is The Willows,' she said, pointing it out.

'It looks very nice, but what is The Willows?' said Alice. 'I never heard Frank speak of it,' which was her standard of interest for everything within her vision.

'I dare say Frank never remembered it,' said Mary; 'it is not a place of any consequence; at least, it never was before. But two ladies have come to it now. They are a mother and a daughter, and they are both widows.'

'Poor things! but that does not sound very important still. Are they nice?' said Alice, in her ignorance. And Mary began to regret the suddenness of her confidence.

'The daughter is very beautiful. She was a schoolfellow of mine once,' said Mary; 'and I'm afraid they are not very nice. If I tell you something, will you never, never say a word to any one,—not even Frank? Oh, it is nothing wrong. I think Ben met her once, and was fond of her. Beauty goes so far, you know, with men. I think he was very fond of her, and she must have deceived him. And think what it will be to him, poor fellow, if he finds her there when he comes home!'

'But how did she deceive him?' cried Alice. 'Oh, tell me! It must be quite a romance.'

'I don't care for such romances,' said Mary. 'He loved her, I am sure, and she went away abroad, and must have married somebody else, for she is a widow I told you; and fancy what he will feel when he finds her here!'

'Well, perhaps he might like it,' said Alice. 'Men are so queer. They are not the least like us. I know by Frank; when something happens that I think he will be in a dreadful way about, he takes it quite calmly; and then for the least little thing, that nobody in their senses would pay the least attention to, he will blaze up! Is Ben nice? Perhaps he will be quite pleased to find her here, to show her he does not care.'

'I don't know if you would think him very nice; but to us, you know,' said Mary, turning away her head, 'he is Ben: and, of course, there is no more to be said.'

'Yes, of course, you are all fond of him,' said simple Alice; and they went on, relapsing into other channels of talk. But though she understood so little the full meaning of what she had heard, Alice was such a relief and comfort to Mary as she had not had for years. Even to have said so much as this relieved her; and to nobody else could she have ventured to say even so much. Not to her own mother, who was too energetic, and might have thought it her duty to come into the field, and break a lance with Mrs. Tracy in defence of her nephew; not to Laurie, who might have seen deeper still, and detected certain secrets of Mary's heart which she would not whisper even to herself. But Alice, who was ready to listen, and give her ignorant, shrewd opinion, was a comfort to speak to. Mary was exhilarated and consoled by her walk, as much as her aunt was by the drive, in which the soft pride and sense of property in Frank's babies had warmed her dried-up soul. When the mother and her babies went back to town by the evening train, Mrs. Renton felt herself able to walk almost to the end of the avenue to see them off, a thing she had not been known to do for years; and Mary drove with them to the station, anticipating joyfully the time when 'Frank's family' should come back to take possession of the apartments prepared for them. The family ark was settling upon the top of the mount. But a few days more, and the doors would open, and the wanderings be over, and the family fate be known.

CHAPTER VIII.

BEN.

THE first who arrived of the family party was the eldest son.

It was on the 15th of September that Ben came home. The day appointed for reading the will was a week later, and none of the others had arrived when Ben's letter came announcing his return for the next morning. Fortunately, the 'boys'' rooms were quite ready, and the house was so wound up to the height of excitement, that the first actual arrival was a godsend. The flutter and commotion of that day was indescribable. As for poor Mary she did not know what she was about. It was cruel on her that he should come alone,—that there should be nobody to break their inevitable *tête-à-tête* at breakfast and during the hours when Mrs. Renton would certainly be invisible. Busy as she was, looking after everything, she found time for a hurried note to Laurie, telling him of his brother's coming. 'He has been so long away that I feel as if it were a stranger who was coming,' Mary wrote, in a panic quite unlike her usual character;—'do come at once and help me to entertain him.' 'Help you to entertain Ben!' was Laurie's reply, with ever so many notes of interrogation. Perhaps the helplessness and fright which were visible in this demand threw some light to Laurie upon the state of affairs, but he either could not or would not help her in her trouble; and with a heart which beat very loudly in her breast, but with an outward aspect of the most elaborate quietness and composure, Mary stood on the lawn in the September sunset watching for the dog-cart to come from the station. The ladies from The Willows had been calling that very morning, and of course had heard what was going to happen, and a glance had passed between the mother and daughter when Mrs. Renton had hoped she would see a great deal of them while the 'boys' were at home. 'I should think Mr. Renton must have forgotten us,' Millicent had said, with a little pathos. Mary took very little part in all this, but noted everything, the most vigilant and clear-sighted of critics. It made her heart ache to look at that beautiful face. Was it possible that those blue eyes which looked so lustrous, and the smiling lips that were so sweet, could obliterate in Ben's mind all sense of falsehood and treachery? And, indeed, Mary only took the treachery for granted. Perhaps there had been nothing of the kind; perhaps he was coming without any grievance against her to fall into this syren's snares. How cunning it was of her to post herself there, on the edge of the river, where 'the boys'' boats would be passing continually, and where they could not escape her! And how deep-rooted the plan must have been which preserved the date for seven years, and made Millicent aware exactly when her victim was coming home! Mary's thoughts were severe and uncompromising. She could not think of any possible tie between Millicent and her cousin but that of enchantress and victim. She did not know how good the adventuress had resolved to be if at last this last scheme of all should be successful; nor what a weary life of failure, and disappointment, and self-disgust, poor Millicent had gone through. Mary could not have believed in any extenuating circumstances. There could be no trace of womanly or natural feeling in the creature who thus came, visibly without the shadow of a pretext, to lie in wait for Ben.

She thought her heart would have stopped beating when the dog-cart dashed in at the gates. But her outward aspect was one of such fixed composure that Ben, as he made a spring out of it, almost without leaving the horse time to stop, and caught his cousin precipitately in his arms, felt as if he had committed a social sin in his sudden kiss. 'I am sure I beg your pardon, Mary,' he cried, half laughing, half horrified. 'I forgot I had been away so long, and you had grown out of acquaintance with me; but still you need not look so shocked.'

'I am not shocked,' said Mary, who had scarcely voice enough to speak; 'it was only the surprise; and, good heavens, what a beard!'

'Well, yes, it is an alarming article, I suppose,' said Ben, looking down with complacency upon one of those natural ornaments which men prize so much. It was an altogether new decoration. And it seemed to Mary that he had grown even taller while he had been away, so changed was the development of the mature man,—brown, bearded, and powerful,—from that of Ben, the young man of fashion, who had been as dainty in all his ways as herself. His frame had broadened, expanded, and acquired that air of activity and force which only occupation gives. His eye had no languor in it, but was full of active observation and thought. The change was so great that it took away her breath, and after the second glance Mary was not quite sure that it was so very satisfactory. He was more like the Rentons than he had been,—his lip curled a little at the corner, as if it might sneer on occasion. His manner had grown a little peremptory. 'Where is my mother?' he said immediately, without giving even a spare moment to look again at the companion of his childhood;—'in her own room?'

'Yes, she is waiting for you,' said Mary. And he went off from her without another word. Of course it was very right he should do so, after an absence of six years and a half, and very nice of him to be so anxious to see his mother. But yet—— Mary went in after him, in two or three minutes, feeling somehow as if she had fallen from an unspeakable height of expectation; though she had not expected anything in reality,—and Ben had been very kind, very frank, and cordial, and cousinly. What a fool she was! And while she could hear the unusual roll of the man's voice in Mrs. Renton's room, running on in perpetual volleys of sound, Mary, in the silence of her own, sat down and cried,—folly for which she could have killed herself. Of course his first hour belonged to his mother. And what did she, Mary, want of him but his kindly regard, and,—esteem,—and,—respect! Respect was what a man would naturally give,—if she did not betray herself, and show how little she was deserving of it,—to a woman of her years. Seven-and-twenty! To be sure Ben was nearly five years older; but that does not count in a man. Moved by these thoughts, Mary went to the extreme of voluntary humility, and dressed herself in one of her soberest dresses for dinner. 'I laid out the pink, ma'am, as Mr. Ben has come home,' said her maid. 'No, the grey,' said Mary, obstinately. He should see at least that there was no affectation of juvenility about her,—that she fully acknowledged and understood her position as,—almost,—middle-aged. Poor Mary was considered a very sensible girl by all her friends, and she thought to herself, while committing this piece of folly, that she would justify their opinion. Sense as her grand quality,—and esteem and respect as the mild emotions which she might hope to inspire,—such were the reflections that passed through Mary Westbury's mind as she put on her grey gown.

'It don't look so bad, Miss Mary, after all,' said her maid encouragingly, as she gave the last twitch to the skirt. And certainly it did not look bad. The sensible young woman who wished her cousin Ben to respect her, had a little rose-flush going and coming on her cheeks, and a lucid gleam of emotion in her eyes, which might have justified a more marked sentiment. Her hand was a little tremulous, her voice apt,—if the expression is permissible,—to go into chords, the keys of half-a-dozen different feelings being struck at the same moment, and producing, if a little incoherence, at the same time a curious multiplicity of tone. The dining-room had more lights than usual, but still was not bright; and when Ben came in with his mother on his arm, he protested instantly against the great desert of a table, which, in deference to old custom, was always spread in the long-deserted place.

'I can't have you half-a-mile off,' he said. 'You must sit by me here, mamma, and you here, Mary. That is better. We are not supposed to be on our best behaviour, I hope, the very day I come home.'

'Why, this is very nice,' said Mrs. Renton, as she sipped her soup at her son's right hand, and stopped from time to time to look at him. 'And one does not feel as if one had any responsibility. I think I shall keep this seat, my dear; it will be like dining out without any of the trouble. And then, Ben, I shall not feel the change when you bring home a wife.'

Mary, who had been looking on, suddenly turned her eyes away; but all the same, she perceived that Ben's obstinate Renton upper lip settled down a little, and that he grew stern to behold.

'I don't think that is a very likely event,' he said.

'But it must be,' said Mrs. Renton; 'it must be some time. I don't say directly, because this is very pleasant. And after being left seven years all alone, I think

I might have my boy to myself to cheer me up a little. But it must be some time,—in a year or two,—when you have had time to look about you and make up your mind.'

'Sufficient unto the day is the evil thereof,' said Ben, with a short laugh; 'if I am to judge of my effect upon English ladies by the impression I made on Mary,—it is not encouraging, I can tell you. I was afraid she would faint.'

'Oh, Ben!' Mary exclaimed, looking up at him with her lucid, emotional eyes; and the rose-flush went over all her face. It was a very pleasant face to look at. And, perhaps, even beauty herself is not more attractive than a countenance which changes when you look at it, and a voice full of chords. Yes; no doubt he had some respect for her, and even esteem, if you went so far as that.

'Mary and I have been living so much out of the world,' said Mrs. Renton. 'We have been quite alone, you know, my dear. My poor health was never equal to the exertion. It is always best for such an invalid as I am to give up everything, I believe. And except just our drives,—your poor dear papa always made such a point of my drives.'

'But Mary was not an invalid,' said Ben, and he looked full at her for a moment, lighting up once more the glow in her face. 'I don't know what you have been doing to yourself,' he said. 'Is it the way she has her hair, mother? It cannot be her dress, because I remember that gown. I suppose she has been asleep all these seven years, like the beauty in the wood.'

'I think I have,' said Mary; but her voice was scarcely audible. After all, the pink gown had not been necessary, and virtue had its reward.

'Asleep for seven years? Indeed, you are unkind to Mary,' said Mrs. Renton. 'You can't think what a comfort she has been to me, Ben. She has always read to me, and driven with me, and talked when I could bear it, and got my worsted work straight, and given the housekeeper her orders. If she had been my own child she could not have been nicer. And never cared for going out or anything. I am sure it is not necessary for me to say it; but if anything should happen to me, I hope you will all be very kind to Mary. You can't think what a good child she has been.'

'Kind to Mary!' said Ben, holding out his hand to her. Well, perhaps there might be something more than even respect and esteem,—affection,—that was the word:—family affection and brotherly-kindness. And what could a woman of seven-and-twenty desire or dream of more?

And when they retired to the drawing-room Mrs. Renton was very eloquent about the change of affairs. 'Not to say that it is Ben, my dear,—whom of course it is a great happiness to see again,—there is always a pleasure in knowing that there is a man in the house,' she said. 'It rouses one up. I am sure there were many days that it was a great bore to go down to dinner. I should have liked a cup of tea in my own room so much better; but a man must always have his dinner. And then they have been about all day, and they have something to tell you, if it is only what is in the evening paper;—and there is always most news in the evening paper, Mary. I have remarked that all my life. And even now, you know, one feels that he will come in by-and-bye,—and that is something to look forward to. It is a great advantage, my dear, to have a man in the house.'

'It is very pleasant, at least, to have Ben in the house,' said Mary; but she quaked a little while she spoke; for what was she to do with him for the rest of the evening after Mrs. Renton went to bed? And if the world was coming to an end, it would not prevent Davison's appearance at half-past nine to take her mistress up-stairs. And there was not much chance that Ben would be inclined for bed at that early hour. Mary tried hard to brace herself up for the evening's work, as she made the tea, pondering whether she might retire in her turn about half-past ten or so, that being a proper young ladies' hour,—though with Laurie she would not have minded how long she sat talking, or letting him talk; and yet Ben had been seeing more, doing more, and had more to tell than Laurie. Thus it sometimes happens that the greater the love the less is the kindness,—though such a word as love had not been breathed in the inmost recesses of Mary Westbury's mind.

But when Ben joined them he was very talkative, and full of his own concerns, and was so interesting that his mother put Davison off, and it was ten o'clock before she actually left the drawing-room. After a little conflict with herself Mary prepared to follow. She would have liked to stay, but felt herself awkward, and uncomfortable, and full of a thousand hesitations.

'Are you going too?' Ben said, as he saw her gathering up her work; and there was a tone of disappointment in his voice that went to her heart.

'I thought you might be tired,' she said, faltering.

'Tired! the first night at home! I suppose the poor dear mother has stayed as long as is good for her; but you are not an invalid, Mary,' said Ben; 'you don't mean to say ten o'clock is the end of the evening for you? And I have a hundred things to tell you, and to ask you. Put on your shawl, and come out for a breath of fresh air. The moon always shines at Renton. I'll ring for somebody to bring you a shawl.'

'I'll run and get one,' said Mary; and she stayed up-stairs for a few moments to take breath and compose herself. It was very silly of her, of course, to be excited; but she reflected that it was not simply the innocent stroll with her cousin in the moonlight for which she was afraid, but the possibility of a return to the subject of Millicent, of which he had spoken to her last time he was at Renton. He was standing outside the window waiting for her when she came down, and they wandered away together, instinctively taking that path towards the river. So many moonlight walks on that same path glanced over Mary's memory as they walked,—childish ones, when the cousins played hide-and-seek behind the great, smooth, shining boles of the beeches,—merry comings-home from water-parties when they were all boys and girls together. And then that walk, which was the last she had taken with Ben.

He did not say much for some minutes. Perhaps he, too, was thinking of all those old recollections. 'When I went away the moon was shining,' he said at last abruptly, 'and I suppose it has been shining and the river running and the branches rustling all this time. How strange it seems! I wonder if I have been dreaming all these seven years?'

'I daresay you have for a great part of the time,' Mary said, with an effort to be playful. 'I am sure I have at least——'

'I hope so, considering my mother's account of what you have been doing,' said Ben. And then he made a pause, and said, as if he did it on purpose to stir up every possibility of discomfort in her, 'Do you remember our last talk here?'

'Yes,' said Mary, and then they went on, stumbling in the dark places, and now and then coming out like ghosts,—two weird figures,—into the silver light. Though he had brought her out on the pretence of having so much to say, in reality he scarcely talked at all. And she kept by his side, with her heart giving irregular thumps against her breast. She had not breath enough to bid him not to go any farther, and the sound of her own foot-steps and his in the utter stillness seemed to wake all kinds of curious echoes in the dark wood. Mary was half frightened, and yet rapt into a curious mysterious exaltation of feeling. What was he thinking of? Were they two the same creatures who had come down that same path together,—was it six years or six hours ago? The darkness among the trees around was not more profound than was the darkness in which Ben's life had been enveloped during his absence. He had written home, it is true, and they had known where he went, and what, as people say, he was doing all the time; but of his real existence Mary knew as little,—just as little and as much, as he of hers. Thus they went on, until they came to the opening, and the green bank upon the river-side, which lay in a flood of moonlight all shut and bounded round by the blackness of the woods.

'What a pity there is no boat!' said Ben. 'I might have taken you up the reach as far as the moonlight goes. We must have a boat. I did not think it was so sweet. And there is Cookesley Church across the fields. I remember so well looking at it the last time through the branches of the big beech. How high the river is! Whose boat is that, I wonder, on the other side?'

'Oh, it is from The Willows, I suppose,' said Mary, with a kind of desperation.

'The Willows? that is something new. Is it old Peters and his sister? But you told me he was dead. What sort of people are at The Willows now?'

'Two ladies,' said Mary, succinctly. Was not this like the very hand of fate? Why The Willows should thus thrust itself quite arbitrarily into the conversation without any word or warning she could not tell. It was like the work of a malicious spirit.

'Two ladies!' said Ben. 'You are very terse,—terser than I ever knew you. And who may the two ladies be who venture on the river in the moonlight?'

'Oh, I do not think they are in the boat.'

'But whether they are in the boat or not, who are they?' said Ben, and there was a sound as of laughter in his voice.

Then there followed a dead pause. The boat lay in the fullest moonlight, and already they could hear the soft plash of the oars and distant sound of voices. It was not coming down the stream, but floating softly on the silvered water, just kept in its place against the current by the oars. Some one was out enjoying the beauty of the night in that magical fashion; and opposite was visible the little margin of lawn which belonged to The Willows, the trees dripping into the water, and the lights in the open windows. A subtle suggestion of happiness, and love, and rest, was in the scene. Was it a pair of lovers, or a young husband with his wife, or——

'Tell me,—this becomes mysterious,—who are they?' said Ben.

'Oh, only some people,' Mary said, with some breathlessness, 'whom I think you once knew. Do you remember speaking to me, the last time we came down here together, about,—some one,—a school-fellow of mine?'

'Yes.'

'It is a very strange coincidence,' Mary said, with a miserable attempt at a laugh. 'It is Millicent, who has gone there with her mother for the summer. We are neighbours now.'

And then silence came again,—silence deeper than before. He started a little, that it was easy to see; but his face was quite in the shade. And after a while he said, with a steady and decided voice, 'You mean Mrs. Henry Rich?'

'Yes,' said Mary; and then they both stood on the rustling grass and watched the boat, which lay caught, as it were, and suspended in the blaze of white radiance. No doubt she was there, enjoying that beautiful moment, not thinking what silent spectators were looking on so near. As for Mary, she stood spell-bound, and gazed full of a thousand thoughts. Since her cousins had been gone, Mary had had no one to row her about the shining river, every turn of which she knew so well; but Millicent had her boatman at once. And who was he? And what could Ben be thinking of that he stood thus on the brink of the full stream, filled more than full by the overflowing of the moonlight? All at once he turned on his heel, as if rousing himself, and drew Mary's hand within his arm.

'Let me help you up the bank,' said Ben. 'After all, the night grows cold. Have you ever walked as far before, so late as this?'

'Never, I think,' said Mary, going with him up the hill at a pace very unusual to her. Though he carried on some pretence at conversation, she was too breathless with the rapid ascent to answer otherwise than by an occasional monosyllable. But when they reached the great beech he permitted her to breathe. Perhaps he paused there only from habit, or perhaps he was curious to look back upon that picture on the river, and gain another glimpse in this strange, unlooked-for, unsuspected way into the life of the woman he had once loved. The boat had disappeared while they were mounting the bank, and on the lawn, before The Willows, stood a white figure, dwarfed by distance into the size of a fairy, but blazing white in the intense moonlight. No doubt Ben saw her, for his face was turned that way; but he went on again without a word. It was only when they had reached the lawn, and were approaching the lights and the open window by which they had come forth, that he alluded to what he had seen. Then he asked sharply, all at once, in the very middle of some other subject which had nothing to do with it, 'How long have these people been here?'

'Three weeks,' said Mary. Not another word was said; but a certain constraint and embarrassment,—at least so she thought,—had come over him. When she lit her candle this time he made no attempt to detain her. She thought even that he gave a sigh of relief as he opened the door for her, and said good-night; and it was hard for Mary to think with any charity of the woman who had thus waylaid him,—waylaid his very imagination,—on the night even of his return. Possibly she was quite wrong in her estimate of Ben's feelings. When she was gone he threw himself heavily into a chair, and sat for an hour or more, doing nothing, chewing the cud of sweet and bitter fancy. But no doubt he had enough to think about without that. It would have been strange had the coming home,—the approach of certainty after his long suspense,—the familiar life that seemed to have taken him up again after casting him out of its bosom,—produced no excitement in his mind. And then there was that curious sense of unreality which comes upon a man when, after an active life of his own, he returns to his father's house, and finds everything, down to the minutest particular, just as it used to be. Is not this life such stuff as dreams are made of? To Ben, who was not a man of thought, this sentiment was bewildering; and the quiet of the house weighed upon him with an irritating heaviness. Talk of noise! There is no such babel as that of silence when it surges round you, when no living thing stirs, and the mysterious air rustles its wings in your ears, and the earth vibrates under your feet. The flutter of moths and invisible insects attracted by the light, the rustle of the leaves outside, the curtains waving in the night air, the mysterious thrills which ran through the furniture, the wavering of the flame of the lamp,—all affected Ben when he was left alone. His life had been so busy and full of action,—and now he had left that existence which was his own, and come back into the midst of those shadows to await the last sentence of a dead man's voice, and have his whole destiny, perhaps, thrown once more into mistiness and darkness. Had there been any need for that boat softly rocking on the curve of the silvered water,—for that white solitary figure in the moonlight,—to complicate matters further? But whether that last incident did count for anything in the multiplicity of his thoughts, or whether it affected him as Mary supposed,—and as Millicent meant it to affect him,—who can tell? He sat a long time thinking, but he uttered none of his thoughts in the shape of soliloquy, which is unfortunate for this narrative; and I am obliged to wait, as most people are compelled to do, for the slow elucidation of events, to show the turn taken by Ben Renton's thoughts.

Mary's mind went more rapidly to a conclusion, as may be supposed. She could no more tell than I can what Ben was really turning over in his thoughts; but one thing was clear to her, that he had not heard of the neighbourhood of Millicent with indifference. It might be indignation, it might be disgust, it might be concealed and suppressed delight; but, at all events, the information had moved him. And at the same time, he had been very nice to herself,—very friendly, almost more than friendly—affectionate; not forgetting to help her even when she had just thrown that bombshell into the quiet. To be sure, he had hurried her up the hill, unconscious of the rapidity of his pace; but that was little in comparison with his kindness in remembering her at all when he had just heard such news. So Mary said to herself, thinking, like a romantic young woman, that Ben must have straightway forgotten everything but Millicent. Well! She was like a sister to him: he was ready to trust her, ready to rely upon her, ready even to admire and praise her in that frank, affectionate way as a brother might. Why should there be any heaviness or sense of disappointment in her heart? Mary said to herself that it was only because of its being Millicent, who was not worthy of him. If it had been almost anybody else,—if it had been half-a-dozen girls she could name to herself, who were good girls, and would have made him happy—but Millicent was no mate for Ben! That was the only reason of the blank, sense of pain and vacancy in her heart. For herself, she was more than content.

And thus the old house closed its protecting doors upon the first instalment of the restored family; and with that received agitation, disquiet, unrest, into the bosom of the stillness. Renton had been lying high and dry, like a stranded vessel, for all those years, and peace had dwelt in it; but now that the tide was creeping up, and life stealing back, the natural accompaniment returned. Sighs of impatience, disappointment, pain,—eager desires for the future, which came so slowly, counting the minutes,—a sense, overmastering everything, of the hardness and strangeness of life. Nobody had thought of life as hard, as troublous, or full of fatal mistakes, during all those years when Mrs. Renton had driven about the lanes, and taken care of her health. The blessed bonds of routine had kept things going, and nobody was either glad or miserable. But as soon as the bigger life came back with chances of happiness in it, then the balancing chances of pain also returned. As soon as it becomes possible that you may be blessed, it also becomes possible that you may fall into the lowest depths of anguish. This was the strange paradox which Mary Westbury contemplated as she heard Ben Renton's unaccustomed step going to his room after midnight, through the profound stillness of the sleeping house.

CHAPTER IX.

THE NEXT MORNING.

RISING full of anxious thoughts of the excitement which must have taken possession of Ben from the revelations of the night, Mary was much taken aback to meet her cousin, in, to all appearance, an extremely cheerful state of mind, next morning. He had been up early, and had taken a long walk, and renewed,—he told her,—his acquaintance with the country. 'If one had it in one's own hands one could do a great deal more with it than has been done yet,' he said, looking more like the portraits of the old Rentons than Mary liked to see.

'I am sure I hope nobody will ever try to improve it as long as I am here,' she said, with a little heat,—for Renton as a parish, and Berks as a county, were to Mary the perfection of the earth.

'You don't like stagnant ponds, I hope,' said Ben, laughing at her vehemence,—'nor cottages falling to pieces,—nor fields that are flooded with every heavy rain.'

'But I like the broad turf on the roadsides, and the old hedges, and the old trees,' said Mary, 'and everything one has been used to all one's life. Ah, Ben, whatever you do, don't spoil Renton! I should break my heart——'

'Probably I shall never have it in my power to spoil Renton,' he said, with a short sigh of impatience. 'I wish I had not come home until the very day fixed for this reading of the will. It is hard work hanging about here and kicking one's heels and waiting. My father was very hard upon us, Mary. It was too much to ask from any set of men.'

'I don't think it has done you much harm,' said Mary, whose natural impulse was to defend the ancient authorities, however much she might sympathise with the sufferers in her heart.

'Don't you?' said Ben, walking away from the breakfast-table to the window, where he stood drawing up and down the blind with preoccupied looks. After a few minutes she, too, moved and went up to him. Her mind was full of anxiety to say something,—to give him to understand that she could enter into his feelings; but it was so difficult to enter upon such a subject with a man, and especially with such a man as Ben.

'Ben, I think I know,—a little,—what you mean,' she said, faltering; 'and I can see how, in some things, it must have been very hard,—preventing you from,—often,—doing what you wished; but now that is over. You need not wait now——'

He turned round and looked at her with some surprise in his eyes. 'You don't know what you are saying, Mary,' he said. 'I am like most men, very glad now to have been prevented doing things which at one time I would fain have done. And you are right, too,—I am my own master now,—not because the will is to be read this day week, but because I have found a trade and can work at it;—but that was not what I meant.'

Mary sat down patiently and raised her eyes to him that he might tell her what he did mean. She was in the way of listening to a great many explanations, and thought them natural. Ben, for his part, stood and looked at her for a minute, and then turned away with a laugh.

'Poor Mary!' he said. 'What wearisome talk you must have listened to all these years,—going into everything! You must have a special faculty for that sort of thing, you women; how have you managed to live through it all and keep your youth and your bloom?'

'There has been nothing dreadful to live through,' said Mary; 'but as for the youth, I don't pretend to that any longer. It is gone, like so many other pretty things; and I am not thinking of myself.'

'Not now, nor ever,' said her cousin; 'but I don't feel disposed to give up the matter as you do. I don't feel very aged——'

'But you are a man,' said Mary, interrupting him, 'which makes all the difference; and, besides, this sort of talk is quite nonsense. I must go and read the paper with godmamma. Have you done with it?' And she took the "Times" from the table, and was about to leave the room.

'I have not done with it,' said Ben, 'I have not begun it even. I am going to read it to my mother, and you shall come and listen, if you like. You have done our duty long enough. It is but fair I should take my spell now.'

Mary made a little protestation, but Ben was not disposed to give in. He was *ennuyé* for one thing, and did not want to be alone and give himself up to troublesome thoughts. There are times when it is better to do even the most humble of domestic duties than to be left to yourself. Mary thought, as she took her work and sat down near the window of her godmother's room, at some distance from the reader and listener, that affairs were wonderfully changed indeed, and that Ben's dutifulness was beyond all the traditions of good behaviour she had ever known. Mrs. Renton herself was a little overpowered by so sublime an act. Ben did not read steadily through as Mary did. He read not the bits of news which were her favourite study, but leading articles and speeches, which were not in her way. And then he would pause and talk in the middle of them, often turning his chair round towards Mary, and defrauding his mother both of the paper and his attention. It was pleasant, no doubt, to have a man in the house, and still more pleasant to have Ben at home; but the great and unexpected condescension of his morning visit to read the papers was not by any means so great a pleasure as it looked. But for the name of the thing she would really have preferred Davison; and Mary's reading was infinitely more satisfactory. When Ben wound up by saying, as it is the proper formula to say, that there was nothing in it, Mrs. Renton could not but echo the words with a little querulousness in her tone. He threw the paper carelessly on to the bed, and the poor lady drew it towards her, and made a feeble search after her spectacles.

'Indeed there seems very little,' she said, 'much less than on most days; but it was very kind of you to think of coming and reading to me, Ben.'

'I mean to come ever morning, mother,' he replied,—at which Mrs. Renton shivered,—'and relieve Mary a little. By-the-bye, I want to know whether you will mind if I have Hillyard here. I told him he was to come on Saturday, if he did not hear from me to the contrary. He is not quite in your way, but he is a very good fellow. I thought you would not mind if I had him here.'

'My dear boy, the house is yours,—or at least it will soon be yours,' said Mrs. Renton. 'It is very nice of you to consult me, and you know I am not very able to receive strangers; but still Mary is there to do all that is necessary, and of course you must have your friends.'

'Mother, I should like you to understand that it is not at all of course,' said Ben. 'The house is not mine,—I am not calculating that it will ever be mine. I want Hillyard, not so much because he is my friend, as because he is with me in business. He is my right-hand man——'

'It was Mr. Hillyard you went to America with at first?' said Mary, from her distant seat.

And Ben, relieved, walked across the room, finding she was easier to talk to than his mother. 'Eh? Yes, it is the same Hillyard,' he said, with a laugh which had some pleasure in it. 'I was his right-hand man then, and now he is mine. That is all the difference; but we have always hung together all the same.'

'Then you have done better than he has,' said Mary, looking up at him with a smile.

And Ben came and stood by the side of the table she was working at, and looked down upon her as he spoke. 'He's a very good fellow,' he said, 'but he does not stick to his work. There are some people who do best to be masters, and some who do best to be subordinate. And when he is not master, poor fellow, he is worth a dozen ordinary men.'

'When some one else is master?' said Mary, with natural female gratification.

'No compliments,' said Ben. 'A man needs to be as hard as iron, and as bold as brass;—though why brass should be the emblem of unpleasant boldness, by the way, I don't know.'

When there had been as much of it as this, Mrs. Renton began to stir uneasily. 'I cannot hear what you two are saying,' she said. 'You have light enough for your work generally at this window, Mary. Why should you go away so far to-day? And, Ben, I can see there are two or three things here you did not read to me. There is a dreadful burglary somewhere, in a country-house like this. It is dreadful to think we might be killed in our beds any nights,—and gives it such an interest;—and there is a great deal out of "Galignani" in the French article. "Galignani" is always amusing. But Mary will read it to me when you go out.'

'I was not thinking of going out,—at present, mother. When is Laurie coming? He ought to be here,' said Ben. 'I don't understand how a man can choose to shut himself up in London at this time of the year.'

'But he is working at something,' said Mary.

'He is always working at something, and I don't know what it is ever to come to. Laurie ought to be the eldest son,—if there is to be an eldest son among us,' said Ben. 'I think that would be the best solution. He could muse about his fields, and paint the trees, and make a very good country gentleman,—don't you think so, Mary?—and marry and make everybody comfortable;—that is how it ought to be.'

'Ben,' said his mother, solemnly, 'I hope you have not been led astray into Radical principles since you have been away. How could Laurie be the eldest son? Your poor dear papa did everything for the best. He thought it was good for you to wait, and no doubt it must have been good for you. But to speak as if he did not care for your rights! Why, you were called Benedict because you were the eldest son. I said to Mr. Renton, "I hate the name,—it is the ugliest name I know." But he always said, "My dear, we can't help ourselves; the Rentons have been Laurence and Benedict for hundreds of years,—and Laurence and Benedict they must continue to be; but you can call him Ben, you know,—or Dick, for that matter." I had a good cry over it,' Mrs. Renton said, dropping back fatigued upon her pillows; 'for, if there is anything I hate, it is those short names like Ben and Dick; but he had his way. And now to think you should talk as if it had been all in vain!'

'Miss Mary,' said Davison with decision, 'my missis has talked a deal more than she ought, and I don't hold with excitement. If you and Mr. Ben was to go out for a walk now,—or something as would take him off his poor dear mamma,' said the careful nurse, lowering her voice. Ben was too much for his mother. After seven years of soft, feminine glidings about her room, softened voices, perpetual consideration of her ailments, this 'man in the house,' thought pleasant at first, was too much for her powers. 'And I don't know how we'll ever do when they're all here,' the faithful Davison murmured to herself, as she sprinkled eau-de-Cologne about the pillows, and mixed some port with the arrowroot. And Ben was banished forthwith from the room. 'He is very nice at dinner, my dear,' Mrs. Renton herself said, 'but men never understand. And they should always have something to do, Mary. They are never happy without something to do.'

'But poor Ben, this is his first day at home!' said Mary, when she had read all about the burglary, and calmed the patient down.

'But, my dear, they are always wretched themselves,' said Mrs. Renton, 'when they are quite unoccupied. You must find him something to do.'

Thus it will be seen that Mary's labours were not much lightened by the arrival of the eldest son. When she went down-stairs after her newspaper-reading, she found him in the library yawning somewhat over a book. 'Come and talk,' he said, setting a chair for her; and then laughed a little over his unsuitableness in the hushed and soft-toned house.

'It is because you have been so long away,' said Mary. 'You have gone off on one current, and we on another. I suppose it is always so when people are long parted. Is it not sad?'

'I don't think that it ought to be so,' said Ben.

'And Laurie has his current, too,—quite different. I should like to find out about Laurie. It is he I know least about,' said Mary, with a little sigh.

And then Ben smiled. 'I should like to hear,' he said, 'what you know about me?'

What did she know about him? Nothing,—and yet everything, Mary thought.

'Sometimes one divines,' she said.

'And sometimes one divines all wrong,' said Ben.

Then there followed a pause. It was a very exciting game of fence so far as she was concerned. But she felt instinctively it was not safe to keep it up.

'Godmamma will not come down to luncheon,' she said, 'but in the evening I hope she will be all right again. And when Alice is here and the children they will be a great help. Alice is not clever, you know, but she harmonises things somehow. I wonder if it is because she is musical.'

'You harmonise things, too, and you are not particularly musical,' said Ben.

'Oh, me!' Mary turned away, not caring to discuss that subject. He was always so nice to her,—so frank and affectionate. 'If he were to marry Ruth Escott now, or Helen Cookesley, how nice it would be to be a sister to her!' Mary thought! but Millicent! Could he be thinking of Millicent now? He had got up from his chair, and was looking out with a certain wistfulness—or at least what would have been wistfulness in a woman, who has always to wait for any one she particularly wishes to see. A man can go forth and seek, and has no call to be wistful; but then it was only according to feminine rules that Mary, so long unaccustomed to anything else, could form her thoughts.

'I have ordered up a boat from Cookesley,' he said; 'and remember, I mean to row you to the Swan's Nest this afternoon. It is clearing up—— ' for it had become cloudy, and rain had fallen during that period of newspaper-reading in Mrs. Renton's room. And then Ben went out abruptly and left her. He stood upon no sort of ceremony, as if she were anything but his natural sister, but went away without any explanation. Going to the Swan's Nest it would be necessary to pass The Willows; and at this moment he was taking the path to the river. Could he be going the very first morning to lay himself again at the syren's feet? Could it be the mere pleasure of passing her house, being in the neighbourhood, that moved him? Mary, without pausing to think, flew up-stairs,—up beyond the servants' floor to a little turret-room which commanded a view of the river. And when she had waited long enough to recover her breath, there, sure enough, was a boat shooting out from the green bank at Renton with one figure in it, which must be Ben. And the course he took was up the river. She covered her face for a moment when she saw it, and a hot, sudden tear brimmed just over, wetting her eyelashes. Mo more. Was it her business that she should weep over Ben's folly? No man can redeem his brother, much less any woman, alas! However dreadful it might be, the man must go his own way.

Mrs. Renton rallied sufficiently that afternoon to go for her drive, and Mary's services were wanted accordingly. But when she had got through that duty, there was still time for the Swan's Nest, to which she had been looking forward with an excitement which was almost feverish. Ben was waiting for them at the door. He took his mother up to her room, subduing his big pace as best he could to quietness, and put her into Davison's hands for her rest before dinner. It was an arrangement very grateful to all parties. While Mrs. Renton was taking her favourite refreshment and being comfortably tucked up on her sofa, the young people were making their way down to the bank with something of the gaiety of former days. 'I once beat you, Ben, running down,' Mary said, for a moment forgetting The Willows and all that was involved in it. 'I defy you to beat me now,' her cousin said, and Mary's heart for one moment felt so light that she made a woman's wild dash down one wind of the path, and stopped short breathless, catching at the great beech to support her. But between the branches of the beech Mary saw a sight which quickly sobered her. Could it be by previous arrangement, or was it by chance? A boat lay at the little steps before The Willows, and some one,— there could be no difficulty in guessing whom,—was getting into it. Mary's heart sank away down to the lowest depths,—a sudden sickness of the light, and the brightness, and the river, and the day, came over her. She turned even from Ben, feeling sick of him too. A certain contempt of him rose up in her tender soul. Yes; there are many pangs in the sensation with which a woman recognises that another less worthy is preferred to herself; but not the least penetrating is that instinctive, involuntary contempt. He had gone and arranged with Millicent no doubt, and then he thought to please all parties by taking her, Mary, to meet the woman he loved. Ben, for his part, with the stupidity of a male creature, saw that some shadow had come over her, and thought she had struck her foot in her rapid descent against the roots of the beech. 'Ah, you should not have gone in for it,' he said in not triumph, but sympathy;—'take my arm. I hope you have not twisted your foot.' I twisted her foot!—when it was he who wrung her heart! But to be sure, Mary did not wish him to divine what was her real ailment; and it was so like a man! But the laughter and the fun were over. The two descended soberly to the river-side and got into the boat. And Mary gathered the cords of the little rudder into her hands, and Ben took up the sculls. They were face to face, and it was difficult for one to hide from the other what emotions might rise or what change come over them. 'I am afraid you have hurt your foot badly,—you look quite pale,' Ben said, bending forward to her with absolute anxiety. 'Oh, no, I am all right,' Mary replied, saying in her heart, What fools men are! How stupid they must be!—a threadbare sentiment which does not bear expression. And then she cried, 'Remember I am strong,' with a certain gleam of wicked glee. She could run him into the weeds if he showed too much interest in that other boat. She could keep him out of speaking distance to baulk Millicent's wiles, or she could run into them to give her a fright. Mary began to feel herself when she pulled that cord which put some power into her hands, and saw the little skiff turn and dart about at her will from one side to another. 'Take care what you are doing,' cried Ben in dismay, thinking his coxswain had lost her wits; but she was only getting possession of them, and beginning to remember that there was no need to be passive, and that she, too, had arms in her hands.

And for a little they shot silently, vigorously, each attending to his work, up the shining river. Mary could not speak, and Ben did not, being moved by a thousand associations. The first break in the silence was made by voices not their own, coming from the boat which Mary kept her eye on with the fixedness of enmity. Distant sounds of conversation and laughter came first, at which Ben pricked up his ears. 'Don't run into any one,' he said. 'I hear voices;—there is somebody coming, and I hope you are keeping a look-out ahead——'

'You need not fear for me,—I see them,' said Mary, with emphasis, and he made no sign as if he knew what she meant, but kept on rowing so quietly that he either did not know who was coming, or thought she was a most accomplished hypocrite. On the contrary, he too began to talk softly like a man absorbed in thoughts and preoccupations of his own.

'The last time you and I were here together was one of my last days in England,' he said;—do you remember? I was full of my own affairs, and indifferent to everything; and, good life, what a fool I was!' he added to himself,—and then paused and sighed. Mary, for her part, saw all, noted all, and in her rashness felt anxious to test his meaning.

'You made me very curious,' she said; 'I was so anxious to know what you meant——' And there was no telling how much further she might have gone had not the other boat suddenly glanced alongside, and some one called her by her name. Some one! Millicent, looking more lovely than she had ever seen her, she thought, with a scarlet cloak lightly thrown over her black dress, lying back upon the cushions, holding gingerly in her hands the steering cords.

'Mary!' Millicent called, softly,—'is it you? Oh, I am sure one of your cousins must have come home! Stop and tell me! What a happy thing for Mrs. Renton! And are not you all in the seventh heaven?'

The picture was one which neither of the cousins ever forgot. She was in the full bloom of her beauty, increased rather than diminished, by the severity of her mourning dress. The river sparkled like a mirror all round the gay little painted boat in which she reclined. An unusual flush of colour was on her cheek, and the young Guardsman who was rowing her gazed with eyes of worship on the lovely creature. No doubt she was excited. It seemed to Mary that even the boy who was with her was part of a plan, the *mise en scène* which she had perfected for Ben's sake; and that her cheek was flushed with the excitement of the meeting and with her unusual anxiety that success might follow. For the first time for seven years Ben and she looked each other in the face. The Guardsman had run the other boat so close that she was almost as near to him as Mary was, confronting him, in a position in which she could watch his face and all its changes. When he looked up her eye was upon him. It was the most curious meeting for those two, who had parted so differently. Was it possible she had forgotten how they parted? She looked at him with an unabashed, smiling, gracious countenance, while Ben, with some agitation, took off his hat.

'Is it Mr. Ben Renton?' Millicent said, softly. And Mary, looking on, saw the colour flash all over Ben's face at the sound of her voice. Then, in her heart, his cousin acquitted him of having arranged this interruption. On the contrary, he was so moved by it that he did not seem capable of finding his voice.

'Mr. Renton, Mrs. Henry Rich,' Mary said, mechanically, attempting an introduction, though she knew how unnecessary that was.

'Ah, we have met before!' said Millicent. 'Did I not tell you, Mary? We used to know each other, though your cousin seems to have forgotten me; but, to be sure, I had then a different name.'

'No, I have not forgotten,' said Ben; 'that would be difficult under any name.'

And then there was a dead pause. Millicent put her arm over the edge of the boat and dipped her pretty hand into the water. She had a certain air of embarrassment, either real or assumed; and Ben looked at her with a curious openness and fixedness of gaze. 'You have just come?' she said at last, not raising her eyes.

'Just come,' said Ben; 'and only for a few days.'

Then Millicent's eyes rose, and turned to him curiously; and Mary, too, bewildered, gave him a frightened, anxious look. There was a whole drama in their glances, and yet the words were very constrained and very few which passed between them. 'So soon?' Millicent said, with a surprised, half-sorrowful tone.

'So soon!' he repeated, with a kind of decision, always looking at her, till Mary, hard-hearted as she thought herself, felt that he was uncivil, and was moved to interfere; but Millicent bore it bravely enough. Her colour grew higher, her composure was a little shaken, but yet she did not betray any symptoms of mortification or fear.

'My mother would be glad to see you before you go,' she said, faltering slightly. 'We cannot forget our obligations to you,—though perhaps you have forgotten;' and then she tried another half-supplicating, anxious look.

'I have forgotten nothing,' said Ben. 'We Rentons have extraordinary memories. I will call on Mrs. Tracy if I can before we go.'

'Then I will not detain you longer,' Millicent said, with a look of relief. 'What a pleasure it must be to you, Mary, to have your cousin to row you about! I am quite grateful to Mr. Horsman, who is so good as to bring me out. How delicious the river is, to be sure! Mr. Renton, it was you who used to tell me of it—first.'

'Then I am glad to have added something to your pleasures,' said Ben. He had adjusted his sculls, and did not manifest the least inclination to stay longer. On the contrary, Mary felt that he was anxious to go on, to get clear of this interruption. And not less anxious was the young Guardsman,—almost a boy,—who had taken his hat off sulkily, and waited his orders with eagerness. Millicent was the only one of the four who had any desire to linger. She gave Ben another long, searching look, to which he made no response, being busy, or appearing to be busy, with his sculls; and then she gave a little nod to her waterman.

'I dare say we shall meet again,' she said, gaily, 'unless you are going a very long way;—*au revoir.*'

'Good-bye,' said Mary. And in another moment, with one pull of the steerage and one sweep of the oars, the Renton boat had shot wide of the other, darting off to one side with a nervous motion, for which Mary alone was responsible. Ben made no remark, which was symptom enough of his agitation too. Had he been as calm as he affected to be, Mary knew well that her illegitimate energy would not have passed without remark. And they went up the river for some time at a tremendous pace, devoting themselves to their work with the energy of professional people. Mary steered beautifully all the way to the Swan's Nest. She steered as if her life depended on it, keeping the due course in every turn, avoiding, as she ought, the side where the current was strongest, which a steerswoman seldom remembers to do, and in every way justifying the old training which had been disused so long. And scarcely a word was spoken between them until they reached the end of their expedition. It was a sheltered little elbow of the river, a very bed of water-lilies in the season. And the green leaves still spread all round like a thick carpet upon the water. Then Ben took breath for the first time. He lay upon his oars and wiped his forehead, and drew a long breath. 'That was hard work,' he said, with a sigh. But which it was that was hard work,—whether the encounter with Millicent, or their long, breathless sweep against the current, Mary could not tell.

CHAPTER X.

AUNT LYDIA.

'LET us run to the Cottage for five minutes, and see mamma,' said Mary, as they made their way back. 'Fancy, Ben, she does not know you have come home!'

'Shall we have time?' Ben asked, making for the bank as he spoke. The path that led to the Cottage struck off from the river-side above The Willows. And it was always gaining time to make this little diversion. He had been so silent, saying nothing,—and a sense of disappointment had crept over Mary after the intense sympathy with which she felt she had been entering into all his thoughts.

But when he thrust the boat into the flowery bank, and helped her to jump out, Ben replied to her, though she had said nothing. 'You are quite right,' he said. 'It is best in every way not to meet them again.'

'Ben! I did not say a word——'

'No,' he answered, 'you did not, and it was very, very kind of you, Mary. I am more obliged to you than I can say. There are some things which it is impossible to talk about. I thank you with all my heart.'

What did this mean? Mary was accustomed to a great deal of talk about everything,—more talk than meaning, indeed. And she was a little bewildered by this absence of all explanation. She would have been comforted had he opened up a little and told her how it all was. But she submitted, of course, concluding it was his mannish, unsatisfactory way. And as they went hurriedly up the lane, in the kindness of her heart she slid her hand through Ben's arm. It was the softest, kindly touch, such as his sister's hand might have given. Was not she his sister, nearer to him than any one else, and, little as she did understand, yet knowing more of what was in his heart,—she thought,— than any other creature in the world?

And Ben was not indifferent to that mute token of sympathy. He drew the timid hand closely through his arm. 'My good little Mary!' he said; but even then he said no more. No explanation came, whatever she might do or say, which was hard, but had to be borne.

And this is how it was that Mrs. Westbury, to her very great amazement, saw her daughter and Ben Renton approaching the Cottage arm-in-arm,—'like an engaged couple,' she said afterwards,—which gave her a curious thrill of admiration and satisfaction at the first glance. When her nephew came up to her, however, nature prevailed, and the recollection of her own agency, which nobody but herself believed in, in sending all the boys away.

'Ben!' she cried, and then kissed him, and held both his hands, and shed some tears of surprise and joy, 'I am so glad to see you! I cannot tell how glad I am to see you! Have you all come home?'

'Only I,' said Ben; 'but the others are coming, and Mary and I have come to fetch you, Aunt Lydia, to dine with my mother. She does not understand my noise and uncouthness, after the long spell of quiet she has had. After dinner Mary and I will bring you back.'

'Mary and you seem to be—full of business,' said Mrs. Westbury, more and more astonished. She had intended to end her sentence differently, but had met Mary's eye, and paused, not quite knowing what to make of it. But she went up-stairs for her best cap, calling her daughter with her. 'What is the meaning of all this, Mary?' she said. 'What does Ben mean by it? For my part, I cannot tell what to think.'

'About what, mamma?' said Mary; but there was a little flutter in her heart which belied her composure. 'Ben has come home, as you see, and he came to see you, as he ought to do, and he wants you to go to dinner. I think it is all very visible what he means.'

'It does not seem to me at all plain,' said Mrs. Westbury; but then she put her hand into her wardrobe to get out her cap, and decided that it was best not to spoil sport by any premature remarks. It was startling to see Mary leaning so confidentially on her cousin's arm. And Ben's talk of 'Mary and I' was very peculiar; and if the will was all right, such an arrangement would be a most sensible, most admirable one. But if things were going on so well of their own accord, it might be best to let them alone, and suffer the affair to take its own course. When she found herself walking down to the river a quarter of an hour afterwards, with a maid behind carrying her cap, and Ben and Mary on each side of her, Mrs. Westbury freely expressed her surprise at the whole business. 'I was just going to have tea,' she cried. 'One can't dine late when one is alone, and Laurence has gone over to Cookesley to see some of his friends. I never thought of seeing any of you, nor of Ben at all, though I knew he was expected. And now to find myself on my way to Renton! Laurence will be struck dumb when he comes home.'

'So Laurence is a parson now,' said Ben. 'How droll it will be to see him so! but pleasant for you. You can keep hold of a parson and keep him at home.'

'Yes. I expect you to give him Renton, you know, Ben, when old Mr. Palliser dies.'

'Well, I suppose one of us is sure to have Renton to give,' said Ben; 'so that Laurence will be safe anyhow. But I have no confidence that it will be me.'

'It must be you,' said Mrs. Westbury, indignantly. And then there came a pause, and she was helped into the boat. 'Who are those new people at The Willows?' she said, as she settled herself. 'That is their boat; they are always on the water. They say she is a young widow; but I don't think that is much like a widow. Somebody told me you knew them, Mary. Was it yourself?'

'She was at Thorny croft at school for a little,' said Mary, giving her mother a look. The look put a stop to the conversation; but it had to be explained afterwards, which was done somewhat at the expense of truth. The Willows' boat had been drawn close to the bank before they passed, and Mary was less particular in steering wide of it. Millicent stood on the lawn, having just landed, with her scarlet cloak dropping off her shoulders, and waved her hand to them. 'Good-night! How pleasant it has been!' she cried, her voice falling softly through the summer air, still full of the slanting sunshine. 'Good-night!' Mary cried across the water. Ben never said a word; he did not even pause in the slow, vigorous, regular stroke which made the boat fly down the shining current. They were yards below The Willows before Millicent had finished speaking her two or three words. "Was he afraid?— was he indifferent? And while Mary's mind was busy about this question, Aunt Lydia was forming her little theories of a very different kind. When a young man passes by a very pretty woman without so much as raising his head, it means,—what does it mean?—that some one else has secured his attention, and taken up all his thoughts. Mrs. Westbury felt as if Providence itself was heaping coals of fire on her head. She it was who had brought about the banishment of the boys, and yet no sooner had the first of them come home than he set about fulfilling her dearest wish. But no doubt it was for Mary's sake. Mary, who had never harmed any one, who had helped and served everybody from her cradle. How bright she had become all at once!— how she had learned to chatter like the rest! It seemed curious to Mrs. Westbury that an important event should be coming about in her child's life in which she herself had not been the chief actor,—especially that Mary should have had the sense to acquire for herself an eligible lover without any assistance. Ben did not look very much like a lover it is true, but Aunt Lydia was aware that a man in such a position is not always possessed with an insane delight, but often has a great deal to think of. She, too, was silent with the stress of her own thoughts. It was Mary who entertained them,—talking as she had never been heard to talk before,—full of wild spirits and fun. Her mother, who knew nothing of the story, did not perceive that Mary's gaiety came on suddenly after they passed The Willows, nor that her eyes had the humid and dilated look which signifies emotion. One finds things out so much more readily when one has an inkling of the *fin mot* of the enigma. Mrs. Westbury did not even know there was an enigma to solve, and set down her daughter's high spirits to what seemed to her the most natural and the most likely cause.

'I congratulate you, my dear, upon having Ben back again,' she said to Mrs. Renton as she kissed her. They were not very fond of each other, the two ladies; but yet, by dint of connexion and contiguity, had come to a certain habit of mutual dependence, though the support was chiefly on one side.

'Yes,' Mrs. Renton said, with an under-tone which was slightly querulous. 'He is a very good boy; but a stranger in the house makes such a difference in one's life.'

'You don't call Ben a stranger, poor fellow! And he is so nice. It is quite a pleasure to see him back,' said Mrs. Westbury. 'I thought you would have been out of your wits with joy.'

'And so I am,' said Ben's mother, with a little indignation; 'but there is nobody that has any real consideration for my weakness except Mary. She knows just how much I am able to bear. I suppose it is difficult for people in health to realise how weak I am.'

'Well, my dear, you know I always said that if you would but make an effort to exert yourself it would do all the good in the world,' said Mrs. Westbury; and then she went up-stairs to put on her cap. 'I have no patience with your aunt,' she said to Mary,—'thinking of her own little bits of ailments, half of which are mere indulgence, when her poor boy has just come home.'

'Poor godmamma! I don't think she can help it,' said Mary.

'Nonsense, child! I have said to her from the first that she ought to make an effort. How do you think I should ever have managed had I given in? And now tell me, please, what you meant by looking at me so, twice over, when I was speaking to Ben.'

'I did not want you to talk about Mrs. Rich,' said Mary, turning away as the exigencies of her own toilette required. 'He used to know her, and I was afraid you might say something——'

'You might have left that to my own discretion,' said Mrs. Westbury, with some offence.

'But, dear mamma, how could your discretion serve when you did not know?' said Mary. 'And, poor fellow! he is so,—so——'

'So very devoted to some one else that he could not even take the trouble to look at Mrs. Rich,—such a pretty woman, too!' said Mrs. Westbury. 'It seems to me, my dear, that you have made the very most of your time.'

'Oh, mamma, how dreadful that you should say so!' cried Mary, turning round again with flaming, crimson cheeks. 'Surely, surely, you know me better! And Ben, poor fellow! has so much to think of. Nothing could be further from his mind. I have been their sister all their lives; it would be hard if I could not try to be a little comfort to him now.'

'My dear, if he needs comfort, I am sure I have no objection,' said Mrs. Westbury, with a smile; and just then Mary's maid came into the room, and the conversation came to an end. It was this dreadful practical turn, which was in the old Renton blood, which bewildered the less energetic members of the family. But it was wonderful to see how Ben and Aunt Lydia got on at dinner. He told her more about his work, and what he had been doing, in half-an-hour than the others had extracted from him in twenty-four. And the Renton spirit sparkled in Mrs. Westbury's eyes as she listened. 'Even if you had not made a penny, Ben,' she said, in her energetic way, 'I should be so much more pleased that you had been making some use of your talents than just hanging on in the old way at home.'

'But I have made a penny,' Ben said, with a kindred glance;—he was pleased with the thought, which gave Mary a momentary disgust;—'though it has cost more than it is worth in the making,' he added, in a lower tone. And then his cousin forgave, and was sorry for poor Ben. It was dangerous work for Mary, especially as there was still the excitement of the return expedition across the river, to convey Mrs. Westbury home to look forward to. But, fortunately, there was no one visible about The Willows when that moment came;—nothing but serene moonlight, white and peaceable, unbroken by any shadow or voice but their own, was on the gleaming river. And the Rev. Laurence Westbury standing on the bank in his clerical coat,—who had been at school when Ben left Renton,—to take his mother home, and bid the new-comer welcome; and then the silent progress back down the stream in the moonlight. It surprised Mary afterwards to think how little Ben and she had said to each other, and yet what perfectly good company he had been. And thus they went on, those curious, rapid days.

CHAPTER XI.

ALL HOME.

LAURIE arrived on the Friday, coming in, in his usual unexpected way, through the window, when they were all in the drawing-room after dinner. The brothers had met in town, where Ben had paused for a day on his way to Renton, so that their greeting was not mingled with any of those remarks on changed appearance and unexpected signs of age which are general after a long absence. But when they stood thus together for the first time for seven years, the difference between old things and new became more perceptible to the bystanders. The surroundings were so completely the same as of old that any variation from the past became more clear to them. The same lamps, shaded for their mother's sake; the same brilliant spot of light upon the tea-table, where the china and silver glittered; Mrs. Renton lying on the same sofa, in the same attitude, covered with the same Indian shawl; the same soft odour of mignonette and heliotrope, and earth and dew, stealing in at the great open window; even the same moths, or reproductions of the same, making wild circles about the lamp. 'And Mary, I think, is the very same,' Laurie said, looking at her with true brotherly kindness. But 'the boys' were not the same. Of the two it was Laurie who looked the elder. He was just thirty, but the hair was getting thin on the top of his head, and his face was more worn than it had any right to be. Ben had broadened, almost imperceptibly, but still enough to indicate to the bystander that the first slim outline of youth was over. But Laurie, though he had not expanded, had aged even in the lines of his face; and then he had grown a little careless, like the society into which he had cast himself. He was dusty with his walk, and his velvet morning-coat looked strange and wild beside Ben's correct evening costume. Lazy Laurence still; but with all the difference between sanguine youth and meditative manhood. Mary, however, was the only one of the party who was troubled by the mystery of Laurie's subdued tone. Mrs. Renton was not given to speculation, and Ben was occupied by his own affairs to the exclusion of all inquiry into those of others. Both mother and brother took it for granted that Laurie was just as it was natural he should be. Only Mary,— sisterly, womanly, anxious always to know how it was,—watched him with a sympathetic eye.

'Well! here we are at home once more, old fellow,' said Laurie, throwing himself into an easy chair near the window, when the mother had been safely conveyed up-stairs.

'Yes, a home that always looks the same,' said Ben. 'I am not so sure as I used to be of the good of that. It makes one feel doubly the change in one's self.'

'These are his Yankee notions,' said Laurie. 'I suppose he has given up primogeniture, and Church and State, and everything. But Mary is an orthodox person who will set us all right.'

'As if women might not think about primogeniture and all the rest as well as you others!' said Mary. 'We are the only people who take any time to think now-a-days. Ben has done nothing but make railways,—and money,—and he likes it;—he is a real Renton,' she cried, pleased to let him know her mind on that subject.

'And very right, too,' said Laurie. 'If there were not Rentons to be had somewhere how should the world get on?'

'But I don't care for the world,' said Mary; 'and I would much rather you were not fond of money, like everybody else, you boys.'

'I am very fond of money, but I never can get any,' said Laurie. 'I say to myself, if I should happen to come into reputation next century, what a collection of Rentons there will be for somebody to make a fortune of,—Ben's heirs, most probably; or that little Mary of Frank's, who is a darling. Now that I think of it, as she is a painter's descendant, it is she who shall be my heir.'

'I think much the best thing would be for you to have Renton, Laurie, and heirs of your own.'

'Thanks,' said Laurie; 'my brothers are very kind. Frank took the trouble to write me a long letter ever so many years ago, adjuring me by all I held dear to marry a certain Nelly Rich.'

'It was very impertinent of him,' cried Mary, 'and very conceited. Nelly Rich would no more have looked at you——'

'Showed her sense,' said Laurie, quietly. 'I am only telling you what actions have been set on foot for my benefit. But I never saw Nelly Rich except once, so I am not conceited; and as for Renton, no such iniquity could ever be, as that it should go past you, Ben.'

'You speak strongly,' said the elder brother.

'That is one result of time, you know. One can see now, without irreverence, how wrong my poor father was. Of course we would have been wretches had we been capable of anything but obedience at the time,' said Laurie; 'but, looking back, one can see more clearly. He was wrong,—I don't bear him any malice, poor dear old father! but he did us as much harm almost as was possible. And if Renton is left out of the natural succession, I shall say it is iniquity, and oppose it with all my power.'

'It would be iniquity,' Ben said, gravely. And then there was a pause. The three sat, going back into their individual memories, unaware what devious paths the others were treading. But for that Laurie might never have fallen into the temptation which had stolen what energy he had out of him, and

- 90 -

strengthened all his dreamy, unpractical ways. But for that Ben might have given the Renton force and strength of work to his country, and served her,—as is the citizen's first duty,—instead of making American railroads, which another man might have been found to do. As for Mary, the paths in which she went wandering were not her own. It did not occur to her to think of the seven years, which for her had been simple loss. Had she been living at home, no doubt, long before this she would have married some one, and been like Alice, the mother of children. But such were not Mary's reflections. She was thinking if this had not happened Ben would have married Millicent seven years ago, and that, on the whole, everything was for the best.

They had but one other day to themselves; but during that day the house felt, with a bewildered sense of confusion and uncertainty, that old times had come back. Mr. Ben and Mr. Laurie had gone back to their old rooms; and their steps and voices, the peremptory orders of the eldest, the 'chaff' of Mr. Laurie, 'who was a gentleman as you never could understand whether he was in earnest or in joke,'—turned the heads of the old servants. They, like their mistress, were upset by the new *régime*; the dulness of the house had been a trouble to them when her reign of utter seclusion commenced; but if it was dull, there was little to do, and the house had habituated itself to the monotonous round. And now they felt it a hardship when the noise and the work recommenced, and dinner ran the risk of having to wait ten minutes, and breakfast was on the table from half-past eight to half-past ten. 'All along o' that lazy Laurie, as they calls him, and a very good name, too,' said the affronted cook. Mary had much ado to keep them in working order. 'There may be further changes after a while,' she said to the old butler, who had carried them all in his arms, and knew about everything, and who would as soon have cut his throat as leave Renton;—'you must have patience for a little, and see how things turn out.' Thus it will be seen that if the return of her cousins brought any happiness to Mary it brought a great increase of anxiety as well. And there was always the sense of Millicent's vicinity to weigh upon her mind. She had been looking forward for years to the family reunion as the end of tribulation and beginning of a better life; but up to this time her anticipations had not been fulfilled. Anxieties had increased upon her,—one growing out of another. Instead of comfort, and certainty, and the support which she had always been taught to believe were involved in the possession of 'men in the house,' Mary found that these tenants had rather an agitating than a calming effect upon herself and the community in general. That she should have more trouble about the dinners was natural; but that even their mother should require to be let softly down into the enjoyment of their society, and that circumstances in general required double consideration on account of their presence, was a new idea to Mary. And then it turned out that Mrs. Renton had spoken very truly when she said a man must have something to do. Both 'the boys' were in a state of restlessness and excitement, not disposed to settle to anything. There was capital shooting to be had, and the partridges were everything a sportsman could desire; but somehow even Ben felt that partridges were not congenial to the occasion. And as for Laurie, he was too indolent to make any such exertion. 'Wait till Frank comes,' he said. 'Frank has energy for two. If we were on a Scotch moor, indeed, where you want to move about to keep yourself warm; but it's too hot, my dear fellow, for stumping about through the stubble. I'll take Mary out after a bit for a row.' And Ben's activities, too, culminated in the same idea. Laurie lay in the bottom of the boat, sometimes puffing gently at his cigar, doing simply nothing, while Ben pulled against stream, and Mary steered him dexterously through the weeds; and then the three floated slowly down again, saying little to each other, lingering along the mid current with scarcely any movement of the languid oars. They were not very sociable in this strange amusement; but still its starts of momentary violent exercise, its dreamy charm of movement, the warm autumnal sun overhead, the delicious gliding water that gurgled on the sides of the boat, and all the familiarity and all the novelty of the scene, chimed in with their feelings. Ben was pondering the future, which was still so dark,—his unfinished work at the other end of the world,—what he would do with Renton if it came to him,—what he would do if it did not come to him,—all the range of possibilities which overhung his way as the trees overhung the river. Laurie, for his part, wandered in a field of much wider fancy, and did not take Renton at all into account, nor the chances which a few days might bring to him. What did it matter? he could live, and he had no more to think of,—no future which interested him particularly,—no hope that would be affected by the tenor of his father's will. Sometimes his eye would be caught by a combination of foliage, or a sudden light on the water, or the turn of Mary's arm as she plied her cords. 'How did Mary keep her steering up while we were all away?' he would say between the puffs of his cigar, and made up his mind that she should sit to him next day in that particular pose. Mary, for her own part, during these expeditions, was too much occupied in watching her cousins to have any thoughts of her own. What was Ben thinking of? Was it The Willows his mind was fixed on as he opened his full chest and sent the boat up against the stream with the force of an arrow out of a bow? Was it the image of Millicent that made his eyes glow as he folded his arms, and let the skiff idle on the current? And what were Laurie's thoughts occupied about as he lay, lazy, in the bottom? Mary gazed at them, and wondered, not knowing what to think, and said to herself how much more difficult it was now to prognosticate what would become of them than it would have been seven years ago, at their first entering upon life. And thus the long day glided to its end.

On the Saturday Frank and his belongings arrived, and all was altered. Frank, so far as personal appearance went, was the least changed of all. His moustache had grown from the silky shadow it used to be into a very decided martial ornament, and he was brown with the Indian sun. Laurie had the presumption to insinuate that he had grown, which touched the soldier to the quick; but though he was the father of a family, the seven years had affected him less than either of his brothers. To be sure, he was but seven-and-twenty, and had lived a comparatively happy life. But it must be allowed that the Sunday was hard to get through. The three brothers, who were all very different men to begin with, had each got into his groove, and each undervalued,—let us not say had a contempt for,—the occupation of the other. What with India, and what with youth, and what with the training of his profession, Frank had all the unreasoning conservatism which was natural to a well-born, unintellectual soldier. And then he had a wife to back him, which strengthens a man's self-opinion. 'Depend upon it,' he would say, 'these Radicals will land us all in perdition if they get their way.' 'Why should I depend upon it, when my own opinion goes directly contrary?' Ben, who had been in America, and all over the world, drawing in revolutionary ideas, would answer him. As for Laurie he would ask them both, 'What does it matter? one man is as good as another, if not better,' and smile in his pococurante way. The children were a godsend to them all, and so was Alice with her youthful wisdom. For Mary by this time, with three men to keep in order, as it were, and Mrs. Renton to hold safely in hand all the time, and all unsuitable visitors to keep at a distance, and the dinner to order, was about as much overwhelmed with cares, and as little capable of the graces of society, as a woman could be. She had to spend with her aunt the hour of that inevitable Sunday afternoon walk, and saw her flock pair off and disappear among the trees with the sensations of an anxious mother, who feels her nursery for the moment in comparative safety. Ben with Alice and little Mary went one way, and Laurie and Frank took another. When she had seen them off Mary turned with a satisfied mind to read to her godmother the Sunday periodical which took the place of the newspaper on this day. It was very mild reading, though it satisfied Mrs. Renton. It was her principle not to drive on Sunday, and the morning was occupied by the Morning Service, which Davison and she read together before she got up, and that duty being over the Sunday periodical came in naturally to take the place of the drive. It was very rarely that she felt able to go to church; and of all days this day, which followed so closely the arrival of her sons, was the one on which she could least be supposed capable of such an exertion. So Mary read a story, and a sermon, and a missionary narrative, and was very tired of it, while the slow afternoon lingered on and the others had their walk.

Ben and Alice, though they were in the position of brother and sister, and called each other by their Christian names, had met for the first time on the day before, and naturally were not very much acquainted with each other's way of thinking. The woods were their great subject of discourse. 'Frank has talked of them wherever we were,' said Alice. 'I am so glad to bring the children here. If we should have to go to India again it will be nice for them to remember. But I need not speak like that,' she added, after a moment's pause, with a sudden rush of tears to her blue eyes; 'for if we have to go to India we must leave little Mary behind,—she is too old to go back. And I suppose if I were prudent, baby too—but I could not bear that.'

'Why should you go back to India?'

'Ah, we must, unless there is some money coming to us,' said Alice: 'you know I had no fortune. I did not think that mattered then; but when one has children one learns. Do you think there will be some money for Frank in the will?'

'I am certain of it,' said Ben.

'Enough to make us able to stay at home,' said Alice, clasping her hands. 'It is not that I care for money, nor Frank either.'

'But it is quite natural you should care. And I promise you,' said Ben, 'if there is anything I can set right, that you shall not go back to India. Whichever of us is preferred, you may be sure of that. I can answer for Laurie as for myself.'

'Oh, I know Laurie,' cried Alice; 'but I did not know you,—and then perhaps Frank would not be willing;—but anyhow, since you say you are sure, I will keep up my heart.'

And in the meantime Frank and Laurie by the river-side were having their confidences too. 'If it should come to me,' Frank was saying, 'I hope I shall do what is right by Ben in any case—but it will be a struggle for that little beggar's sake.'

'I would let the little beggar take his chance,' said Laurie; 'there is time enough. I don't think you need begin to consider him yet.'

'I should do my duty, of course,' said Frank, 'by Ben, who has been badly used; but I don't deny it will cost me something, Laurie. A man does not get ties about him for nothing. If I had the chance of a home for Alice and the little ones,—even if it were not a home like this, by Jove! it would be an awful temptation,—a temptation one would scarcely know how to resist.'

'Then it is to be hoped it will never come,' said Laurie. 'I don't see how we could stand in doubt for an instant. I don't speak of natural justice. But Ben was brought up to be the heir. There was never a doubt of his being the heir till my poor father's will had to be read. Therefore he must be the heir now. I don't care whether it falls to you or me. It's as clear as daylight, and I can't believe you would find the least difficulty in doing what was right.'

'I should do it,' said Frank, but he made no further protestation. In his heart he could not but say to himself that it was easy for Laurie, a man with nobody dependent on him, with no question before him such as that of returning or not returning to India, and with,—so far as any one knew,—no prospects of future happiness which depended on this decision. And Ben, too, was unmarried, and likely to be unmarried. 'Unless he marries Mary,' Frank said to himself. Of course if Renton fell to him he would marry, and they had all pledged themselves that Renton must fall to him, and Ben accordingly would sit down in his father's seat, and bring in some stranger to rule over the place, and Alice and the children would have to go away. Back to India! If that were the only alternative Frank felt as if it would be impossible to do his duty by Ben. The excitement of the moment, and the fundamental simplicity of his mind, thus brought him to the strange notion that all secondary justice must have been set aside, and that it would be a question of everything or nothing to the victor. Thus the Rentons awaited, with thoughts often too deep for words, with a restrained excitement wonderful to behold, with hopes and sinkings of heart, the revelation of their father's will; and that was to take place next day.

CHAPTER XII.

SUSPENSE.

WHEN the Rentons were all seated together in the drawing-room after dinner, doing their best to get through the Sunday evening, a note was brought to Mrs. Renton, to the amazement of all the family assembly. Mrs. Westbury and her son Laurence, who was curate of Cookesley, had joined them at dinner; and they were all seated in a circle round the room drinking their tea and trying to talk, and suppressing an occasional yawn with the true decorum of a family party. Sometimes there would get up a little lively talk between Mary and her mother and brother touching the gossip of the district, or Alice and Laurie would brighten into a familiar discussion of something belonging to Fitzroy Square; but then they would suddenly remark that the others were uninterested and taking no part, and the talk would come to a stop, and Mrs. Westbury would make a commonplace remark to one of her nephews, and Alice would ask the curate if he went often to the Opera, and a uniformity of dulness would fall upon the party. The Rentons were all well-bred people, and it was certainly not well-bred to enjoy one's self in an animated way in a corner with two or three, while the rest of the company sat blank and did not know what one was making merry about. To be sure, there was Alice's music to fall back upon; but, except to two or three of the company, that would not much mend matters; so that when the note was brought to Mrs. Renton there was immediately a little movement of interest. Ben brought one of the shaded lamps to his mother that she might read it, and Mary drew near in case her services should be wanted to write the answer, for which the butler stood solemnly waiting erect in the midst of the fatigued group.

'It must be something very urgent indeed to write about to-day,' Mrs. Westbury said. 'I am old-fashioned, and I don't think the family quiet should be disturbed on Sunday unless it is something of importance.'

'My dear, I can't read these dreadful hands that people write now-a-days,' said Mrs. Renton. 'I can't get the light on it, and I am too tired to sit up. If you would read it aloud, Ben——'

Ben took the little note in his hand, and put the lamp down on the nearest table. His face was in shade, and it was impossible to tell what his feelings were. He glanced over the note for a second, and then read it aloud as his mother bade. It was a prayer to be allowed to visit the woods next morning with a friend who was going away, and it was signed 'Millicent Rich.' 'I would not have dreamt of asking, knowing that you have all your people about you, and do not want to be troubled with strangers,' she wrote; 'but our friend is going off by the three o'clock train. We shall keep strictly to the woods, and not come near the house to worry you, when your attention must be so occupied with other things; but please let me come.' This was what Ben read out with a perfectly expressionless voice, not even faltering over the name.

'Of course she must come,' said Mrs. Renton. 'Mary, you must write a note for me. Say that the boys being here makes no difference, and that if she will come to luncheon and bring her friend——'

'But, godmamma, Mr. Ponsonby is coming,' said Mary, while Ben took up the lamp, and stood like a monument, holding it in his hand.

'Mr. Ponsonby will not eat her, I suppose,' said Mrs. Renton; and then there was a pause.

'But, godmamma,' Mary resumed after that interval, 'don't you think so important a day as to-morrow is,—and so much as there will be going on——'

'Any stranger would be a bore,' said Frank. 'How are we to go and talk and be civil, when an hour more may see us set up or ruined——'

Here Alice plucked at his sleeve, indicating with a look of warning the stolid countenance of old Willis, who stood listening to everything. 'If it would be any pleasure to grandmamma, I would attend to them,' she said.

'And I think it would be a very good thing for you all,' said Mrs. Westbury, 'and take your minds off yourselves a little. It is a blessing to have a stranger for that,—you are obliged to exert yourselves, and kept from brooding over one subject. I think your mother is quite right.'

'Let us have them,' said Laurie. 'What does it matter? Old Ponsonby is always late.'

'He will surely never be late on an occasion of such importance,' said Laurence Westbury.

Mrs. Renton looked from one to another with an anxious countenance, and they came round the sofa, glad of the little interruption to that family quiet which was almost too much blessedness. Ben, who said nothing, lighted up the circle in a curious Rembrandtish way, holding his lamp so as to screen his mother; and outside stood old Willis, erect as a soldier, with unmoved countenance, waiting for the answer.

'Ben, what do you say?' said Mrs. Renton, with all the earnestness of a last appeal.

'That you must do just what you like, mother,' said Ben.

Upon which she wrung her hands in despair. 'How can I tell what I shall like if none of you will advise me?' she said.

'I will attend to them, if grandmamma would like it,' said Alice, coming to the head of the sofa. 'And I am sure you would like it, dear grandmamma; it would give you something else to think of.'

'So it would, my dear,' said Mrs. Renton, ready to cry; 'and how I am to get through to-morrow without some assistance is more than I can tell.'

'It will take all your minds off the one subject,' added Mrs. Westbury; 'and of course there must always be luncheon. Mary, go and do what your aunt tells you. It will be good, my dears, for you all.'

And Ben gave a little gesture with his hand, Mary caught his eye over the glowing darkness of the shaded lamp, and went and wrote her note without a word. Ben's face had said, or seemed to say, 'Let them come,—what does it matter?' And if it did not matter to him, certainly it mattered nothing to any one else. When the note was despatched, Alice sat down at the piano and played to the entire satisfaction of her husband, his mother, and Laurence Westbury. Ben settled down in a corner and took a book, till his aunt Lydia went and sat beside him, when an earnest conversation ensued; and Laurie stood idling by the window, beating back the moths that came in tribes to seek their destruction in the light, and sometimes saying a word to Mary, who, half occupied by the music and more than half by her own thoughts, sat near him within the shadow of the curtains.

'What sort of people are those that are coming to-morrow, and why don't you like them?' said Laurie, under cover of a fortissimo.

'I never said I did not like them,' said Mary.

'No; but I know you don't. Who are they?'

And then the music fell low into tremulous, dying murmurs, and all was silent in the room except for a shrill 's' now and then of Mrs. Westbury's half-whispered energetic conversation with Ben. When the strain rose and swelled into passion, the talk at the window was resumed.

'It is not they,—it is she I don't like;—one of my old school-fellows, and the most beautiful woman you ever saw.'

'Hallo!' said Laurie, 'is that the reason why?'

'Yes, of course. We should all like to strangle her because she is so pretty,' said Mary, with a certain rancour in her voice.

Laurie sent a great night-moth out with a rush, and then he stooped towards his cousin's hiding-place. 'Granted in the general,' he said, 'but there is something particular about this.'

What could Mary say? Her heart was quivering with that poignant sense of weakness and inability to resist fate which sometimes overcomes a woman in those secret machinations for somebody else's good, which are so seldom successful. 'I have done,' she said; 'I will try no more.' And that was all the answer that was given to Laurie's curiosity.

Alice had not fallen off in her playing. The piano, under her fingers, gave forth such sounds as wiled the very hearts out of the bosoms of the three who were listening. Mrs. Renton lay back on her sofa, with the tears coming to her eyes and a world of inarticulate, inexpressible feeling in her heart. Had it been poetry, the poor lady would have yawned and wished herself in bed; but now she had floated into a serene Eden,—a Paradise full of all vague loveliness, and sweetness, and unspeakable, indistinct emotions. As for Laurence Westbury, he dared scarcely draw breath, so entirely did the witchery seize him. The music to him stormed and struggled like a soul in pain, and paused and sank to give forth the cry of despair, and swelled into a gathering hope, into a final conflict, into delicious murmurs of sweetness and gratefulness and repose; there was a whole drama in it, moving the real listener with such a rapid succession of feeling as the highest tragic efforts of poetry call forth in others. While in the meanwhile Ben and Aunt Lydia talked quite undisturbed in their corner of railways and investments, and of how much Renton might be improved, and how fast Dick Westbury was making his fortune out in India; and Laurie was driving out the moths, and moralising over their eagerness to enter, and thinking of anything in the world rather than the music. Such were the strange differences of sensibility and feeling among half-a-dozen people, all of one race.

A forlorn hope that it might rain next morning, and so prevent the threatened invasion, was in Mary's mind up to the last moment. She felt as if, having thus failed in her own person, Providence must aid her to save her cousin, the head of the house, who was of so much importance to the family, from such a snare. But Providence refused, as Providence so often does in what seems the most heart-breaking emergency, to aid the plans of the schemer. As lovely a September morning as ever shone brightened all the park and the trees under her windows as she gazed out, unable to believe that she was thus abandoned of Heaven. But there could be no mistake about it. It was a lovely day, enough to tempt any one to the woods had there been no purpose of the kind beforehand; and as if to aggravate her sense of the danger of the situation, Ben himself was visible from her window, coming up the river-path in boating costume, though it was only half-past seven in the morning. Had he been on the river already at this ridiculous hour? Passing The Willows no doubt, gazing at the closed windows, pleased with the mere fact of being near her, though at such an hour no one, Mary assured herself with a little scorn, had ever seen Millicent out of bed; and on such a day as this, when all his prospects for life hung in the balance! But, strangely enough, it never occurred to Mary in her womanish pre-occupation to think that it might be the feverish excitement of the crisis, and not any thought of Millicent, which had roused Ben and driven him to try the tranquillising effects of bodily exertion. Notwithstanding the atmosphere of family anxiety by which she was surrounded, the fact was that Millicent's visit was ten times more important in Mary's eyes than that of Mr. Ponsonby. The one did not cost her a tenth part of the anxious cogitation called forth by the other. No doubt the will would be read and everything settled, ill or well. Ben would have

Renton, as he ought; or Frank would have it, or it would be settled somehow; but the effect of Millicent's appearance would be to unsettle everything. It would rouse up those embers of old love which she felt were smouldering in Ben's mind. Smouldering! How could she tell that they were not blazing with all the warmth of present passion? Else, why had he sallied out in the dawn of the morning only to pass by the sleeping, shut-up house which contained the lady of his dreams? For that he had gone out for this purpose, and no other, Mary felt as certain as if she had watched him every step of the way. But there was nothing now to be done but to submit, and to put the best face that was possible upon it. Perhaps, indeed, if anything should occur so as that Ben should not have Renton, it would no longer be an unmixed misfortune, for it would take him out of Millicent's way.

It was hard to tell whether it was a relief or an annoyance to find a stranger at the breakfast-table when they all met down-stairs. 'What a nuisance!' Frank said to his wife, feeling that Ben's right-hand man was not the sort of person to be admitted to familiar intercourse with the family at such a moment. But Mary felt, on the whole, that Hillyard's unexpected appearance was a good thing for Ben. The stranger, who ought to have arrived some days before, had been detained, and got down to Cookesley on Sunday night, from whence it appeared Ben had gone down early to fetch him, thus explaining, to the great consolation of his guardian and watcher, his early expedition. Hillyard was very carefully dressed, too carefully for the morning, and a little impressed by the house and the circumstances. His beard had been trimmed and his wardrobe renewed before he would follow his once *protégé*, and now patron, to the Manor, and he was very anxious to make himself agreeable, and justify his presence.

'I know I should not have come at such a time,' he explained to Mary; 'I told Renton so. Of course we have been so much together that I could not but know why he was coming home.'

'I do not think it makes any difference,' said Mary. 'I am sure my aunt will always be glad to have any of Ben's friends.'

'It is very good of you to say so,' Hillyard answered gratefully. And then he began to tell her what a fine fellow her cousin was, and what a head he had, and how he had mastered his profession while other men would have been gaping at it. 'He is master and I am man now,' he said, unconsciously using Ben's words, 'though I was brought up to it; and I should just like you to see the beautiful work he puts out of his hands.'

'I daresay I should not understand it if I saw it,' said Mary, smiling behind the urn; but she lent a very willing ear, and thought Hillyard a very nice person. Unquestionably he was a relief to the high strain of suppressed feeling which appeared in every face at the table, except, perhaps, Laurie's, who, late as usual, came in, carrying the baby in his arms, and did not mind.

'Here is a little waif and stray I found wandering about the passages,' he said. 'Little Laurie, your mamma does not care about you to-day; you had better stay with me.'

'Doesn't mamma care for him, the darling!' cried Alice. And then the child was picked up, having made a rush to her arms, and set up beside her at table.

'The heir-presumptive, I suppose?' Hillyard said behind the urn; and Mary began to think he was not quite so nice as she had thought him before.

Then the members of the family dispersed, to kill this lingering, weary forenoon as they best could. Ben and Hillyard went out together in earnest conversation, and Laurie established himself in a shady corner of the lawn, and made a group of Alice and her children, and began to draw them; while Frank started off, as he said, for a long walk. Mr. Ponsonby had announced that he was to come by the one o'clock train; but there was another three-quarters of an hour later, and nobody who knew him expected him to arrive by the first. And at half-past one Millicent and her friend would come to luncheon. Such a conjunction of events was very terrible to think of; though, perhaps, not so alarming to any one as to Mary, who alone knew of the motives of the latter visit. She had to go about her usual occupations all the same. She could not cheat the sick expectations of her heart by joining the group on the lawn and chatting with the children, nor could she rush forth to still her anxieties by bodily exertion, like the boys. A woman, she thought to herself, is always tied to the stake. She had to fulfil all her little peaceful household occupations as if her heart was quite at ease, and had not even any sympathy to support her, for what was it to her any one could have said? They were all three her cousins, and it could not matter very deeply to her which of them got Renton; and as for Millicent, that was mere feminine jealousy, and nothing else,—so Mary had to lock up her troubles carefully in her own breast.

It was only about a quarter past one when Millicent arrived at Renton, and with her came her mother and her 'friend,' who was the young soldier they had seen rowing her on the river. Mrs. Renton had just come down-stairs, with Davison carrying her shawls and her worsted work, and it was to her the visitors made their way. 'Mr. Horsman is a connexion of my poor husband's,' Millicent said with a decent sigh. 'He is a brother of Sir George Horsman, whom Nelly married. Nelly is my sister-in-law, Mrs. Renton; but I suppose you know?'

'Indeed I know very well,' said Mrs. Renton. 'It was she who we once thought would have married Frank. Not that I am not perfectly satisfied with Frank's wife. She is certainly nice, and suits him admirably, which of course is the great thing. But she had no money. And there was once a time when he saw a great deal of Miss Rich.'

'She was quite a catch,' said Mrs. Tracy,—a word which wounded Mrs. Renton's ear.

'I cannot say I looked upon it in that point of view; but the young people were thrown in each other's way a great deal,' Mrs. Renton said with some stateliness; and Millicent immediately rushed into the field.

'I thought the Mr. Rentons had all arrived,' she said, 'and yet you are alone;' and cast an angry glance at Mary, as if demanding of her where they were.

'What has become of the boys?' said Mrs. Renton, looking round her. 'I have only just come down. The fact is, it is a very exciting day for them; we expect Mr. Ponsonby down immediately to read the will.'

Millicent and her mother exchanged glances. 'Then the time is up?' Mrs. Tracy said meditatively, and bent with increasing solicitude over the invalid on her sofa. 'What a trial for you!' she said, clasping her hand in sympathy. And Mrs. Renton raised to her eyes that said unspeakable things.

'Ah! yes,' she murmured; 'but nobody thinks of me;' and this balm of consolation was sweet to her heart.

They all came dropping in a few minutes later to luncheon, and Ben and Hillyard were among the first. 'Ponsonby has not come by this train,' said Ben, 'but Frank is waiting at the station for the next.' It was hard not to feel as if Frank was doing the rest an injury by waiting to have the first word with the lawyer; such, at least, was Mary's instinctive feeling. But her heart was weighted now with a more painful anxiety still. She saw Ben give a brief, contemptuous glance at young Horsman, whose position was not a comfortable one, and her heart sunk. But then he turned away from Millicent,—avoided seeing her, indeed, in a curious, visible way, and that was a consolation. Mrs. Tracy, however, got up with effusion to shake hands with dear Mr. Renton, begging that she might have a good look at him, to see if he was changed. 'Not at all changed,' was her verdict. 'Just the same generous face that once came to our help in our troubles. Mr. Renton, do you know I may say you saved my life?'

Then Millicent, too, rose, and, with a whole drama in her eyes, held out her hand to him. There was regret, remorse, and a tender appeal for pardon, and a sweet self-pity in those blue, shining eyes. They seemed to say, 'Be kind to me! Be sorry for me! I am so sorry for myself!' But it was hard to make out whether there was any answer in Ben's looks. She stood so turned towards him, holding out her hand, that he had no choice but to draw near, and then she turned meaningly towards a vacant chair at her side. He could not have gone away without rudeness, and Ben was not disposed to be rude to anybody at such a moment of fate. He took the seat accordingly, though with grave looks, and then there came a gleam of triumph into Millicent's eyes.

'How curious we should have chanced to come here on this day of all others,' she said, her voice sinking to its softest tones. 'You told me of it the very last time we met; but, perhaps, Mr. Renton, you forget?'

'Did I tell you of this?' said Ben. 'What a good memory you must have! but there are some things I do not forget.'

'Ah! something unkind about poor me, Mr. Renton! but if you knew what I have had to go through since, you would not think anything unkind.'

'I suppose we have all had a great deal to go through since,' said Ben. 'Seven years! it is a large slice out of one's life; one's ideas about most things change immensely in seven years.'

'Do they?' said Millicent, looking at him with soft, appealing eyes.

'Very much,' said Ben, with a smile; 'so much that one looks back with amazement upon the follies one has been guilty of. A man says to himself, "Is it possible I could have been such an ass?" Are ladies not subject to the same effect of time?'

'No;—ladies are more constant,' said Millicent. 'When our thoughts have turned one way, it does not matter what happens, they always keep the same. We may be obliged to change in outward appearance. We are not so free as you gentlemen are. One's friends or one's circumstances sway one sometimes, but in the heart we never change,—not half, oh! not a quarter so much as you.'

'That may be. I have no experience,' said Ben.

'But I have,' said Millicent, 'and I do so want to tell you. You know I never was very happy in my circumstances, Mr. Renton. Mamma is very kind, but she does not understand one's feelings; and when she got me abroad, she had me all in her own hands. Yes, you are quite right about the change time makes. When I look back I cannot think how I could have done it. But I was so young, and so used to obey mamma.'

'And a very laudable principle, I am sure,' said Ben, with a polite little bow. 'I beg your pardon—I thought I saw my brother and Mr. Ponsonby coming up the avenue. You were saying,—something about obedience,—I think?'

'You do not think it worth while to listen to me,' said Millicent.

'Oh, yes, surely,—pray go on. I am full of interest,' said Ben.

And then the poor creature looked at him with eyes which were pitiful in the eagerness of their appeal. She was a mercenary, wretched woman, ready to barter her beauty for comfort and wealth, and a fine house and a good position; and yet there was still in Mrs. Henry Rich the same redeeming possibility that there had been in Millicent Tracy. If he would have taken her out of that slough of despond, she would have been good, have made him a true wife, have grown a gentle lady, so far as it was in her. To the bottom of her soul Millicent felt this,—just as many a poor criminal feels that in other circumstances he would have been a model of all virtue. And for her the matter was not one without hope;—marriage to a woman may always be a new life,—and the seven years had not dimmed her eyes, nor taken the roses from her cheeks. And by those roses and bright eyes and lovely looks are not a woman's fate determined continually? Again, it was her last hope. For though admiration was always sweet, yet to be troubled with a boy like this young Guardsman, was irksome to Millicent in her maturity. And to go through a round of such boys,—flattering, wooing them, being wooed,—good heavens! was this all that fortune had in store for a woman? Therefore she made one more effort before she yielded to fate.

'You were more interested, Mr. Renton,' she said, with soft reproach, 'when we talked together last,—oh, so much more interested! If I did not know you so well, I could scarcely think it was the same.'

'That is true,' said Ben; 'but you taught me some things, Mrs. Rich, and I profited by the lesson. I doubt whether but for your assistance I could ever have been the man I am.'

'Ah! then I have at least something to do with you?' said Millicent. 'Come and tell me, will you? It is not like London, where one was always being interrupted. In the country there is so much time for talk.'

'But I have no time,' said Ben. 'After to-morrow I shall probably go away again; and when I tell you I have profited by your instructions, I think that is all I have to say.'

'You are angry with me because of,—because of,—poor Henry,' said Millicent, with tears coming to her eyes. 'But ah, Mr. Renton!—ah, Ben, if you only knew!'

Ben sprang impatiently to his feet. To him, as to any other generous man, it felt like a personal pang and shame to see a woman thus humiliate herself. He made a long step towards the window, with a flush on his face. 'Here they come!' he said, though at the moment he was not thinking much of their coming. And then there ensued a sudden inevitable flutter in the family which affected the guests. Alice, who had been charitably talking to the Guardsman, jumped up with a little cry of excitement, and sat down again, ashamed of herself, but with all possibilities of conversation quenched out of her; and Mrs. Renton, whom Mrs. Tracy had been occupying to the best of her ability to leave Millicent free for her important interview with Ben, was suddenly overcome, and cried a little, lying back on her pillows. 'Oh Ben, my dear! I don't know how I am to bear it,' she said, holding fast by her son's hand. Laurie was the only one who was perfectly steady. He came forward immediately from the background, and raised his mother up, supporting her on his arm. 'You will bear it beautifully, mamma, as you always do,' said Laurie. 'Come and give us our luncheon. You forget we are not alone.'

And he supported her into the dining-room, holding her hand caressingly in his. As for Ben, he turned and gave his arm to Millicent, 'As if I had been a cabbage,' she said afterwards, indignantly. None of her pathetic glances, not the soft little pressure of her hand upon his arm, gained the slightest response. His face was set and stern, full of thoughts with which she had nothing to do. Mrs. Tracy ventured to whisper as she followed, 'Ah, how sweet it is to me to see you two together again!' But Ben did not even hear what she said. He waved his hand to Mr. Ponsonby in the distance as he went across the hall. The beautiful face at his side had no more effect upon him than if it had been a hideous mask. He was absorbed in his own business, and careless of her very existence. Millicent, in her fury, could have struck him as he took her into the dining-room. Was this to be the end?

CHAPTER XIII.

THE WILL.

IT was Hillyard's behaviour at this meal which gained him the regard of the various members of the Renton family. He took such pains to attend to the strangers, and give to the agitated group the air of an ordinary party, that all of them who were sufficiently disengaged to observe his exertions felt grateful to him. Millicent sat next to Ben on one side, but Hillyard had placed himself between her and Mary Westbury on the other, and in all the intervals of his general services to the company Mrs. Rich had his attention, for which Mary blessed him. She herself, overcome by many emotions, was but a pale spectator, able to take little part in what was going on, saying now and then a languid word to the unfortunate Guardsman, but capable of nothing more except watching, which she did with a sick excitement beyond all description. Mary was so pale, indeed, and watchful and excited, that her mother was alarmed, and made signs to her across the table which she did not feel capable of understanding. 'She will cry if she does not mind, and make a scene,' Mrs. Westbury said to herself; and set it all down to the score of Ben, which was true enough, but not as she thought. As for Ben, he inclined his ear specially to Mrs. Tracy, who was at his other hand, and hoped she liked The Willows, and that her rheumatism was better, and a hundred other nothings. There was, it is true, nothing very remarkable about this party, looking at it from the outside. They were well-dressed people, gathered round a well-appointed table, getting through an average amount of talk, smiling upon each other like ordinary mortals; but yet underneath how different it was; Mrs. Renton was consoled, and ate her luncheon, sustained by her son Laurie's attentions; but Mrs. Frank Renton trembled so that she could scarcely keep up the fiction of eating, and grew pale and flushed again six times in a minute, and nervously consulted the countenance of her husband, who, very silent and self-absorbed, drank his sherry, and more of it than he wanted at that hour, taking little notice of any one; then, at the other end of the table, there was Mrs. Tracy, hanging with ostentatious, artificial interest on every word uttered by Ben; and Millicent, very pale, with an excited gleam in her eyes, casting tender, wistful looks at him, which he never saw; and Hillyard talking enough for six, helping everybody, introducing a hundred indifferent subjects of conversation, which ran a feeble course half-way round the table and then died a natural death. Mrs. Westbury, one of the few people who was calm enough to remark upon the appearance of the others, concluded within herself that, after all, the strangers were a mistake. If the family party had been alone, their excitement would have been nothing beyond what was natural; but her own child, Mary, who ought at least to have been one of the calmest of the party, sat by that unhappy Guardsman pale as a ghost, once in ten minutes saying something to him, and looking as if she were about to faint; and all the others were equally under the sway of agitation and self-restraint. When this uncomfortable meal came to an end, everybody rose with an alacrity which showed how glad they were that it was over. And then there ensued another moment of supreme embarrassment. If the strangers had any sense of the position they would go away instantly, the family felt; but instead of that, Millicent moved at once to the upper end of the room, where there stood upon a crimson pedestal a bust of the last Benedict Renton, and humbly begged of Ben to explain to her who it was; and while the others stood about waiting, he had to follow and describe his grandfather, and fulfil the duties of showman, Mrs. Tracy rushing to join the group.

'Benedict Renton—your name!' Millicent said, with again another attempt upon his feelings, while Ben stood angrily conscious of the effort and contemptuous of the fooling, scarcely concealing his eagerness to be at liberty. 'And this portrait, Mr. Renton? I can trace the family resemblance,' said Mrs. Tracy. And all this while Mr. Ponsonby's blue bag waited outside, and the family murmured, standing round in agonies of suspense to know their fate. Then once more Hillyard stood forth, vindicating his claim to be called Ben's right-hand man.

'Let me be cicerone,' he said, 'Renton, I know you are anxious to see to your business. Mrs. Rich will take me for her guide to the pictures for the moment. You know Mr. Ponsonby cannot wait, and you are losing time.'

'If Mrs. Rich will excuse me,' said Ben.

'Oh, please don't think of excuses; we can wait,' said Millicent. 'Mayn't we wait to learn the news?' and she clasped her hands softly, unseen of the bystanders, and gazed into his face. 'Nobody,' she murmured, lowering her voice, 'can be more interested than I.'

'So long as you can find anything to amuse you,' said Ben, half frantic. 'Hillyard, I confide it to you;' and he had turned away, before any further dart could be thrown at him. Then there was a hurried consultation between Mrs. Renton and her sister-in-law. 'I shall stay with them; never mind. Of course I am anxious too; but half-an-hour more or less don't matter,' Mrs. Westbury said, with the voice of a martyr; and when Millicent looked round she found herself standing alone with her own special party, Hillyard at her right hand, and Mrs. Westbury, with a smile of fixed politeness, behind. Ben was gone. He had made no answer to her appeal,—he had shown no inclination to linger by her side. She had put forth all her strength for this grand final *coup*, and it had failed.

'I don't think Mr. Renton has improved in politeness in his travels,' she said to Hillyard, unable altogether to restrain the expression of her despite.

'He has not been in polite regions,' said Hillyard; 'and everything, you know, must give place to business, now-a-days, even the service of ladies. You must forgive him, when you consider what it is———'

'I have nothing to do with him,' said Millicent, angrily. 'I hope I never shall have anything to do with so rude a man;' and then she paused, thinking she had gone too far. 'You know it is not a way to treat an old friend———'

'Poor Renton!' said Hillyard. 'He is so unlikely to be any the better for this anxiety, you know,—that is the worst of it; and I don't think he has any hopes to speak of. He has made all his arrangements for going back to his work———'

'You don't say so!' cried Mrs. Tracy, with a look at her daughter. 'And I can't believe it!' cried Millicent.

'But I assure you it is true. No one can know better than I, for I go with him,' said Hillyard; 'all our arrangements are made. But let me show you the pictures. This was Sir Anthony Renton, who was a—Master in Chancery in Queen Elizabeth's time,' pointing to a respectable merchant in snuff-coloured garments of the days of Queen Anne. But the visitors cared nothing for the family portraits, and Hillyard's last shaft had told. If Ben was unlikely to have Renton, it was of no use spending more trouble upon him. They consulted together hastily for a moment, and then they turned their backs upon the pictures. 'I have the pleasure to wish you good morning, Mrs. Westbury,' said Mrs. Tracy. 'Since our friends are so much occupied we will take our leave. Pray give Mrs. Renton my best sympathies.'

'It is to be hoped some one will get the money at the end,' said Millicent, with less civility, sweeping towards the door. And thus the strangers were got rid of at last.

'I flatter myself I did that,' said Hillyard, with a chuckle of satisfaction. And then he, too, took his departure, and left Aunt Lydia free to join the party in the library, where the great revelation of the future fate of the family was about to take place.

The air of restrained excitement in this room was such that it would have communicated itself to the merest stranger who had entered. It was a dark room by nature; and a cloud had just passed, as if in sympathy, over the brightness of the day. The window was open, and the blind beat and flapped against it in the wind, which was a sound that startled everybody, and yet that nobody had nerve enough to stop. Mrs. Renton had been placed in an easy chair near the vacant fireplace. Alice and Mary sat formally on two chairs against the wall; and the three brothers stood up together in a lump, though they neither spoke nor looked at each other. Mr. Ponsonby was seated at the writing-table, arranging his papers and holding in his hand a large blue envelope, sealed. There was complete silence, except now and then the rustle of papers, as the lawyer turned them over. The members of the family scarcely ventured to breathe. When Aunt Lydia entered they all turned round with a look of reproach; their nerves were so highly strung that the least motion startled them. In the midst of this silence, all at once Mrs. Renton began to sob and cry, 'I feel as if you had just come home from the funeral!' she said, with a wail of feeble grief. There was a little momentary stir at the suggestion, so true was it; and Alice, being at the end of her strength, cried too, silently, out of excitement. As for the brothers, they were beyond taking much notice of the interruption. They were now so much wiser, so much more experienced, since the day of the funeral, the last time they had all met together in this solemn way. Now they did not know what they were to expect: their confidence in their father and the world and things in general was destroyed. By this time it had become apparent to them that things the most longed for were about the last things to be attained. Had they been all sent away again for another seven years, or had the property been alienated for ever and ever, the brothers would not have been surprised. Whether they would have submitted, was a different question. Their opinions about many things had changed. Their unhesitating resolution to obey their father's will seven years ago, without a word of blame, appeared to them now simple Quixotism. They were scarcely moved by their mother's tears. He had done them harm, though they had been dutiful to him. He might now be about to do them more harm for anything they could tell. The uncriticising anxiety and expectation which filled the women of the party was a very different sentiment from the uneasy, angry anticipations of 'the boys.' Few dead men have ever managed to secure for themselves such a vigorous posthumous opposition. In short, he was not to them a dead man at all, but a living power, against which they might yet have to struggle for their lives.

Mr. Ponsonby looked round upon this strange company, with the big envelope in his hand and an excitement equal to their own. He looked at them all, after Mrs. Renton's crying had been quieted, and cleared his throat. 'Boys,' he said, hoarsely, 'I don't know what's in this any more than you do. He did it without consulting me. If it is the will of '54 that is here, it is all just and right; but if it is any new-fangled nonsense, like what I read to you here seven years ago, by the Lord I will fight it for you, die or win!'

This extraordinary speech, it may be supposed, did not lessen the excitement of the listeners. Alice crossed over suddenly to her husband, and clung to him, taking it for granted that disappointment and downfall were involved in these words. 'Dear, if there is nothing for us, I shall not mind!' she cried, gazing at Mr. Ponsonby with a kind of terror. 'Quickly, please; let us wait no longer than is necessary,' said Ben, with a certain peremptoriness of tone. Mr. Ponsonby had settled down in a moment, after this outburst, to his usual look and tone.

'I need not trouble you with many preliminaries,' he said; 'you all remember how everything happened. He sent for me a week before his death, and gave me this,' holding up the envelope, 'and this letter, which I have also here. When I remonstrated his answer was, "If the one harms, the other will set right." My own impression now is, I tell you frankly, that his mind was affected. Have patience one moment. Nothing in the shape of a will, even in draft, was found among his papers, so that there is nothing whatever to set against this, or explain his intention. If it is that of '54 it is all right——'

'No more!' cried Ben; 'let us know what it is at once.'

Then the lawyer tore open the envelope. Not a sound but the tearing of the paper and crackling sound of the document within was to be heard in the room, except one sob from Mrs. Renton, which seemed to express in one sound the universal thirst of all their hearts. Mr. Ponsonby rose up as he unfolded the paper; he stopped and gazed round upon them blankly, with consternation in his eyes. Then he opened the sheet in his hand, turned it over and over, shook out the very folds to make sure that nothing lurked within,—then caught up the torn envelope and did the same. And then he uttered an oath. The man was moved out of himself,—he stamped his foot unconsciously, and clenched his fist, and swore at his dead antagonist. 'D—— him!' he cried fiercely. This pantomime drove the spectators wild. When he held up the paper to them they all crowded on each other to see, but understood nothing. It was a great sheet of blue paper, spotless—without a word upon it. Mr. Ponsonby in his rage tossed it down on the floor at their feet across the table. 'Take it for what it is worth!' he shouted, almost foaming with rage. Frank, at whose feet it fell, picked it up, and held it in his hands, turning it over, stupid with wonder. 'What does it mean?' cried Ben, hoarsely. Surprise and excitement had taken away their wits.

'Give it to me!' said Mrs. Renton, from behind; and her son, upon whom the truth was beginning to dawn, threw it into her lap. It flashed upon them all at once, and a kind of delirium, fell on the party,—flouted, laughed at, turned into derision, as it seemed, by the implacable dead.

'It means that there is no will. I have been keeping a blank sheet of paper for you,' said Mr. Ponsonby bitterly, 'for seven years.'

And then there was another pause, and they all looked at each other, too much bewildered to understand the position, as if the earth had been rent asunder at their very feet.

'We never did anything to him to deserve this!' said Laurie suddenly, with a voice of pain. 'Is there no mistake?'

As for Ben, he said nothing. His eyes followed the gleam of the paper, which his mother was turning over and over in her helpless hands, as if the secret of it might still be found out. But by degrees his eyes lighted up. Almost unconsciously he made a step apart, separating himself, as it were, from the audience, placing himself by Mr. Ponsonby's side as a speaker. There was a certain triumph in his eye. After all, he was but a man, like other men, and the heir; and his rights had been debated and questioned by everybody, himself included. There was a flush and movement of satisfaction about him,—a sudden warm blaze out of the absorbing disappointment, baffled hopes, and bitter resentment which were rising round him.

'If there is no will,' he said, with a deep flush on his face, and nervous gesture of his hand, 'Renton is mine, as it ought to be. I am in my father's place; and what has been done amiss, it is my place to undo. I cannot believe that there is any one here who doubts me.'

While he was speaking, Alice uttered a little cry. She had turned to him her white face, but without seeing him or any one. 'Must we go back to India?' she said, with a voice of anguish. That was the shape it took to the young pair. She was pale as marble, but Frank's face was blazing red.

'Hush, Alice!' he said, fiercely; 'that is our own affair.'

Ben made a movement towards them in his impatience. 'I have told you you should not go back!' he cried. 'I am here in my father's place to set all right.'

'Stop a little,' said Mr. Ponsonby, suddenly coming forward with a chair in his hand, which he placed in the midst of them, sitting down upon it, amid the agitated group. 'You have not done with me yet. We have not come to such simple means yet. Mrs. Frank, my dear, don't be angry, and don't give way to your feelings. Things are not so bad as you suppose. I lost my head, which is inexcusable in a man of my profession. It was a dirty trick of him, after a friendship of thirty years. My dear young people, sit down, all of you, and listen to me.'

No one made any change of position, but they all turned their eyes upon him with looks differing in intensity, but full of a hundred questions. Frank was defiant; Alice wild with despairing anxiety; Mrs. Renton crying; Laurie soothing her; Ben very watchful, eager, and attentive. Mr. Ponsonby, however, had entirely recovered his composure, which unconsciously had a calming effect upon them all.

'Yes,' he said, 'I lost my head, which I had no right to do; but I am coming to myself. Now, listen to me. There is no will; and Ben from this moment is master of Renton, as he says. But stop a little. The personal property remains, which is worth as much as Renton. I don't know what I could have been thinking of to forget that. After all, there is really nothing to find fault with but the look of the thing. The money has been accumulating these seven years;—it has been as good as a long minority;—and some of the investments have done very well. The land, of course, goes to the eldest son; but the personality, as some of you ought to have known, is divided. It comes to just about the same thing. God forgive me if I said anything I ought not to have said in the excitement of the moment. It is shabby to me, but it won't harm you, thank God! I lost my head, that was all, and more shame to me. The will of '54 would have come to much about the same thing.'

'Oh, Mr. Ponsonby,' cried Alice, with streaming eyes, thrusting herself, unconscious of what she was about, in front of them all; 'tell me, will there be enough to keep us from going to India again?'

'There will be twenty thousand pounds, or more,' said Mr. Ponsonby, 'if you can live on that; and I could, for my part.'

Alice, like the lawyer, had lost her head. She was too young to bear this wonderful strain of emotion. She threw her arms about his neck in her joy, and wept aloud, while they all stood by looking on, with such feelings as may be supposed.

She was the only one who spoke. Her husband drew her back at this point, half angry, half sullen, with his disappointment still dark in his face. 'You had better go,' he said to her, almost harshly; 'you have heard all that there is to be heard. It is best we should discuss the real business by ourselves.'

'Yes, come along,' said Laurie, 'all you ladies. You have heard it is all right. You don't want to hear the accounts, and all that legal stuff. We will manage the business. I will take you back to your sofa, mother, now you know all's right.'

'But is it all right?' said Mrs. Renton. 'I don't seem to understand anything. Ben, will you come and tell me? Have they all got their money,—all the boys? And what is Frank to have for his children? Till you have children of your own, it is his boy who is the heir. Laurie is always telling me it will come right. I would rather hear it from the rest. Oh, boys! your poor father meant it for the best.'

'It is all right, mother,' said Ben; 'better than we thought.'

'Ah, but Frank says nothing,' said the mother. 'I will not go away till I am satisfied about Frank.'

'You heard Alice, I suppose,' said Frank, somewhat sulky still. 'I do think it is a shame there is no will; but if we are to have our shares, as Mr. Ponsonby says, I suppose, mother, it is all right.'

'Of course it is,' said Laurie. 'Come, and I'll see if the carriage is round for your drive. You know how important it is you should have your drive.'

'Your dear papa always made such a point of it, Laurie,' Mrs. Renton said, holding her handkerchief to her eyes, 'or else I am sure I never could have the heart to go out on such a day.'

And thus the ladies were dismissed, and the brothers held their meeting, and settled their business by themselves. It would be vain to say that they were satisfied. Frank, whose mind had been vaguely excited,—he could not tell why,—and to whom it had begun to seem inevitable that some special provision should have been made for the only one of the three who had 'ties' and a family to provide for, had experienced a most sharp and painful downfall. And it took him a long time to accustom himself to the idea that after all he was not wronged. It was a personal offence to him, as it had been to his wife, that Ben should look satisfied. 'When he has Renton, I do not see the justice of Ben having his share of the money too,' he said, with a little bitterness in his unreasonable disappointment. And Ben was half displeased to feel that it was not to be his magnanimous part to provide for his brothers, but that their own right and share remained to them as indisputably as Renton was his. His proposal was that they should return to the will of '54, of which Mr. Ponsonby still possessed the draft, and a great deal of discussion took place between them. It was half-past six o'clock before any of the party emerged out of the dark library, where they had spent between three and four hours. Mr. Ponsonby came out, declaring that he was tired and thirsty and half dead, and demanding sherry from the butler, who was preparing the table for dinner. They all went in and stood by the sideboard, and swallowed something to refresh themselves. 'And, my dear boys, give me the satisfaction of hearing you say you are contented,' said Mr. Ponsonby, 'before dinner comes on; for I should like to be jolly, if I may.'

'I am perfectly satisfied,' said Laurie; 'and Ben is happy for the first time for some years. As for Frank, he must speak for himself; he has been dreaming, and it is sometimes unpleasant to wake up.'

'If I have been dreaming, it was not for myself,' said Frank; 'a man with a family is so different from you fellows; but if it will be any satisfaction to you, I think I may say I am content, since better can't be.'

And then he went up-stairs abruptly to dress. Alice had been waiting for him long, trembling a little, and not daring to believe anything till her authorised expositor of external events came to deliver the judgment to her. It did not seem right to Alice that Frank should not be the first in any distribution of prizes or honours. And yet she was not insensible to the claims of natural justice. 'We should never have been able to give it up if it had come to us,' she said to herself; 'and it would have been contrary to all traditions of the family to disinherit Ben.'

'You always told me he was to have it,' she said, when Frank came in, with the remnants of his sulkiness still hanging about him. 'You used to say if it came to you, you would give it up to Ben.'

'And so I should, of course,' said Frank; 'the thing is, the fellow was so self-satisfied,—with a kind of look of pleasure that we were all cut out. That was what I could not stand.'

'But don't you think he meant to be good to us?' Alice said, trying hard to smoothe her savage down.

'Good to us, by Jove! but fortunately that's all over,' said Frank. 'We are safe enough. No need to worry yourself over those blessed children any more. Poor little beggar! he won't have much to look forward to; but still you may bring him up at home, and that is all you care for, you little goose,' the young husband said, softening over the happiness in Alice's eyes.

'How much shall we have, Frank?' she asked, with a sudden relapse into prudence.

'Let me dress now,—and go and make yourself pretty,' he said. 'We shall not be so badly off; there will be something like a thousand a-year.'

And thus Frank Renton too acknowledged to himself that things might have been worse, and that he was content.

But perhaps the strangest thing of all was that Mrs. Westbury withdrew into her daughter's room, and locked the door, and had a cry, in which Mary, over-worn and over-excited, was quite disposed to share, though for a different reason. 'I cannot understand your uncle Laurence,' said Mrs. Westbury. 'I am sure I am not mercenary. I have given you up to your aunt, and never grumbled, much though I wanted you; and you have given up seven years of your life to her, and he has not left you so much as a gown. I do feel it, my dear, for you.'

'I am sure, mamma, I don't feel it for myself,' said Mary, with a smile. 'One does not mind so long as all is right with the boys.'

'The boys are all very well,' said Mrs. Westbury, 'but he might have left something, my dear, to you.'

'I did not want anything, mamma,' said Mary. 'But godmamma will not want me so much when she has Ben, and oh, I do so long to get home!' Poor Mary was over-done, over-worn, excited by so many diverse feelings that her power of self-command failed her at last. She put her arms round her mother's neck, and threw, as it were, all her weight of unexpressed cares and griefs upon her. 'Take me home, mamma!' she said, and wept in the abandonment of weariness and disappointment, and that overwhelming despondency for which one can give no reason, on her mother's neck.

Mrs. Westbury was a woman fond of explanations from other people, but she understood her child by instinct, 'Yes, yes, you shall go home, my darling!' she said, soothing her, but without any intention of carrying out her promise. It was early days, as she said to herself. Before any change was made, it must be made plainly apparent what the rest of the family meant to do.

On the whole, the dinner-table was more cheerful that night. They were all worn out with excitement, it is true, and signs of tears were about the women's eyes; but still there was the sense that, after all, justice was once more in force, and natural law ruling their affairs. One man's will, fantastic and unaccountable, was no longer supreme over them. Ben took his place at the head of the table with a certain glow of satisfaction. 'I know none of you would have seen me wronged,' he said when they were sipping over their wine. It was the first time that he had taken any notice of the often-repeated declaration of his younger brothers.

'Not if the prize had been Great Britain, instead of Renton,' said Laurie; 'though, to tell the truth, the one would have been as great a bore as the other, had it come to me.'

'Of course I should have given it up to Ben,' said Frank; 'but it would have been a struggle; therefore I'm very glad things have been settled as they are without my help.'

'Bravo!' cried Mr. Ponsonby, 'that is the best sentiment I have heard to-night.'

'Shake hands, old fellow,' said Ben, holding out his hand. Laurie somehow did not count. The world would indeed have been coming to an end had he been out of temper about his rights. It was the younger and the elder who exchanged the grasp of peace and mutual amity. 'And, remember, Renton is home to us all,' Ben said, with moisture in his eyes. 'Of course my mother remains here; as it has always been, with room for all.'

'Bravo, bravo!' said Mr. Ponsonby, 'now is the time for generous feelings! My dear fellows, prosperity is the thing that opens men's hearts. Don't talk to me of the benefits of misfortune! Let a man feel he has his thousand a-year, or his five thousand a-year, safe in his pocket, and then is the time his heart warms. But I'd have Mrs. Frank come to an understanding with Mrs. Ben before I would take the invitation in too literal a sense,' said the old lawyer, with a chuckle over his own wit.

'I do not expect there will ever be a Mrs. Ben,' said the heir, with an impatient movement of his head.

'Tell me that this time twelvemonths,' said Mr. Ponsonby; and then they all went out to the lawn to smoke their evening cigar.

CHAPTER XIV.

THE END OF A DREAM.

IF I do not enter very particularly into the family arrangements which were made after this settlement, it is because, in the circumstances, so much detail is unnecessary. Had Ben been in Frank's position, a married man with a family, it would of course have been needful that some arrangements should have been made about Mrs. Renton's future habitation. She herself was provided for by her marriage settlements, and had a little fortune of her own, settled on herself, which was something for the babies to look forward to; and there was a jointure-house on the estate, known by the name of the Dovecote, a pretty, small house, with a view on the river, and only a mile's drive from Cookesley, where there can be no doubt Mrs. Renton, had there been any need for it, would have been very comfortable. But as Ben was not married, what did it matter? It was better his mother should keep house for him, as she said in her innocence, than leave him to servants. There was a consultation held in her room next morning, to the interruption of the newspaper-reading; but as this was a crisis, full of events, for once in a way she did not mind.

'I would go to the Dovecote, my dear boy, if you thought I should be in your way,' she said; 'but I think I had much better stay and keep house for you, till you have a wife of your own to keep your house.'

'I don't think that is a very likely event,' said Ben. 'Of course you will keep house for me. And I think you should give the Dovecote to Frank,—that is one thing I wanted to speak to you about. I will have it fitted up, and do what I can to make it comfortable, and then you can have the children always at hand to amuse you while I am away.'

'But you are not going away?'

Mary was quite at the other end of the room, working by the window. It was only her aunt's worsted-work she was doing—not a very serious occupation—but it always wanted a remarkable amount of light when Ben was in the room. She was sitting there by herself, listening eagerly, with a sore feeling in her heart, as of being excluded,—she who had sacrificed so much to the comfort of the family. After all, though she was so nearly related, and had spent her life with them, she was not a Renton. Not like a daughter of the house, whose opinion would have weight and whose comfort had to be consulted. Talk of Mrs. Renton keeping the house! The meaning of that of course was that Mary was to keep house. But of Ben's house she never would be the honorary housekeeper,—of that she was sure. When she heard her aunt's frightened exclamation, she too looked up a little,—of course it must be only a figure of speech about his going away. Or he meant going to

London perhaps, or to the moors, or something temporary. Ben came to the window, with his hands in his pockets, before he answered. Not as if he were coming to Mary. It was only the restless habit men have of wandering about a room. 'Yes,' he said, looking out, and addressing nobody, 'I am going away. Of course I must go back to my work. You forget that when I came home I had not the least idea of what was to become of me. And to throw away the work I had been making my bread by for six years, would have been a great piece of folly. Indeed, the fact is,—and I hope you won't be vexed, mother, I assure you it is quite necessary,—I am going to-morrow. I must finish what I've got to do.'

'Going to-morrow!' said Mrs. Renton, with a little shriek. Mary did not even lift up her head from her work. She kept on bending over the worsted roses as if they were the most important things in the world; but her heart suddenly had taken to flutter in the wildest way against her quiet breast.

'Yes, Mary,' said Ben, suddenly, 'don't you see that it is necessary? I must finish my work.'

Mary made him no answer, being intent on the shade of a pink, and he took a few turns about the room in his impatience; for his mother had begun to cry softly in her bed.

'That is always the worst of talking to you women,' he said. 'Mother, can't you understand? You can't go breaking off threads in life, as you do it in your sewing. I must wind up my affairs. There are some things I must see after for myself.'

'Oh, Ben, after I had made up my mind to something so different!' said his mother. 'I did not sleep a bit last night for making up how it was to be. I had quite settled in my mind what parties it would be necessary to give. We have not entertained since your poor dear father died, not once,—but now I had been thinking there ought to be a series of dinners, and perhaps a ball, to give Renton its proper place again in the county, and prove that everything is settled. And now you come and break my heart, and tell me you are going away!'

'But, dear godmamma, he will soon come back,' said Mary, coming to the rescue. 'He does not mean he is to go on making railways all his life. He is going to finish his work,—that is what he said; though it is disappointing of course.'

'Because of the ball?' said Ben, looking at her across his mother; but Mary was not able at that moment to take her part in any encounter of wit.

'No,' she said, almost angrily, 'not because of the ball. I am not young enough now to care very much for balls; but because I thought it was your turn now to take care of godmamma, and——' Mary could trust herself no further. She went back abruptly to her work, leaving both mother and son in a state of the utmost surprise and consternation.

'I think you are all bent on driving me wild,' said poor Mrs. Renton. 'It seemed as if everything was over yesterday; but now here is Ben going away, and Mary is disagreeable. And who have I to fall back upon? Laurie is very kind, but he will be going too; and Alice is nice, but I am not used to her. If Mary is to be sharp with me like this, what am I to do?'

'I will never be sharp with you, godmamma,' said Mary, who for the first time in her gentle life felt herself driven further than she could bear. 'But you must remember sometimes that I have a home and people of my own. You have wanted me very much for these seven years, and you know I have never said a word,—but now that the boys have all come home, I did hope———'

She would not break down and cry,—not for the world, while Ben kept gazing at her from his mother's bedside. But she stopped short abruptly, in the middle of her sentence, which was the only alternative, and applied herself with a kind of fury, with trembling fingers, and eyes blind with unshed tears, to the worsted work. Calculating upon her services as if she were a piece of furniture! Making all these arrangements without any reference to her! It was more than Mary could bear.

'Ben, speak to her,' said Mrs. Renton, faintly. 'Oh, my dear, the boys! Of course I am fond of the boys; but what can boys do for a poor woman like me? Oh, Ben, speak to her! You would not go and forsake me, Mary, when I want you most?'

Ben did not speak, however. He was startled, and out of his reckoning. He went to the window again, and stood opposite to his cousin, and gazed down upon her, with his hands in his pockets and a look of profound concern and uncertainty on his face.

'I won't forsake you, godmamma,' said Mary, with a trembling voice; 'but surely you might think,—plan out something,—make some arrangement.' How hard it is for a woman to assert herself, to speak out of a heart sore with the consciousness of being made no account of, and not to cry! It would have been easier for Mary to put herself down under their feet and allow them to walk over her,—as, indeed, it seemed to her she had been doing. And they did not know it! They had endured their seven years' bondage, and it had come to an end, and all was right again; but for her the same round was to go on for ever, and nobody even was aware for what poor hire she had sacrificed her life and her youth.

'Davison, Miss Mary says she is going to leave us,' said Mrs. Renton, as the maid came in. 'No, no; take it away. I could not swallow it. I am sure if I thought there was anything in the world she wanted, I would have got it for her, Davison. And I always thought she was so happy with me. No, it would choke me, I tell you. And if she was not happy with me, there are years and years that I might have got used to it; but to go and tell me now, just when I want her most———'

'You'll take your arrowroot, ma'am,' said Davison, soothingly. 'It's just as you like it, neither too hot nor too cold. Miss Mary agoing away! That's a fine joke. Miss Mary couldn't stay away, ma'am, not if you was to send her. She's a deal too fond of you. It's just nice now, just as you like it. It's all her fun, that's what it is!'

'I don't see any fun in it,' said Mrs. Renton, feebly. But she was consoled by the fuss, and the re-arrangement of her pillows, and the arrowroot. 'You'll speak to her, Davison, won't you?—and tell her I couldn't bear it. I am sure it would cost me my life.'

'To be sure, ma'am, I'll tell her,' said the maid.

While this little scene was going on, Ben stood by the window, always with his hands in his pockets, gazing at his cousin, who worked with fury, with hands that trembled, and eyes blind with tears. She kept them from falling with a superhuman effort, but she could not see anything but great blurs of mixed colour on the piece of embroidery before her, harmless bits of worsted all dilated and magnified through the tears.

'Do you really mean it, Mary?' he said, looking down upon her with a look of grief, which she did not see, and yet knew of, and was stung by to the bottom of her heart.

'I don't know,' she said, 'Ben. I can't tell. I don't want to give you more trouble. I don't know what I am saying. It has all been too much,—too much!'

'Come out into the air,' said Ben. 'I see it has been too much. We are all such selfish wretches, thinking only of our own concerns. Come out into the air.'

'I think I am more fit to go to bed,' said Mary, and the tears fell in spite of her. 'Never mind me. I have got such a headache,—and,—a bad temper. Never mind! I think I shall go to bed.'

'Come out to the woods instead,' said Ben, with a brother's tender sympathy. 'Never mind, mother,—she will come round. It is only that she is worn out and over-done. I am going to take her out into the air.'

And so he did, though there was nothing she less desired. He took her out, giving her his arm, and suiting his steps to hers as if she had been ill. She was moved to a weary laugh, half of exasperation, when she had been thus led forth. 'There is nothing the matter with me, Ben. Don't make all this fuss. You make me ashamed of myself,' she said.

'There is something the matter with you,' said Ben. 'Come and sit down here, where we can have a good talk. I see now, though I was such a selfish ass as not to think of it before. You see, Mary, you have always been so much one of ourselves, that it never occurred to me to think of the sacrifice you were making in living here.'

'It was no sacrifice!' cried Mary. 'Don't make me wretched, Ben. I lost my temper, that was all. I thought you were making all your plans, as if it were to go on for ever and ever; and that I was only a piece of furniture that nobody thought of. Don't pay any attention to me.'

'My poor little Mary!' said Ben, taking her hand into his. He made her sit down on the root of the beech, and bent his eyes wistfully on her, holding her hand in one of his, and with the other stroking his moustache, as is the wont of men in trouble. He saw there was something in it, more than met the eye; and he looked at her with a certain blank wistfulness. What did Mary want? If it had been anything he could fetch for her from the ends of the earth, he would have done it. If he had only known what it was!—or what would please her,—or how to soothe the nerves, which were evidently all ajar. Mary could not bear that gaze. Shame, and a sense of humiliation, and all the sensitive pride of a woman, overwhelmed her. Was there something in her heart which she would not have him discover? She put up her other hand and covered her face with it, turning away from him; and whether any sort of enlightenment might by degrees have penetrated the blank anxiety of his gaze, I cannot tell; for at that moment they were interrupted in such a way as Mary remembered to the end of her life.

All at once a rustle was audible as of some one coming,—indeed, of some one quite near; and then there was a little, light laugh. "Oh, good gracious! we have come at an unlucky moment,' said Millicent's voice, close at their side. Mary sprang to her feet, drawing her hand away from Ben's, raising her flushed face in a kind of desperation. Mrs. Tracy and her daughter had just turned the corner round the beech-tree, from which Ben rose, too, with more surprise than delight. Millicent had put on a white dress, with no sign, except in the black ribbons, of her mourning. She was in the full splendour of her beauty, excited into more brilliancy than usual. 'I am sure I am very sorry if I have interrupted anything,' she said, with the colour rising into her cheek, and a laughing devil of malice in her eyes.

'Yes, you interrupted a serious discussion,' said Ben. 'Mary is worn out, and I have been questioning her about her health. She has been shutting herself up a great deal too much, and she denies it, as all women do.'

'How sorry I am! and you were feeling her pulse, I suppose?' said Millicent. 'It looked the prettiest scene imaginable, seen through the trees. You did not hear us coming, you were so pleasantly,—I mean seriously,—occupied. And have you found out what is the matter with her, Mr. Ben?' This was said with the air half-malicious, half-friendly of the discoverer of a secret. And on the score of this pretended confidence, Millicent approached him closely, and used all her weapons against the man who had once knelt at her feet. She looked him in the face with eyes as much brighter than Mary Westbury's as they had been in the earlier days,—with the sweet tints of her complexion increased by exercise, and by, perhaps a little excitement over this supposed discovery,—with the morning air puffing out the white frills and trimmings of her dress, and ruffling a curl which, after the fashion of the day, fell over her shoulder. The mother had immediately appropriated Mary, who, wild with shame and confusion and anger, stood at bay, and was now with difficulty restraining her inclination to burst away from the intruder, and go home and bury herself in her room, where nobody could see her hot blushes and angry tears. Ben was moved by a certain confusion, too, against his will. It was an awkward attitude, certainly, in which to be seen by any stranger eye.

'I am not much of a physician,' he said; 'but we have all had a great deal of excitement lately, and Mary is worn out. I trust it is nothing more.'

'Ah, yes,' said Millicent. 'I know that; indeed, I had thought I might come and inquire this morning as an old friend. You forget that you told me all about it,—once. I thought I might ask, for the sake of old times, if all was right at last.'

'You do me a great deal of honour to remember anything about my affairs,' said Ben. 'Are you going to the river?' and he turned with her to go down in the direction she had been taking. 'Have you a boat?'

'Yes; the old gardener put us across,' said Millicent. 'You do not give me credit for any friendly feeling, and you always try to get rid of me, Mr. Renton. Oh, indeed, I can see it very well. I do not feel angry, for perhaps you have had provocation; though I can see it very well. But it would not do you any harm, nor me much good—except for old friendship's sake,—if you were to answer my question. Is it all right?'

'It is perfectly right,' said Ben, with a little bow. 'I don't know that there was ever any doubt on that subject. I must thank you for taking so much interest in us and our affairs.'

'That is all you say now,' cried Millicent, with ready tears springing to her eyes; and tears come as readily from mortification and the passion of anger as from any other cause. 'You would not have answered me like that once. Ah, Ben Renton, how much you are changed!'

'I think it is very natural I should be,' said Ben. 'You are changed, too, Mrs. Rich; though not in anything external,—unless it may be for the better, if that were possible,' he added, with a certain grudge in his words. The man was but a man, and they were extorted from him by the beauty which could neither be mistaken nor overlooked.

'If I am not changed in externals, you may be sure I am changed in nothing else,' said Millicent, turning upon him with a smile of such eager sweetness and hope, that it almost reached his heart. She, poor creature! believed she was winning him back. The thought quickened all her powers, quickened the very springs of being in her. She forgot Mary, and the attitude which for a moment had driven her to despair. So much the better if he had been Mary's lover,—a touch of triumph the more! 'I have had a great deal to endure since we parted,' she went on. 'Oh, you cannot tell all I have had to bear! And I thought time had worn me and aged me, and that you would scarcely have known me again. But nothing has ever changed me at heart.'

'Mrs. Rich, you forget that this conveys very little information to me,' said Ben, moved with sudden vindictiveness. 'In those days of which you speak,—and I don't know why you should speak of them, the recollection cannot be a pleasant one,—I remember clearly enough what a fool I made of myself. My heart was open enough,—ass as I was,—but I don't know now, and I did not then, what were the sentiments of yours,—if indeed——'

'I had one!' cried Millicent. 'Oh, that you should say this to me! And yet I feel that I deserve it. I acted as if I had none. What can I say or do to make you know how sorry I am? Sorry is too poor a word. Oh, Ben, I know I ought not to say it; but if either then or now you could have seen into my heart——'

Her eyes were shining through her tears; her cheeks glowed with soft blushes; her look besought, implored, entreated him. Poor soul! she said true. If he could have seen into her heart, then or now, this is what he would have seen there:—If Ben Renton will lift me out of all the necessities of my scheming, wretched life,—if he will give me plenty, money, luxury, comfort, what my soul sighs for,—then I will do my best to love him. I will be a good wife to him,—I will be good in my way,—I will,—I will,—I will! She had said all this to God many a time saying her prayers, and this is what her heart would have said to Ben, with a kind of desperate ingenuousness,—innocence in the midst of guile. And he looked at her, and the man's soul was shaken within him. Something of the truth became visible to him;—not the ineffable charm of love. If it had been very love that shone in her eyes,—however his finer sense had been revolted by its over-frankness,—no doubt he would have fallen a victim. For he had loved her once, and she had never been more beautiful, perhaps never so beautiful in her life. He was touched by her loveliness, by her eagerness, by the pitiful intensity of expression in her eyes. Take me,—save me!—she seemed to be crying to him: and, good heavens! to think what one gleam of this fire, one such look, would have been to him once! Ben grew confused in himself, half with recollections, half with pity; and the softness of success and restoration was in his mind,—even of triumph,—for had not he won a victory, and silenced all opposers? His voice faltered as he answered her, if answer it could be called.

'It is a long time ago,' he said; 'one's very body and being alter you know, they say, completely in seven years.'

'But one's heart never changes,' murmured Millicent. And that was the moment when Mrs. Tracy, feeling that the conflict was not progressing, chose to come in like a watchful goddess, who sees that her champion's arms do not prevail.

'My dear, we are taking Mr. Renton away from his cousin,' she said, 'and from talking over family matters; but since we have done so, could you not persuade him, Millicent, to come over to us to luncheon? You might go on the water a little; you are so fond of it; and then lunch would be ready. Mr. Renton, you must not think it strange that we are anxious to see a little of such a kind friend as you are. I always say your ready kindness saved my life.'

Millicent turned sharp round, and involuntarily clenched her hand, as if she would have struck her mother. 'It is all over now!' she said to herself; and never had the battle been so nearly won. As for Ben, the sound of the new voice woke him up in a moment. He gave himself a little shake, and recovered his self-command. Good heavens! to think how near a step it had been to falling helpless into the syren's snare!

'Thanks; but we must turn back when we have seen you to your boat,' he said; and lingered to let Mrs. Tracy join them. 'I have no time for any such pleasures. My mother thinks it hard enough already, and I must give her what little time remains. I am going away to-morrow.'

'To-morrow!' said Mrs. Tracy, with a half-sneer and a look at her daughter, to which Millicent, flushed, and pouting, and angry, made no reply. 'Then is it a mistake, after all? I thought I heard you say all was right. I beg your pardon, I am sure——'

'About the property it is all right,' said Ben; 'but I am not the idle fellow you once knew me. Those were the only six months I ever absolutely threw away in my life. And I can't give up my work in a moment because I have got back my rights.'

'It was a pity you threw away those six months you speak of,' said Millicent. 'Come, mamma; why should we trouble Mr. Renton to go with us to the boat? Of course he must have a great deal to talk of,—to his mother,—and to Mary,—his own people. We are strangers, and have no claim upon him.'

'There are some things which one gives all the more freely because there is no claim,' said Ben, with good-nature. 'The path is rather rough here. Mrs. Tracy, give me your hand.'

'Thank you, I want no help!' Millicent cried, when he turned to her, and she sprang over the gnarled mass of roots, and ran down the path to the green river-bank. She stood there, framed in by the thick foliage, her white figure standing out against the light of the river,—a picture not to be easily forgotten. Emerald green below,—green, just touched with points of autumnal colour, here and there a yellow leaf above;—gleams of blue sky looking through;—one long line of light reflecting all the darker objects, the river, with one boat lying close to the grassy margin; and in the midst the beautiful, flushed, brilliant creature, full of passion, and mortification, and an angry despair. She did not think it worth while now to hide the strong emotions in her mind, but stood with her face turned to them as they followed, humiliated, yet defiant,—the crown of all the scene, and the only discord in it. Poor Millicent! her eyebrows lowered, her eyes shone; her colour was high with the shame of her defeat; and yet, beyond the angry glance in her eye, there was a tear, and the corners of her mouth drooped; and, scarcely concealed by the hard, little laugh of artificial gaiety, a sob was sounding in her throat.

'Good-bye,' she said, almost roughly, 'Ben,—I will never call you so again! I wish you luck of your good fortune. It makes a great difference to most people in this world.'

'Good-bye,' said Ben, taking her hand almost against her will. 'It makes little difference to me. What has been done has been done by nature and years. If you should ever want help or counsel that I can give—— Well, let us say nothing about that. Good-bye——'

'For a time,' Mrs. Tracy added, with her bland smile, taking his hand in both hers,—'till our meeting again.'

And Mary, whose feelings all this time had been more overwhelming than can be described, and who had followed mechanically, with an instinct of being there to the last to see what direful harm might happen, stood passive by his side, not knowing if she were in a trance or a dream; and saw the boat push off into the shining river. Mrs. Tracy turned and waved her hand to them, bland to the last. But Millicent never turned her head. Once only, just as the boat shot past the long drooping branches of the willow which closed in the view, she looked round sharply and saw them; and the rowlocks sounded hollow and loud, and with another stroke the boat was gone. Neither of them have ever seen that beautiful face again.

Ben stood for some time after they had disappeared on the same spot, forgetting everything, gazing out upon the vacant stream and vacant sunshine, in a curious vacant way. If it had been put to him, he would never have confessed how much moved he had been. Perhaps he was himself unconscious of it. But nature made a pause in him, manifesting the convulsion, in her own way, when this woman, who had influenced it so strangely, passed for ever out of his life.

'Are you fond of Coleridge, Mary?' he said to her without any preface, quite suddenly, as they went up the steep bank.

'Of Coleridge, Ben? What an odd question! Why do you ask?'

'Do you remember what he says? And what a curious sense he had of the things that are inexpressible,—

'How there looked him in the face
An angel beautiful and bright,
And how he knew—'

'No, I don't mean that,—not so bad as that!'

'I don't know what you mean,' said Mary, with a little shiver; and she took hold of his arm with an instinctive desire to show him her sympathy. Very well did she know what he meant; or at least thought, hoped she did; but denied it with characteristic readiness. He pressed the soft, sisterly hand to him when he felt it on his arm. Certainly, there was a great sympathy between them, though nothing more. And he did not say another word to her of the subject of the conversation which this last meeting had blotted out as if it had never been. They did not talk of anything, indeed, but went home together, with a silent understanding of each other in which there was certainly some balm.

Understanding each other! which meant that the woman,—partly,— understood the man, and had it in her heart to be a little sorry for him in respect to the conflict through which he had come; and a little, a very little,— which was more remarkable,—sorry for the other woman thus finally foiled and done with; but that the man had no comprehension at all of the woman, and gave no particular thought to her, except so far as was conveyed in a tender, kindly sympathy for poor little Mary. Her life must not be made a burden to her any longer by his mother's drives and her worsted work. That was all the progress Ben had made in the comprehension of his cousin's heart.

CHAPTER XV.

AN UNEXPECTED VISITOR.

ON the next morning Ben went away without a word, no repentance of his intention or lingering desire to postpone it having apparently crossed his mind. He took leave of his mother the night before, for he was going away early. 'It will not be for seven years this time,' he said, as he kissed her, and was going to kiss Mary, too,—a formula which his cousin, with a pang of mortification in her heart, felt might be better dispensed with. 'Nay; I shall see you in the morning,' she said, half terrified lest the blood which she felt to be scorching her cheek might 'make him think anything.' What should it make him think? She puzzled him a little, it must be allowed; but he was not the kind of man who can think of many different things at one time. His mind had been absorbed with the business which brought him to Renton. It was absorbed now with thoughts of what he had to do in the winding-up of his own affairs. Now and then it flitted vaguely across his perception that Mary had something on her mind which, one time or other, it would be his business to see into. Dear little Mary! Ben was very fond of his cousin. If she had wanted a hair from the beard of the Cham of Tartary, or a golden apple from the Tree of Bliss in the gardens of the Enchanted Isles, he would have done all a man could do to get it for her. But he did not know now what she wanted, or if she wanted anything,—and that was one of the matters which could wait till he came home.

Laurie, too, was going away with Ben, though only to town; and the night before they left was a night of talk and recollections more than the separated family had yet permitted themselves. It was true that Hillyard put himself singularly in their way. Perhaps he had not had all the advantages of the Rentons; but still he was a gentleman, though much knocking about the world had taken some of the outside polish off him, and he had never shown any inclination to intrude upon their private talk, or make himself a sharer in the family communings,—never till now. Perhaps it was because they were just setting off again, and Ben's family came in for the *attendrissement*, which might have been more justly bestowed upon his own. But it was ridiculous that he should plant himself by Mary, occupying her attention, and pouring forth his confidences upon her, as it seemed to him good to do. They were all gathered together in the drawing-room as they had been so many times before, after Mrs. Renton went to bed, with the windows open as usual, the lights shaded, the languor of the night and its wistfulness and soft content and melancholy stealing in; the half-darkness and the soft breathing of the night air, and the fluttering moths about the lamp, were all accessories of the picture which nobody could forget. And there was a mysterious gloom about the walls and the roof, owing to the shades on the lamps, which gave a more distinct character to the half-visible faces, each in its corner, and to the brilliant circles of illumination round every light. They had begun to talk of their father, and this last event in the story of his will, which was so strange, and so unlike all his previous life.

'One would like to know what he meant by it,' said Laurie. 'Poor, dear old father! If there had been something dependent on the issue of our probation; if there had been a reward for the man that had used his talent best, like you, Ben; or for the man who had given him an heir, like Frank; but all to end in this aimless way! We have always thought ourselves very sound in the brain, we Rentons, or I know what one might be tempted to think.'

'That is what I have thought all along,' said Frank.

'It is not for us to say so, at least,' said the elder brother. 'I believe illness coming on had confused his mind. They say it does. I don't think he can have been quite clear what he was doing. And then he remembered at last, and was sorry,—don't you recollect?'

'My poor father!' said Laurie. And then there was a pause; and in this pause, through the dimness and the stillness, came the sound of Hillyard's voice, too low to be distinguishable, coming from Mary's corner, addressed to her with a volubility and eagerness which struck them all with amazement. He had not meant to be so audible; and when, after the first silence, a little laugh burst from Alice at the one voice thus brought into prominence, he faltered and stopped too, as people do under such circumstances. What could he be finding to say to Mary? and what could Mary be thinking of to listen to him? were the half-angry thoughts that flashed over Ben's mind. Of course he was a guest here, and everybody's equal. Yet still, it seemed to Ben as if, on the whole, this was bad taste, to say the least, on Hillyard's part.

But Alice, though she had laughed at the sound of the solitary voice which continued when they all dropped, was eager to let loose her opinions, too, on the other subject. 'I cannot see what other will could have been just, now,' she said. 'If he had told you something to do, it would have been different. But he gave you nothing to do; and how were you to know what he wanted? It was not Laurie's three princes, after all.'

'And, now I come to think of it, I don't believe in my three princes,' said Laurie. 'I have not a doubt they fought it out when papa was out of the way. Fancy two elder brothers giving in to a fellow because he had the marvellousest little dog that ever was seen! It came to natural justice, you may be sure, at the end, and the strongest had it. And it has come to a kind of natural justice with us, so far as law allows. Poor old father! One used to feel as if he must be so much wiser than we were. And it proves he was as confused as the rest, and saw just as short a way before him, and stultified himself, half-knowingly, like one of his own sons.'

'Don't!' said Ben, with a voice of pain. He was more angry with his father than soft-hearted Laurie ever could have been, and consequently was less able to talk of it. 'Thank heaven!' he cried, suddenly, 'I don't suppose it has done any of us any lasting harm.'

'No,' said Laurie, out of the silence, after a pause, 'no more harm than we should have done ourselves, anyhow, for our own hand.'

And somehow, in the room, there was the sound of a sigh; whom it proceeded from it would be hard to tell—six people all gathered together of a soft autumn evening, and not too much light to betray them, it would be strange if there was not more than one who sighed. But Alice, in the shade, slid her hand through her husband's arm, and said joyously, 'It has done us no harm, Frank!' 'Because we would not let it,' he whispered back again, brushing her soft cheek with his moustache. Yes, that was the secret. Have your will, anyhow, whether fortune permits or no; and in the long run the chances are you will come out just as well as your neighbour, who allowed fortune to constrain him, and will have had your will and your happiness into the bargain; bad social morality, perhaps, but just as good fact as any other. The young soldier and his wife had their little triumph unsuspected by the others, who heard but a momentary whisper in that corner, which was drowned by Hillyard's more forcible whisper, always conversing with Mary. What did the fellow mean by it? Ben was so disgusted by this 'bad taste' of his friend, that he got up and stepped out on the lawn, with some murmur about a cigar. And the other men all rose and joined him, though not with any enthusiasm. When they had all trooped out, he stepped back for a moment, and held out his hand to his cousin.

'Is it really the case, Mary, that I am not to bid you good-bye to-night?'

'No,' Mary said, drawing back, with a shy hesitation which he did not understand; 'do you think I would let you go away,—so far,—and not make your breakfast for you the last morning? This is only good-night.'

'Good-night, then,' he said, but held her hand still. 'What was that fellow, Hillyard, so voluble about?'

'That fellow!' said Mary. 'I thought he was your great friend. Indeed, it was mostly you he was talking about.'

'A poor subject,' Ben said, only half satisfied; and then she drew her hand away from him, and he went off with a half-suspicious glance at her, and a certain sense of uneasiness, to join the men outside.

A parting in the morning is of all things in the world the most detestable. He who would have a tender farewell, and leave a soft recollection behind him, let him depart by the night train,—the later the better,—when there is no inquisitive light to spy out, not only the tear, but even that humidity of eye which tells when tears are coming. Mary's eyes were in this condition when Ben rose from his hurried breakfast, and came up to her in the full light of day, and of Mr. Hillyard, who lingered, though nobody wanted him. She had kept behind the urn, feeling that, after all, had she stayed up-stairs and watched him going away from her window, it would have been less unsatisfactory. 'You'll write and let me know how things are going on,' Ben had said, not feeling particularly cheerful himself, but yet approaching the best part of the wing of a partridge to his mouth. 'Oh, yes, of course I will write, as usual,' Mary said, and he gave a nod of satisfaction as he ate. To be sure, he had to eat before he started. And then she added, 'You'll let us know as soon as you arrive.' And he nodded again over his coffee-cup. It was to give him his breakfast she had got up,—and what else was there to be expected? And when the dog-cart was at the door, Ben wiped the crumbs carefully from his moustache, and went up to his cousin, and took her hand, and bent over her. 'Good-bye, Mary,' he said, kissing her cheek, 'take care of yourself. I'll write a line from town before we start. I'm very sorry, now it has come to the last. Good-bye!'

'Good-bye, Ben!' she said, unable to articulate another word. The blood seemed all to stagnate about her heart. Up to this moment there had always been a possibility of something happening,—something being done or said. But now it was all over. A certain haze came over her eyes, and yet she could see him looking back at her as he went to the door, with an indefinable expression. She stood and held by the back of the chair, looking out of the window before which the dog-cart was standing, forgetting for the moment that there was any one else in the world.

'Good-bye, Miss Westbury,' said a voice at her ear.

Mary turned round with an impatience it was scarcely possible to disguise. 'Oh, Mr. Hillyard, I beg your pardon! I thought you were gone. Good-bye!' she said. He was standing holding out his hand with his eyes bent on her, and a glow in them such as even a woman agitated with feelings of her own could scarcely mistake.

'Good-bye, Miss Westbury. I shall never forget the days I have spent here,' he said, and stooped over her hand, as if——

'Hillyard! do you mean to stay all day?' cried Ben from the dog-cart, in a tone which was not sweet.

'Indeed, you will be late for the train; you have not a moment to lose,' cried Mary, withdrawing her hand.

He muttered something, she could not tell what,—nor, indeed, did she care. 'Not farewell yet,' was it he said? But what did it matter? The interruption had so far roused her that she felt able to go to the window and smile and wave her hand to Ben. Hillyard was still holding his hat in his hand, trying to attract her attention, when the dog-cart disappeared down the avenue. Then Mary sat down and gazed straight before her, with that poignant sense of unreality which such a moment gives. Five minutes ago he was there; and now here was vacancy, silence,—a blank in which life lost itself. Five minutes, and all the world changed! Her brow was burning and heavy with tears unshed,—an ache which seemed physical, so hard the strain and pain it produced in her, went through her heart. And a whole long day to go through, and the birds singing merrily, and the sun shining, and old Willis on his way to remove the remains of Ben's breakfast, and to spread the table for the family that remained! 'It don't seem no good, do it, Miss Mary, to have master home so short, and he been so long away?' Mary started to her feet at the words. No good indeed?—perhaps harm, if one dared say so!—deeper blank and silence after the momentary movement and the light!

And now to think it was all over, and that there remained nothing but the old life to be taken up again and gone on with just as before! If it had been night, when one could have shrouded one's-self in one's own room, and cried or slept, and forgotten one's-self! But it was day,—early morning,—with a whole heap of duties to be performed, and people to look on while she was performing them. And Mary felt sick of it all,—the duties, and the daylight, and the life. Laurie, who thought early rising idiotic, went by a much later train, at what he called a rational hour. And then the house was left in its old quiet, but for the presence of Frank and Alice and the children, which no doubt made a great difference. When Mary went to her godmother with the newspaper she was questioned minutely about Ben's departure and his looks. 'Did he eat any breakfast, Mary?' Mrs. Renton said, putting her handkerchief to her eyes.

'He ate a very good breakfast,' said Mary, with a slight sense of humour, but on the whole, a greater sense of something like displeasure. Yes, he had been quite able to eat breakfast, though he was going away!

'And enjoyed it, poor fellow?' said his mother. 'Ah, if one only knew when he would eat his next meal at Renton? And was he cheerful, my dear, or did he feel it very much? Poor Ben! None of you think how hard it is upon me!'

'You have Frank, godmamma,' said Mary, 'and if he settles in the Dovecote it will be very nice for us all. And there is Laurie close at hand whenever you want him, and no one could be more kind than Laurie——'

'But neither Laurie nor Frank is Ben,' said Mrs. Renton with decision, drying her eyes—which, alas! as her niece felt to the bottom of her heart, was most true. And then Mary read the papers, all the bits of news, as she had done any day these seven years. Had there been any break in the endless round, or had she only dreamed it? It seemed so hard to know: for the interruption, with all its agitations and pleasures, had vanished, and everything was as it had been before. Except, indeed, that Frank and Alice made the dinner-table cheerful, and took the heavy duty of the drive off Mary's hands, which was a relief for which she should have been more grateful. But even that showed the difference between her own life and that of Frank's wife, though Mary, had she not been driven to it, was not given to such comparisons. For her there was but the usual monotonous promenade over the well-known, too well-known country; but Alice was taken to the Dovecote, and even the invalid grew interested about the changes necessary, and the furnishing and decorations of that abode. 'The Frank Rentons' had all the pleasant excitement of settling down before them. And Mary felt that it was very wicked and unwomanly of her to desire any excitement, or to feel so wearily conscious of the want of interest in her own existence. Would it be much better in the cottage with her mother, who in all these years had learnt to do without her, and whose whole mind was absorbed in her curate-boy? Perhaps that would not be any better. And, anyhow, it was evident that there was nothing to do in the meantime but to submit.

There was, however, an excitement awaiting Mary much nearer than she had any expectation of. It came to her just two days after Ben's departure, in the afternoon, when once more Alice and the children had gone to accompany Mrs. Renton in her drive, and she was alone in the drawing-room, with the window open as usual,—that window by which everybody went and came,— everybody, that is to say, belonging to the family. Mary was reading, seated in her favourite chair, half buried in the curtains, when it seemed to her that a shadow fell on her book,—a very familiar accident. It must be Frank, she thought, looking up; but to her great amazement she saw it was Hillyard standing with a deprecating, anxious look before the window. She made a spring from her seat with that one thought which fills the mind of a preoccupied woman to the exclusion of all personal courtesy and consideration. Something must have happened to Ben! 'What is it? for God's sake, tell me! tell me!' she said, rushing out upon him, dropping her book, and holding up her clasped hands.

'Nothing, Miss Westbury,' he said, putting out his hand to take hers, with the humblest, softest tone,—a tone amazing in its gentleness from such a big-bearded, unpolished man. 'I was only waiting to ask you whether I might come in.'

'But you are sure there is nothing wrong with—my cousin?' Mary cried; and then recollected herself, and was covered with confusion. 'I beg your pardon; but seeing you so suddenly it was natural to think of Ben. I felt as if you must have brought bad news, Mr. Hillyard; don't think me very silly—but godmamma may come in any moment from her drive—you are sure there is nothing the matter with Ben?'

'Nothing at all. I left him a few hours ago, very well and very busy,' said Hillyard; and then once more he added in the same soft, subdued, disquieting tones, 'Will you let me come in?'

'Yes, surely,' said Mary, though she was trembling with the sudden fright. 'But it is so strange to see you. Is there any change in your plans? I thought you were to go to-day.' And then a wavering of light and colour came over her face suddenly in spite of herself. This man, who had no possible business at Renton, surely could not have come alone!

'I begged for another day,' said Hillyard, following her into the room. 'I daresay I was a fool for my pains. It may be years before I return again. I asked for another day.'

'I am sure godmamma will be very glad,' said Mary, courteously; 'but somehow it was very startling to see you, and not Ben.'

And she gave a momentary glance out, as if still she expected the other to appear. Such a reception to a man who had come on Hillyard's errand was like frost to a brook. It bound him, shrank him up within himself. He stood looking at her with a half-stupefied, wistful gaze, saying nothing. Ben; always Ben! Was that the only thought in her mind? Was it possible she could see him thus, and meet his eye, and not see his errand was altogether apart from Ben?

Mary, however, was so much occupied with her tremor and start, and curious little flutter of expectation, that it did not occur to her as strange for some minutes that her present companion said no more. She took his silence with the composure of perfect indifference. She was not even curious about him, further than concerned her cousin. Why should she be curious about Mr. Hillyard? But at last it did strike her that politeness required that she should speak to him. And, looking up, she caught the expression of his face and of his attitude all in a moment, and the ardent light in his eyes. Such a look is not to be mistaken. With a sudden rallying of all her blood to her heart, and steadying of her nerves for an utterly unforeseen but unmistakable emergency, Mary faltered and stopped in her intended speech, waiting for what was to come.

'Miss Westbury,' he said, 'I might as well tell you at once that I see what a fool I am. I have my answer before I have spoken. You think no more of me than if I were Ben Renton's horse, or his dog, or anything that belonged to him. I see it quite plain, and I might have seen it before I went away on Wednesday; but there are things in which a man cannot be anything but a fool.'

'I don't know what you mean, Mr. Hillyard?' said Mary. 'I hope I have not been rude. You are a stranger to us all. It is only through Ben we have known you; and it was natural when I saw you that I should think of my cousin. If I have hurt your feelings I am sure I beg your pardon.'

In all this she was talking against time, hoping that Frank or somebody would come in.

'No,' he said; 'I know I had no right to think of anything else. Of course I am a stranger. Ben's dog,—that is about it! I am not sneering, Miss Westbury. I should not have minded your calling me so when I came.'

And there he stood, turning his eyes away from her, a big strong man of the woods as he looked, abashed and disconcerted, like a chidden child. He gazed out blankly, pulling his beard, with a flush of such quick mortification and downfall as a boy might feel when he sees his hasty projects fall to nought, and yet a deeper pang underneath than any boy could bear. Altogether the man looked so humbled and sore and sad, silenced in the very moment of effusion, that Mary's heart was moved. She was sorry for him, and remorseful for her own indifference. It seemed almost needful to let him say out his say by way of consolation.

'We all called you Ben's friend,' she said; 'his best friend, whom we have heard of for years. Nobody else could have come among us at such a time. You must not think I mean anything disrespectful or unkind.'

Then there came a great burst of words from him. 'That was what I thought,' he said; 'that you had been used to hearing of me; that I might have been to you as an old friend. I too have heard of you for years. And look here, Miss Westbury; you may scorn me, but I must say it, I have been in love with you for years. I used to see your letters, and think there was a woman, if one could ever hope to get within speech of her! And then I came here. I ought never to have come. My heart was full of you before, and you may think what it was when I saw you. Don't stop me, please; it is better now that it should all come out. You were kind to me, as you would have been to any stranger; but you did not know what was in my mind, and I did, and went on fire like a fool. There now, I see how it is. I won't grieve you by asking anything. Only give me your hand and say you forgive a rough fellow for taking it upon him to love you, before he ever saw you; and behaving himself like an ass when he did.'

'Mr. Hillyard, I am so sorry,' said Mary, with tears in her eyes. 'I did not mean,—I never thought,—It is me whom you must forgive,—if you can.'

'You!' said the strange man. 'God bless you! that's what I say. You and forgiving have nothing to do with each other.' And then he took her hand between both his, and gazed down upon her with a fond, lingering, sorrowful look, as if he were getting her face by heart. 'I don't know why I came,' he said, muttering to himself; 'I knew it would be exactly so,—just so. And yet I wanted you to know——'

And then the man seemed suddenly to forget her presence altogether. Standing there, holding her hand, he might have fallen into a dream so perfectly still was he. But her hand was lost, buried between both his, held fast, while she stood perforce by him. And yet there was no force in it, no rudeness, but only a profound melancholy silence,—a sacrifice of the hidden sweetness he had been cherishing in his life.

'Mr. Hillyard,' she said, softly, 'you must say good-bye to me and let me go.' And then he woke up and came to life.

'The other hand too,' he said, 'for this once. Good-bye, and God bless you! It's all I'll ever have for my love. God bless you! Good-bye!'

He did not even kiss her hands, but held them fast; and then let them drop, and turned, stooping his tall head through the white curtains, and went out as he came in. Mary stood looking after him with an indescribable sensation. Was he really gone, this man who had been nothing to her barely an hour since, and now was part of her life? or was it a dream altogether, an invention of her fancy? His heavy foot ground upon the gravel for two or three steps while she stood in her amazement looking after him; and then he stopped, and turned round, and came back. But he did not attempt to come in. She on the one side of the white curtains, and he on the other; stood for another moment and looked at each other, and then he cleared his throat, which was husky. 'I am not coming back,' he said, 'I have just one word to say. If there should ever be a time when you might think,—not of me, I don't mean of me, for I'm a stranger as you say,—but that a man's love and support might be of use to you,—they say women feel that sometimes, if things don't go altogether as they wish,—then let me but know, hold up only your little finger, Mary,—there! I've said it for once,—and I'll come if it were from the ends of the earth!'

And then, without another word or look, he went away.

Was this the excitement she had been wishing for, and blaming herself for wishing? Mary ran up to her room in terror of meeting any one, with her heart beating wildly in her breast. Here was an incident indeed, to diversify a dull afternoon, a dull life with! She was so touched and excited, and moved by compassion and surprise and regret, that the effort upon her was not much less than if Hillyard's extraordinary suit had been that of a man to whom her heart could have responded. She sat down and hid her face in her hands, and got rid of some of her excitement in tears, and went over the strange scene. How strange a scene! For all these seven years,—her best and brightest,—Mary had never heard the voice of love. Now and then a tone of that admiration and interest which might have come to love had just caught her ear from the outside world, but she had been drawn back into her retirement and the deeper tone had never followed. And now, all at once, here was passion of such a kind as seldom startles a woman's ears in these days. An utter stranger an hour ago, and now,—happen what might, should she never see the man again,—a bit of her life! Mary's head swam, and the world went round with her. 'They say women feel that sometimes, if things don't go altogether as they wish.' What did he mean? Had he read in her heart more than others could? Was she one to fall into a longing for some love and support, some awakening and current of activity in her life, after all youthful dreams were gone? The suggestion moved Mary with a humbling sense of her own weariness and languor, and senseless disappointment, and longing for she knew not what. She was not one of those women to whom somebody's love is indispensable,—if not one, then another. With a cheek burning with shame, and eyes hot with tears, she rose up and went down again to her duties, such as they were. Henceforward she was determined she should suffice to herself. This, after the first shock of emotion, was all the effect poor Hillyard's sacrifice upon her altar had on Mary. That he should have seen that all was not going altogether as she wished! After all, what better had most women to do with their lives, than to tend a real or imaginary invalid, to order dinners, to read newspapers, to go out every afternoon for a drive? And she had perfect health, and a beautiful country, and plenty of books, and all the poor people in Renton parish, to occupy her. To think with all that, there might come a time when she would want a man's,—any man's,—love and comfort! The counter-proposition, that a man should some time in his life long to have a woman by him, does in no way shock the delicacy of the stronger creature. But what woman is there who would not rather die than acknowledge personally for herself that a man is necessary to the comfort of her existence? In the abstract, it is a different matter. Poor Hillyard! the immediate result of his pilgrimage of love, and hopeless declaration, was to move Mary Westbury, in a wild flame of indignation at her own unwomanliness, to the task of contenting herself, energetically and of set purposes, with all the monotonies of her life.

CHAPTER XVI.

WHAT IT ALL MEANT TO LAURIE.

WHEN Laurie Renton arrived in town, he went with the story of his family's fortune and his own, as was natural, to the padrona, who had now a double interest in the tale. She had already heard of it in a letter from Alice; but such a narrative is naturally more full and satisfactory by word of mouth.

It was in the same house, up the same stairs, in the same studio, that Laurie sought his friend. Everything was seven years older, and the hair growing thin on the top of Laurie's head, and Alice the mother of children; but neither Mrs. Severn nor her studio was much changed. She had attained, when we saw her first, to that table-land which lies in the centre of an innocent and healthful life, and on which Time, if he does not stand still, moves with such equal and steady steps, that it is difficult to trace his progress; and as many more years were probably before her ere there would appear in the padrona any such marked signs of the passage of years as those which had already left their stamp on Laurie in his youth. There might be a few white threads among her hair, at least she said there were; but for all that any one could have told, she might have been wrapped in some enchanted sleep for all those years, instead of working, and thinking, and sorrowing, and taking such simple pleasures as came to her. The pleasures had been less and the sorrows greater since Alice left her; but now Edie had grown, as everybody said, a great girl, and the mother's heart was stirring into life in her development, to prepare for herself another crisis and sacrifice. It was years now since Laurie had returned from his first self-banishment to Italy. He had come back and he had been away again from time to time, but he had always returned here,— 'home' as he liked to call it,—and for a long period there had been nothing in the character of his feelings which made it painful to him to come. How this was he could not tell. When he went away on that forlorn journey to Rome he had felt as if he never could look again upon the woman whom he loved with all his heart, but who, as nature herself indicated, could never be more to him than a friend. She could not be his,—never,—though everything in heaven and earth were to plead for him,—and the only thing for him to do was to rush away from her, and bury himself and his unhappy love out of sight for ever. These had been his feelings when he went away;—but, somehow, they did not last. Slowly, by degrees, he and his heart came back to her without any anguish or despair in them. When he returned, and went half-tremblingly to see if he could bear the sight of her, Laurie found, somewhat to his astonishment, that the sight, instead of driving him wild with disappointed affection, soothed and consoled and softened him as nothing else could do. Perhaps, had it been possible that she should become any other man's wife the sensation would have been different; but there had long ago ceased to be any strong wish on the matter in Laurie's mind. The old custom of hanging about her house came back upon him. He would come and talk to her of all his own concerns, and of a great many of hers, by the hour together; and not of realities only, but of fancies,—everything that came into his head. There was the strangest transposition of ordinary rules in their intercourse. While he lounged about, and talked and poured out all his mind, she would be working on steadily, pausing to note her effects,—now and then calling him into counsel on some knotty point, responding to his thoughts, understanding him even when he but half-uttered his meaning, giving him a certain proof of perfect sympathy and friendship, more soft and tender than ordinary friendship,—and yet never stopping in her work. Had they been of the same age, such a thing of course could not have been possible; but on the vantage-ground of a dozen additional years the woman stood calm and steadfast, and the man too, his boyish fit of passion over, was calm. No doubt there was a whisper at one time in the artists' quarter that Mrs. Severn was going to make a fool of herself and marry a man young enough to be her son. But as time disproved that matter, the world, which after all is not such a stupid world, but acknowledges, after due probation, the privileges that can be safely accorded to the blameless, held its tongue,—or only jeered innocently by times at the friendship. 'Such things are impracticable generally, and dangerous, you know, and all that. It is all very well to talk of friendship; but one knows it always falls into love on one side or the other. I really do believe an exception ought to be made for the padrona and Laurie Renton,' was what was said in Fitzroy Square. And as the two took matters with perfect composure, and never looked as if they supposed either the world or the Square to have anything to do with it, the unusual bond between them soon came to be considered a matter of course. It was not such a bond that the man was always at the woman's apron-strings. He went away, sometimes for months together, and travelled about in that half-professional, half-dilettante way that suited Laurie; and then he wrote to her, and next after Alice's, Laurie's letters were looked for in Mrs. Severn's house. And I will not say that there was not now and then just a word in them which the padrona passed over when she read these epistles to the boys, and which made her half smile, half sigh with a curious mingled sense of regret, and amusement, and pleasure. He would say, when he was describing something to her, 'If you were but here, padrona mia, I should want no more.' Foolish fellow! as if she ever could be with him, as if it would not be the height of folly and weakness, and overturn of the whole rational world and all the modesties of nature. But yet, so long as it evaporated in a harmless sigh like this, it hurt no one,—not Laurie, who perhaps loved his wanderings all the better for that soft want in them; and not her, as she doubled down the page at that point with a half-laugh. And when he came home the first place he went to was the Square. To be sure, such a friendship put all thoughts of marrying out of Laurie's head, as Mrs. Suffolk, who thought everybody should marry, sometimes deplored. 'Unless you send him away, padrona, he will always be just as he is. He will never think of any other kind of life,' she would say to her friend. 'My dear, he has no money to marry on,' the padrona would say,—and so Laurie's heart had always found a home and every kind of support and consolation and sympathy in Fitzroy Square.

And, to tell the truth, the money had been rather a difficult point with him now and then. To live upon two hundred a-year when you have been brought up a Renton of Renton, is a matter which requires a great deal of consideration. But Laurie, fortunately for himself, had no expensive tastes, and he painted some pictures, and, what was more remarkable, sold some; and even found himself on the line at the Academy, thus carrying out his highest dreams. But it did not give him the gratification, nor cause the stir he had once anticipated. It was a small picture, a little bit of Italian air and sunshine, and Slasher gave it a little paragraph all to itself in the 'Sword;' but the people whom he had once pictured to himself finding out his name in the catalogue, and calling heaven and earth to witness that Laurie Renton had done something at last, had by this time forgotten all about Laurie Renton, or he had forgotten them, which came to the same thing. And candidly in his soul, Laurie allowed, that had not old Welby been on the hanging committee, probably it never would have reached 'the line;' and had not Slasher been a friend of his, would never have been noticed in the 'Sword.' But it sold for a hundred pounds, which was always an advantage. The picture was called 'Feliciello, on Tiberio,' and was the picture of a dark-faced Capriote guide, on one of the highest points of his island, pointing out to a fair English girl the points in the wonderful landscape round. It was Edie Severn, who had never been there, with her golden hair streaming round her, who was the English girl. But handsome Feliciello had been studied on the spot. And Mr. Rich of Richmont,—always a great patron of the fine arts,—gave Laurie a hundred pounds for it, and thought it one of his greatest bargains. 'This picture has a story,' he would say to his guests; 'it was painted by a gentleman, the son of one of my neighbours in the country, a man who had never been brought up to make his living by art. It is quite a romance; but I hear matters are settled, and that he has come into his share of the money, and will paint no more, and I think I was very lucky to secure this. My daughter, Lady Horsman, will tell you all about it.' 'About the picture painted by a gentleman?' Nelly would say, on being questioned. 'Most painters that I know are gentlemen. Papa means to infer that he is not much of a painter, I suppose.' For Lady Horsman was not fond of the Rentons, and had never cared to cultivate their society. 'If you get my lady on painters she'll talk till midnight,' Sir George said out of his moustache. He did not know the difference between a sign-post and a Titian, and thought the one quite as pretty as the other; but he was the head of one of the oldest families in Christendom, and Master of the Hounds in his county, and a great many other grandeurs; and, so far as I know, Nelly had the full value for her fifty thousand pounds.

This, however, is a digression a long way out of Fitzroy Square. Laurie went to the padrona with his story, and found her still in a state of excitement over Alice's letter,—the second since the event,—with something in it about Dovecote, which was the last new possibility. She had just been taken to see it, and her letter was full of an enthusiastic description of its beauties. 'Think, mamma, of a lovely little house close to Renton, with a lawn sloping to the river, and a cow, and a pony-carriage, and I don't know what,' the young wife wrote in her delight. 'And Frank thinks he may afford himself a hunter, and there is the sweetest honeysuckle room for Edie and you!' The padrona, being mother to the being upon whom this glorious prospect was opening, was more interested at first in the Dovecote than in anything Laurie had to say.

'To think one has only to take the train and be with her in an hour,—after being so far away for,—a lifetime!' the padrona said, with tears in her eyes.

'Only six years,' said Laurie; 'but never mind; after Alice has had her turn perhaps you will think of me.'

'When you know I always think of you!' said Mrs. Severn, 'it becomes you to be *exigeant*, Laurie! and you are not going to have a cow, and a pony-carriage, and everything that is most delightful on the face of the earth. Think of Alice having a cow! You are so terribly *blasé*, it does not seem to strike you. And Edie is out, the child, so that there is no one to be glad but me.'

'It does not strike me at all,' said Laurie. 'If she had a dozen cows, I think I could bear it. But some day I must take you to see Dovecote, padrona, since you like it so much.'

'I wish they had had Feliciello,' said Mrs. Severn, 'if one had known you were all to be so well off,—it would have pleased Frank.'

'Frank will like some of those vile chromos just as well,' said Laurie. 'I'll buy him a few, I think. And I mean to bring Ben to see you to-night; then you will know us all. Not that there will be any intense gratification in that; but you'll like Ben. He is made of different stuff from the rest of us. There is more in him. He is not so cheeky as Frank; and he is another sort of fellow, to be sure, from a good-for-nothing like me.'

'Laurie, there is something the matter,' said the padrona, turning upon him with her palette in her hand. She knew all his tones like the notes in music, and heard the far-off quiver of one of his fits of despondency already vibrating in the quiet. 'Is not this as good for you as for the rest?'

'Oh, yes, quite as good,' he said abruptly, with his eyes on her work. 'You are putting too much yellow in that light.'

'Am I? but that is not the question. Laurie, never mind the light, but tell me what is wrong.'

'I must mind the light,' he said. 'If I can't put you right when you get into a mess, what is the good of me? It's all wrong and it's all right, padrona mia, and I don't know that it matters much one way or another; but I don't quite like your shadows. With that tone of light they should have more blue in them,' he went on, gazing at the picture and shading his eyes with his hand.

'But it will make a great difference in your life,' said Mrs. Severn, putting down her tools and drawing a chair near to where he sat.

'That is just it,' he said; 'it will make no difference to speak of. It is a great thing for Ben; and for Frank, too, it will be everything. You can see that clearly. But what difference will it make to me? More money to spend, perhaps, and better rooms to live in; but no sort of expansion or widening-out of life. That's not possible, you know. It was put a stop to once, and no change that I know of can effect it now.'

'You cannot mean to reproach me, Laurie?' said the padrona.

'No,' he said, still fixedly gazing at the picture; 'I don't reproach you. Being you, perhaps you could have done nothing else. I am not complaining of anybody; but this is how it is,—you see it for yourself.'

'Laurie, listen to me,' she said, with eagerness, laying her hand on his arm. 'I have wanted to speak to you for long, and never liked to begin the subject. You must make an effort to break this spell. I did not say a word as long as you were poor,—for what could you do?—and I thought I was always some consolation to you; but now that you have money enough, and can make a new beginning,—Laurie, do you know, I think it would be better for you to go away from me.'

'What, go away again?' he said, with a half-smile, 'as I did when I went to Rome? No, there is no such occasion now.'

'Of course there is no such occasion now,—that dream has passed away, as all dreams do,—but, Laurie, for that very reason I speak. Even what you were so foolish as to wish then you don't wish now.'

She made a momentary pause, but he gave no answer. It was quite true. He was not in love with her any longer,—though she was the creature dearest to him in the world. Nor did he any longer want to appropriate or bind her closer to himself. He would not have admitted this change in words, but it was true.

'I don't think in the least that you have ceased to care for me,' she continued; 'but it is different,—it is not in that way. And you are getting not to care much what happens. We talk over it, and come to our conclusions; and after that, good and evil are much the same to you. That is why I think you should go away,—not to Italy, as you did before, but out of this neighbourhood, to some place like the one you used to live in, and go back into the world.'

'Why, I wonder?' said Laurie. 'The world and I had never much to say to each other. And at least I have some comfort in my life here.'

'Too much, a great deal,' said the padrona, with a smile. 'You know you can always come to me, whether it is a pin that pricks, or a storm that overtakes you. I am fond of you; and you can always reckon on my sympathy.'

'Always!' said Laurie, stooping to kiss the hand she had laid on his arm.

'Yes; but that is not good for you,' said Mrs. Severn, hastily withdrawing her hand. 'Now is the moment to preach you Helen Suffolk's little sermon. She says you will never marry so long as you are constantly here.'

'Marry!' said Laurie, looking at her, and then turning his head away with a half-contemptuous impatience.

'Well, marry. Why should not I say so? If I have stood in your way, unwillingly, unfortunately, once, why should that shut up all your life? Laurie, if I were to ask you to reconsider all this, and make a difference,—for my sake?'

'I could not marry even for your sake,' he said, turning to her with a sudden laugh; 'though there is no other inducement I would do so much for. Tell me something else to do to show my devotion, and let everything go on as it was before.'

'Not as it was before,' said Mrs. Severn. 'This atmosphere might be good enough for you when you were poor. At least, it did you no harm; but now I want you to go back into the world.'

'You want me to be wretched, I think,' said Laurie. 'I have got used to this atmosphere, as you call it; and it suits me. But I have forgotten all about the world. What have I done that I should be sent back among people who have forgotten me, to mix myself up with things in which I take no interest? Padrona, in this you do not show your usual wisdom. Let us return to the question of the light.'

'Not yet,' she said. 'It is because I am anxious about you that I speak. This is such a point in your life; a new beginning,—anything you please to make it,—and you feel yourself how hard it is to think that it will make no difference. Laurie, what I want you to do is to break this thread of association, and turn your back upon the past.'

He turned and looked at her as she spoke, and their eyes met;—hers earnest and steady; his with a smile, which was full of tenderness, and a kind of playful melancholy dawning in them. 'But that is not what I want you to do,' he said, the smile growing as he met her gaze. She turned away with a little impatient exclamation. It was not the kind of reply she had looked for.

'You are provoking, Laurie,' she said. 'You have regained the ground you stood on seven years ago, and why should you refuse to recall the circumstances too?'

'And make the seven years as if they had never been?'

'I think you might, in a great measure,' said the padrona, with a little flush on her cheek, 'though you laugh. Nothing has happened in those seven years. Yes, I grant you, you have felt some things as you never did before, and learned a great many things. But nothing has happened, Laurie. Nothing has occurred either to tie up your freedom in any way, or to leave rankling recollections in your mind. There has been no fact which could fetter you. Indeed,—for all that has come and gone,—your life might be safer to begin anew than that of any man I know.'

'Well, that is hard!' said Laurie, with more energy than he had yet shown; 'the present is not much, the future I take no particular interest in, and you ask me to agree that there is nothing in the past! What has been the good of me altogether, then? Nobody will say that it has been worth a man's while to live in order to produce 'Feliciello.' Padrona, this is very poor consolation,—the poorest I ever knew you to give.'

'I did not mean it so, Laurie.'

'No, you did not mean it,' he said; 'you did not think that the past,—such as it is,—is all I have. Of course I might now go back to Kensington Gore, as you tell me, or somewhere else; and go to a few parties next season, perhaps. Fine fate! Didn't I tell you how I used to anticipate people finding my name in the Academy catalogue, and standing and staring at Laurie Renton's picture? and now I can't, for the life of me, remember who the people were I so thought of! That's encouraging for a return to old ways. Let's say no more about it,' said Laurie, getting up and following his friend to her easel. 'After all, the boys and Edie shall have some pleasure out of the money, and then it will not be quite lost.'

'The boys and Edie must not get into the way of looking to you for pleasure,' said the padrona, quickly; 'neither for you nor them would that be good.'

'There it is now!' cried Laurie, 'proof upon proof how little I am the better for what has happened. You cannot work for ever, padrona; but if I had all the gold-mines that ever were dreamt of you would not take anything from me; and what is the good of my having it, I should like to know?'

'No, I would not take anything from you,' she said, with a momentary smile; but it was a suggestion that made her tremble in her fortitude whenever it was made. 'Laurie,' she said, with a little gasp, turning to him for sympathy, 'when I cannot work I hope I shall die.'

'But one cannot die when one pleases, that is the worst of it,' said Laurie. 'I hope you will, padrona mia,—and I too,—and then, perhaps, one might have a better chance for a new life.'

This was not cheerful talk for a new beginning; but the amusing thing about Laurie, and, indeed, about the pair thus strangely united, was, that after all this had been uttered and done with they both became quite cheerful; and, a quarter of an hour afterwards, were planning an expedition to Dovecote, taking Renton by the way, with all that enjoyment of the idea of a country excursion which is so strong in the laborious dweller in towns. The vision of gliding rivers and autumnal trees swept over Mrs. Severn's mind like a refreshing wind, carrying away all the vapours. For a time, she thought no more either of that twilight life which Laurie had chosen for himself, and of which she felt herself partly the cause, nor of her own anxieties, but went on painting, reducing the yellow tone in her light, and modifying her shadows, and full of cheerful discussion of the day and the way of going. To the moment its work or its thought; and to the next, why, another thought, another piece of work; and so forth, as pleases God. This blessing of temperament,—special gift of heaven to its beloved,—belonged more or less to both. The artist-woman had it in its perfection, which was the reason why she had got through so much hard labour and so many struggles with eye undimmed and spirit unbroken; and Laurie had it in a degree which had done much to lead to the unsatisfactoriness and imperfection of his life, which is a strange enough paradox, and yet true. For in the padrona, this power of dismissing care and living in the hour was accompanied, as it often is, by the strongest vitality and energy of constitution, by a natural delight and pleasure in exertion, and by the perpetual, never absent spur of necessity. Whereas in Laurie's case it was associated with the meditative, contemplative soul; the mind that is more prone to thinking than to doing; a slower amount of life in the veins, and an existence disengaged from necessities and responsibilities. Temperament had more to do with the matter than had that early blunder in his life for which the padrona never forgave herself. 'If I had not stood in his way he would have made a life for himself, like other men,' she would say to herself, with an ache in her heart, yet with that touch of tender gratitude to the man who had it in him to pour himself out like a libation on her path, which a woman cannot but feel, however undesired the sacrifice may be. I am afraid to acknowledge it, but the truth is that such a libation is very grateful to a woman. There is in it the most exquisite, tragical, heart-rending pleasure. Not that one would not regret it with all one's heart and soul, and do everything that one could, like Lancelot, to turn aside the rising passion. But even to Lancelot was not that self-offering of the lily-maid, though he would have given his life to prevent it, an exquisite sweetness and sorrowfulness, a combination of the deepest pain and gratification of which the soul is capable? Such an act raises the doer of it,—

be it man or woman,—out of the level of ordinary humanity, and envelopes the receiver of the offering in the same maze of tenderest, most melancholy glory. Something of this feeling the padrona had for her Laurie, who had given her his life like a flower, without price or hope of price in this world. And yet, I think, temperament was at the bottom of it, and the sacrifice, and the sweetness of it, and all the subdued tones of his existence which had followed, were more to him than the brighter daylight colours of ordinary existence, even though he might feel the absence of those fuller tones now and then, once in a way.

But to some extent Laurie acted upon Mrs. Severn's advice. As luck would have it, his old rooms at Kensington Gore, having passed through many hands in the interval, proved to be vacant about this time. And Laurie secured them, and fitted up all his old fittings, his carved brackets and velvet hangings, and all the contrivances that had been so pleasant to him; and had his bow-window once more full of flowers, and looked out once more upon the gay park and the stream of carriages as from an opera-box. But the ladies who looked up at his window once had passed away and given place to others, who knew not Laurie, or had forgotten him, and asked each other who was the man who stared so from that window? And from Kensington Gore to Fitzroy Square is a very long walk to be taken every day. And though, to be sure, there are plenty of studios about Kensington, into which an amateur may drop, yet these are grand studios, flanked by drawing-rooms, with ladies to be called upon, and the flavour of society about. It is true that Suffolk lives in that refined neighbourhood now, having made very rapid progress since the days when Mr. Rich bought 'The Angles,' and Laurie put the studio in order for the reception of the patron, and got cobwebs on his coat. 'They were very nice, those old days, after all!' Mrs. Suffolk says, when they talk it over; but they have now a spruce man-servant,—more spruce, though not so well instructed as old Forrester, Mr. Welby's man,—to move a picture that has to be moved, and open the door to the patrons and patronesses. And Laurie for one, to whom a man-servant is not the badge of grandeur and success which it is to Mr. Suffolk, rather preferred, I fear, the state of things in the old days, when they all clustered about Fitzroy Square.

But the padrona has not removed from No. 375, though she has been tempted and plagued to do so on all sides. Frank, who would prefer to have a mother-in-law (since such a thing he must have) in a habitable part of the town, is very energetic as to the advantage it will be to Edie when she grows up. And Alice recommends it with wistful eyes, as so much nicer for the air, not liking to say a word against the home of her youth. Mrs. Severn thinks it would be unkind to Mr. Welby to withdraw from him; and it would cost a great deal of money; and then there would be new carpets wanted for new rooms, and quantities of things; and, last of all, would not it be a still greater clog upon Laurie and hindrance to him, in the possibility of his heart disengaging itself from all the pleasant bonds of the past? I think, however, that the thing which will finally resolve the point will be Frank's success in the competition for a Foreign Office clerkship, for which he is going in. None of his people have any doubt of his success; and, in that case, the boy may be trusted to make his mother's life a burden to her so long as she remains in Fitzroy Square. But what is to be done with Mr. Welby, and Forrester, to whom it would now be impossible to live out of sight of Edie and the boys, and withdraw themselves from the gradually increasing authority of the padrona, I don't know.

Laurie's sketch of the 'Three Fairy Princes' turned up out of a packing-box when he took back his belongings to Kensington Gore; and he hung it in the placer of honour over his mantelpiece. There anybody may see young Frank pushing forth towards the Indian towers and minarets, with a coronet hanging in a haze over the distant prospect; and Laurie himself, with his goods and chattels hung about him, and his lay-figure gazing blank over his shoulders, trudging towards the pepper-boxes of the National Gallery; and Ben scaling the rocks, like Mr. Longfellow's Alpine hero, with the nymph on the summit beckoning him,—not to eternal snows and supernatural excellence, but to Renton and the House of Commons. Frank has not got the coronet; nor Laurie, except in the very mildest accidental way, the glories of the Academy. But who is to tell what is waiting for Ben? At least, there is only another chapter to do it in, and the story is all but told.

CHAPTER XVII.

CONCLUSION.

THE day of Hillyard's visit was full of trial and excitement to Mary. To live in a household where everything is talked of freely, with the consciousness of having various matters of the deepest interest entirely to yourself, is not an agreeable position in any case; and to feel yourself thrilling through every vein with the concussion of a recent shock, while yet you are compelled to put on the most commonplace composure, is more trying still. Mary, however, had been used to it for some time back, if that was any alleviation. She only had known, or rather suspected, the ancient connexion between Ben Renton and the beautiful Millicent. She alone had had the excitement of watching their meeting after so long an interval. She only had understood the passage of arms between the two; and she had witnessed their parting, which to her was of ten-fold more interest than even the great interest which the family had in common. And now, her spectatorship in Ben's romance being over, here had suddenly sprung up a romance of her own, so completely beyond all expectation that even now she could scarcely believe it had been real. Mary could not have betrayed Ben's secret to any one; but had her mother been at hand, or even had her godmother been less pre-occupied, I doubt whether she could have kept poor Hillyard's to herself. For it was her own, and in the excitement of the moment she might not have remembered that it was the man's also, and a humiliation to him. But, as it was, poor Mary had not the opportunity of relieving her mind. Mrs. Westbury was away, and Alice took her share in nursing Mrs. Renton, entering into it with a certain enjoyment of the task. There were even moments when she thought Mary unsympathetic, and was sorry for 'poor grandmamma,' bringing with her a fresh interest in the ailments and the alleviations, such as was scarcely possible to the nurse who had been going through it all for seven years. Mary consequently at this extraordinary moment of her existence had lost all her habitual quiet, and all those possibilities of communication which had ever been open to her. She herself and her personal being was floated away, as it were, on the current of 'the Frank Rentons.' They had come into the house like an inundation, and left no room for anything but their own cheerful beginning of life,—their arrangements, their new house, their children, what they were going to do. The two women who had lived there so long in the silence were carried away by the vigorous young tide; and Mary, hiding her individual concerns in her own mind, lived for the rest of that evening a strange, abstracted, feverish sort of existence, like a creature in a dream, hearing the cheerful voices round her, and the lights shining, and figures flitting about, but only awaking to take any part in it when she was called upon energetically to come out of her abstraction. The position altogether was so strange that she kept asking herself which scene was real and which was a dream;—either this was the reality,—this evening picture, with Frank talking to his mother on the sofa, and Alice working in the golden circle of the lamplight, and the urn bubbling, and gleams of reflexion shining from the tea-table in the corner; or else the other scene, with Hillyard standing sunburnt, and bearded, and impassioned, telling her he had loved before he even saw her,—saying, if some time, any time she should want a man's love and support—— One thing was certain, they could not both be real; she had been dreaming them,—or else she was dreaming now.

Nor yet was Mary's excitement over for the night. When the evening post came in, a letter was brought to her, which at the first glance she saw was in Ben's handwriting. Well! there was nothing surprising in that. Of course Ben would write, though she had not expected it so soon. But the contents of the note were such as to raise to a climax her sense of being in some feverish dream. This is what Ben said:—

'DEAR MARY,—I want to speak half-a-dozen words to you before I go. I have heard something to-day which has taken me very much by surprise, and I cannot leave England without seeing you. But I don't want to disturb my mother with a hurried visit and another parting. If you will be at the beech-tree on the river-walk to-morrow morning at eight, I will come down by the first train and meet you there. Don't refuse me. It is of great importance. In haste,

'Yours, B. R.'

Mary's head went round and round as she sat,—hearing Frank's voice talking all the while, and Alice pouring out the tea,—and read this note. The question changed now, and seemed to be,—they or Ben; which was the phantom? But the paper and the writing were very real,—so real that she could see it had been written in excitement, and was blurred, and betokened a scratching and uncomfortable pen, which is a thing that no imagination would be likely to invent. When she had put the extraordinary note away in her pocket,— fortunately she had not said out loud, 'Here is a letter from Ben,' as on any other day she would have done,—Mary's mind went hopelessly into abstraction. She gave up the tea-making to Alice gratefully and without an effort, though in general she did not like her prerogatives invaded. She never uttered a word to help on the conversation. She had to be recalled as from a distance, when anybody spoke to her. Things had come to such a pitch that she seemed to lose her individual consciousness altogether. To have violent love made her one day by a man whom she scarcely knew, and to meet her cousin Ben clandestinely the next morning by the great beech, to talk over something of importance, which concerned only her and him, and nobody else in the family,—the earth seemed to be going off its pivot altogether to

Mary. She felt that now nothing would surprise her. If Mrs. Renton had suddenly proposed to her to walk to town, or Frank that she should swim across the river, it would have seemed to her perfectly natural. But to meet Ben by stealth at the great beech at eight o'clock! Could she have mistaken the words? For one moment a sort of gleam of eldritch fear came across her, and a reminiscence of the amazing manner in which the familiar forms of the nursery arranged themselves in the mind of little Alice in Wonderland in the story. Could it be that Ben was to start on his long journey to-morrow by the first train, and could the great beech be the name of the ship? Mary was so completely thrown off her balance, that this idea actually occurred to her. And then she felt that they must all have remarked that she had got a letter, and had thrust it stealthily into her pocket. Altogether, the evening swam over her somehow, she could not tell how. And then there was the stir of Davison's entrance, and Mrs. Renton's going to bed. And then Frank disappeared to smoke his cigar, and Alice, finding her companion uncommunicative, sat down at the piano, and began to play softly to herself, as she had been wont in the old days at home; and silence, broken only by sounds which helped to increase all the mists, and made her feel a safety and comfort in the retirement of her thoughts, fell upon the quiet house.

Next morning Mary was awake and up before any one was stirring. She did not herself think that she had slept all the night; but she was still young enough to consider an hour or two's wakefulness a great matter. And she was as much afraid of Ben's visit being found out, as if he had been the most illegitimate of visitors. She was out soon after six, while the grass was still quite wet with dew, and went wandering up and down the river-walk like a ghost, under the cloistered shade of those great trees which, as yet, let no sunshine through. There was something in the air at that early hour which told that summer was waning, and Mary was chilly with nervousness, which had all the effect of cold. She went all the way down to the river-side, and basked in the sunshine which lay full on the open bit of green bank, by way of overcoming the shivering which had seized her. The world was so still, the birds so noisy,—which rather heightens than impairs the stillness,—the paths so utterly vacant and suggestive, that fancy continually caught glimpses of something disappearing behind the trees. Now it would seem a gliding dream-figure, now the last sweep of a robe just getting out of sight. The ghostliness of the early morning is different, but not less profound, than that of the night; and at six o'clock the Renton woods were as mysterious, as dim under the great shadows of the trees, as any enchanted wood. The sunshine went all round them, drying up the dew on the open bank, and chasing the mists and chills of night; but the river-walk was all brown and grey, and full of clear, mystical distances and windings, broken by upright shafts of trees. Any one might have appeared suddenly at such an hour in such a place. People out of books, people out of one's own straining fancy, people from the other world. And though it was Ben, and no other, for whom Mary Westbury was waiting, yet her imagination, over-excited, was ready to see anything. And she was alarmed by every waving leaf or bough that swayed in the morning air. If anybody should discover this tryst! If it should be known that Ben had come in this sweet inconceivable sort of way to see her! Had he been a tabooed lover, whose discovery would have involved all sorts of perils, Mary could not have been more afraid.

It was half-past seven before he came,—as indeed she might have known,— since that was the earliest moment at which any one could come by the first train. She could see him coming for a long way, making his way among the trees. He had not come in by any gate, but through some illegitimate byway known to the Renton boys and the poachers, so lawless were all the accessories of this extraordinary stealthy meeting. He came along rapidly, making himself audible by, now and then, the sound of the gravel sent flying by his foot, or the crackle of a fallen branch on the path. And then he came in sight, walking very quickly, with a look of abstraction, wrapped in his own thoughts. He was close upon the bank before he caught sight of Mary, whose grey gown was easily lost sight of among the branches,—then he quickened his pace, and came forward eagerly.

'You here,' he said, 'Mary? I thought I should be too early for you,' and held out both his hands for her.

'I was so much surprised,—so anxious to know what it was. I have been out for nearly an hour, I think,' said Mary. 'I could not sleep.'

'Did I startle you?' said Ben. 'Not half so much, I am sure, as I was startled myself. But if I have made you uneasy I will never forgive myself,' he went on, looking closely into her face.

What could have made that difference in his look? He had always been kind,—certainly he had always been kind,—but he had never looked at her before in that wistful, anxious way. He had been protecting, superior, affectionate; but such was not his expression now.

'Oh, it does not matter!' said Mary; 'but, of course, since it is something important enough to bring you from town like this,—and at this hour—— Tell me, please, and put me out of pain.'

What he did was to draw her arm closely through his own. 'Come this way,' he said, 'I don't want to be seen or interrupted. There is a corner down here where we shall be quite safe. It was very good of you, Mary, to come.'

'Oh, Ben,' she cried, 'don't talk so, you frighten me! You never were so gentle, so soft to me before. Tell me what it is. It must be something terrible to make you look like this. What is wrong?'

'I don't know if there is anything wrong,' he said. 'It depends upon your feelings altogether, Mary; only I never had thought of,—anything of the kind,—never! It came upon me like a thunder-clap. To be sure. I might have known. You could not but be as sweet and as pleasant in the eyes of others as you were in mine——'

'Ben, don't talk riddles, I entreat of you,' said Mary. 'I cannot make this out to-day. A shadow would frighten me to-day. I have had too much to bear,—too much,—'

'Sit down here,' he said, tenderly; 'you must not be frightened. There is nothing to hurt you. It is only me that it can hurt. Mary, Hillyard came to me yesterday, and said,—I suppose by this time you must know what he said?'

'Yes,' she answered, first with a violent blush, and then growing suddenly hot.

'Of course, I ought to have known it,' said Ben. 'I used to read him your letters, like an ass, never thinking. I was furious yesterday; I thought it presumption and insolence. But, of course, that was nonsense. The man is as good as I am. The fact is, I suppose I thought that no other man but myself had any right to think of you.'

'Ben!' Mary cried, trembling with a sudden passion, 'you never thought of me! How can you say so? or what is it you would have me understand? I feel as if you were mocking me,—and yet you would not come all this way, surely, to mock me!'

'Then, I did not think at all,' he went on, without any direct answer. 'I felt that no man had any right,—and I was a fool for thinking so. Mary, the fact is, it ought to be you and I.'

'What ought to be you and I?' she faltered, lost in confusion and amazement.

He was standing before her, not lover-like, but absorbed, pressing his subject, and paying no special regard to her. 'It ought to be you and I to build up the old house. No. I cannot think any man has a right to come in and interfere. But only just there is this one thing to be said. Whatever is for your happiness, Mary, I will carry out with all my might. If you should set your heart on one thing or another, it shall be done; but still that does not affect the question,—it ought to be you and me.'

'For what?' she asked again.

'For what? Oh, for more than I can tell,' said Ben; 'to build up this old house, as I told you,—to get through life. I must always have felt it, though I did not know. And here is this fellow come in with his wild backwoods way, and thinks he can win you off-hand. I don't say a word if it is for your happiness; but I know it should be you and me.'

And then there was a pause, and Ben walked up and down the little vacant space in front of the seat he had placed her in, with his eyes bent on the ground, and his face moody and full of trouble. As for Mary, she sat and gazed at him, half-conscious only, worn out by excitement and wonder, and the succession of shocks of one kind and another which she had been receiving, but with a soft sense of infinite ease and consolation stealing over her confused heart. It was that relief from pain which feels to the sufferer like positive blindness. She had not even known how deep the pain in her was until she felt it stealing in upon her,—this ineffable ease and freedom from it, which is more sweet than actual joy.

'Ben,' she said at last, when she could get breath. 'It is very difficult for me to follow you, and you confuse me so that I don't know. But, about Mr. Hillyard you are all wrong. I never saw him till Monday. I never thought about him at all. I was very sorry. But it is not as if I could blame myself. I was not to blame.'

'To blame! How could you be to blame?' said Ben, and he came and stood before her again, gazing at her with that strange look which Mary did not recognise in him, and could not meet.

'I should never have mentioned it to any one,' she said. 'I would not now, though you question me so. But only it is best you should not have anything on your mind. Is,—that,—all?'

It was not coquetry which suggested the question; it was her reason that began utterly to fail her. She did not seem to know what it was he had said besides,—though he had said something.

'Ah!' he cried vehemently, and then paused and subdued himself, 'all except my answer, Mary,' he said, softly stooping over her.

'Your answer? You have not asked me anything. Oh, Ben,' she cried, suddenly getting up from her seat, with her cheeks burning and her eyes wet, 'let there be no more of this. It was all the feeling of the moment. You thought something had happened which never, never could happen, and you felt a momentary grudge. Don't tell me it was anything else. Do you think I forget what you told me once up at the beech about her?' Mary cried, waving her hand towards The Willows. 'You did not mean to tell me; but I knew. And the other day—— When you say this sort of thing to me it is unkind of you; it is disrespectful to me. I have my pride like other women. Let us speak no more of it, but say good-bye, and I shall go home.'

'Then you do not even think me worthy of an answer?' said Ben; and the two stood confronting each other in that supreme duel and conflict of the two existences about to become one, which never loses its interest; she flushed, excited, suspicious; he steadily keeping to his point, refusing to be led away from it. And why Mary should have resisted, standing thus wildly at bay,— and why, when she could stand no longer, she should have sunk down on the seat from which she had risen, in a passion of tears, is more than I can tell. But that finally Ben did get his answer, and that it was, as anybody must have foreseen, eminently satisfactory to him at last, is a matter about which there can be no doubt. I do not know even whether he offered any explanations, or justified himself in the matter of Millicent. I am inclined to think, indeed, that at that moment he took no notice of it whatever; but only insisted on that reply, which, when nature was worn out and could stand against it no longer, came. But the victor did go into certain particulars, as with Mary's arm drawn closely through his he led her again up that bank which, in so much excitement and uncertainty, half-an-hour before he had led her down.

'I can't tell you the fright I was in yesterday,' he said. 'It suddenly flashed upon me in a moment how mad I had been. To leave you here so long, open to any assault, and to be such an ass as to bring a man down who had eyes in his head, and was not an idiot?'

'I wish you would not swear,' said Mary. 'The strange thing is that you should like me, and yet think me of so small account that any man,—a man I had only known for three days——'

'Hush!' he said, drawing her to him. 'When a man's eyes are opened first to the thought that another man has gone off express to rob him of his jewel, do you think he pauses to be reasonable?' and then they looked at each other and were silent, there being more expression in that than in speech.

'But the jewel was no jewel till yesterday,' said Mary, making the kind of objection which women love to make, 'and who knows but it may be paste to-morrow?'

'My dear,' said Ben, 'my only woman in the world! might not a man have been beguiled to follow a Will-o'-the-wisp till he cursed and hated such lights, and chose darkness instead,—and then all at once wake up to see that his moon had risen, and that the night was safe and sweet as day?'

I suppose it was the only bit of poetry which Ben Renton was ever guilty of in his life; and it was perfectly successful. And they went on and continued their walk to the beech-tree. Mary's eyes were blind with sweet tears; but then, what did it matter? was not he there to be eyes to her, through the winding of the tender morning path? And as they reached the trees, the sunshine burst into the wood all at once with something like a shout of triumph. If it was not a shout, it came to precisely the same thing, and caught a branch here and a twig there, and made it into burnished gold, and lit up the far distance and cloistered shade into all the joyous animation and moving stir of life.

'Must you go now?' Mary said, clinging to him a little closer, 'must it still be secret? is no one to see you now?'

'I must still go away,' he said, 'no help for that, Mary; but in the meantime I am going home with you to tell them all about it. I shall still catch my ship if I go by the next train.'

He was received with subdued consternation by the household, which jumped instantly to the conclusion that something had happened; but there is an instinct in the domestic mind which is almost infallible in such matters; and before Mrs. Renton had even been told of the unexpected arrival of her son, Davison had said to the housekeeper, 'He's come down at the last to settle it all with Miss Mary. Now didn't I tell you?' and Willis had recorded his opinion that, on the whole, there wasn't nothing to say again it. 'A little bit of money never comes amiss,' he said; 'but she was used bad in the will, never to have no compensation. And, on the whole, I agrees with Ben.'

Such was the decision of the house, conveyed in language, kind, if familiar, just five minutes after the entry by the window into the dining-room, where the breakfast-table was prepared for the family, of the betrothed pair. Mary's gown was wet with the dew, and she ran up-stairs to change it, leaving Ben alone to receive the greetings of his brothers, who appeared at the same moment. 'I thought you couldn't resist coming down again, old fellow, before you left for good,' Frank said in her hearing, as she rushed to the covert and sanctuary of her own room. He was not so discriminating as the intelligent community below stairs.

And then, in that strange golden forenoon, which seemed at the same time one hasty moment and a long day, full of events, Mrs. Renton, amazed, found her son again stooping over her, and received the astonishing news. It was some time before she could take it in. 'What,' she said, 'Mary? I will never believe it is Mary. You are making fun of me, Ben.'

'It is a great deal better than fun, mother,' he said. 'I could not go till it was settled; and now there is only ten minutes or so to kiss us and bless us, and thank me for giving you such a daughter. She has been a daughter to you already for so long.'

'Of course she has,' said the bewildered woman. 'Mary! it's like your sister. I can't think it's quite right, do you know, Ben. I should as soon have thought of you marrying Alice, or——'

'Frank might object to that, my dear mother,' said Ben.

'But, Mary—you are sure you are not making one of your jokes? And after all, I can't think what you see in her, Ben,' Mrs. Renton said, with a little eagerness. 'She was never very pretty,—not like that beautiful Mrs. Rich, you know, or those sort of women,—and not even very young. She must be seven-and-twenty, if she is a day. Let me see, Frank was born in July, and she in the December after. She will be seven-and-twenty on her next birthday. And nothing to make up for it—— '

'Except that there is nobody else in the world,' said Ben, smiling at Mary, who had just come into the room.

'Nobody else in the world! I don't know what you mean. Not to say a word against Mary, but you might have done a great deal better, Ben.'

'And so he might, godmamma,' said Mary, with the gravity of happiness, though Ben had her hand in his.

'Yes, my dear,' said Mrs. Renton, in perfect good faith, 'a great deal better. You always have the sense to see things. If I were you, I would reflect a little longer before I announced it, or did anything more in the matter, Ben.'

The answer Ben made to this proposal was to draw his betrothed close to his mother's bedside within his own supporting arms. 'Give her a kiss, mamma, and say God bless you,' he said, bending down his own face close to Mary's. And the mother, quite confused and bewildered, did as she was told, crying a little, and not knowing what to think. And before any one knew, Ben was gone again, off by express to join the steamer which sailed from Liverpool that night. He had just time; everything belonging to him having gone on before with poor Hillyard, who knew nothing about this morning's expedition. And before noon the episode was all over, and the Frank Rentons once more in the foreground, and Mary reading the newspaper as if such a wild inroad of romance into the midst of reality had never been.

'My dear, it is not that I am not as fond of you,—fonder of you than of anybody,' Mrs. Renton said, when poor Mary, for one moment, owing to a paragraph about a shipwreck, fairly broke down; 'but it does not seem somehow as if it were quite proper. And we can't shut our eyes to it that he might have done better. It feels as if there was never to be any satisfaction in the boys' marriages. I had a fortune of my own, and so had your grandmother; but everything now is going to sixes and sevens——'

'Don't say anything more about it, godmamma,' said Mary, with an outburst of pent-up agitation, and the nervous panic that seizes a weakened mind. 'Oh, how can we tell what may happen in the meantime? Let us say nothing more till he comes home.'

'Well, to be sure, he might change his mind,' said Mrs. Renton, as Davison came in with her arrowroot. And for half-an-hour or so that satisfactory conclusion, and the adding of another teaspoonful of port, on account of the excitement she had been going through, put a stop to the conversation, and gave Mary time to draw breath in peace.

But if the reader of this history hopes to be humoured by a shipwreck at this late period of the narrative, it is a vain expectation. The winds blew, and the sea rose, but Ben Renton got safely out to Canada, and came safely home. I am sorry to have to say that his last great piece of work did not pay nearly so well as he had expected it to do; and the business, which he made over to Hillyard, was, owing to the state of the colony at that moment, of less value than had been anticipated; but at the same time patience alone was wanted to realise all possible hopes. I have been obliged to ask the reader to take Ben's success for granted all along, as it would have been simply impossible to introduce details of engineering enterprise into a work of this description;

and, indeed, to tell the truth, I fear I should not have sufficiently understood them to set them forth with any distinctness. But whether Hillyard will have patience, and keep up the energy which Ben put into the business, is a very doubtful matter; and it is just as likely as not that he may turn up again at the old club, which is the only luxury he keeps up, as rough, as *insouciant*, as careless what becomes of him, as on the first day Ben met him, after the weird of the Rentons had begun. Mary might have made another man of him perhaps; but who knows? Temperament is stronger than circumstance,—stronger than fortune,—stronger even than love.

Ben Renton came home, as I have said, as safely as most men come home from Canada. And everything occurred as it ought to have occurred. I would add that they lived happy ever after, if there had been time to make such a record. But the fact is, that it is too early yet to be historical on that point; and for anything anybody can tell, the Rentons may yet come to be very wretched, and give occasion for other chapters of history; though, in common with all their friends, I sincerely hope not. Benedict Renton of Renton stood for the county of Berks, in the late election, with politics perhaps slightly tinged by his life in the other world, but failed by a few votes, notwithstanding the interest attaching to him,—Berks, like many other counties, being of the opinion that a good, steady, reliable bumpkin, who will do whatever he is told, is a more satisfactory legislator than a man who has spent his youth in objectionable exercises, such as writing, and thinking, and moving about the world. Frank Renton, true soldier and constitutional Tory, is one of those who hold this opinion. But I do not despair of seeing Ben in Parliament yet.

And thus the story ends; being like all stories, no history of life, but only of a bit out of life,—the most amiable bit, the section of existence which the world has accepted as its conventional type of life, leaving all the profounder glooms and the higher lights apart. As in heaven there can be no story-telling of the present, for happiness has no story,—there, perhaps, for the first time, the mouth of the minstrel may be opened to say or sing what is untellable by the frankest voice on earth. But till then we must be content to break off after the fairy chapter of life's beginning, the history of Youth.

THE END.